T0162824

JERK
Magnet

Katy Franklin

iUniverse, Inc.
Bloomington

Jerk Magnet

iUniverse books may be ordered through booksellers or by contacting:

iUniverse
1663 Liberty Drive
Bloomington, IN 47403
www.iuniverse.com
1-800-Authors (1-800-288-4677)

ISBN: 978-1-4759-1358-3 (sc)
ISBN: 978-1-4759-1359-0 (e)

Printed in the United States of America

iUniverse rev. date: 5/2/2012

The author would like to thank:

Jamie Oslawski-Lopez: The best editor and friend a girl could wish for. Thank you for your hard work, patience, ideas and advice. This book would be nothing without your input and expertise.

Christy: For being the best sister, best friend and (second) editor a girl could wish for. Thank you for always being the first person to read my books, and for being the best buddy eva.

My friends: Namely Erin, Natalie, Mary, Grace, Kelly, Keri, Sandra, Heather, Melissa, Shannon, Eden and Ashley for forever encouraging me and always being interested in my work. Thanks for the memories that made this book what it is.

My family: For always supporting me

My fans: Namely Bucket, for believing in me

The Jerks: Without whom there would be no book. Ironically, thank you.

His name was Greg. His swingy blond hair sashayed across his electric blue eyes as if in a sexy, slow motion music video. His lopsided, silly smile could break your heart. He had a come hither dimple in his right cheek that caught your attention and wouldn't let you go. His creamy white skin was unmarred by blemishes and his posture was always erect. He was cocky and that was sexy. He was sure of himself and magnificent. He had an aura about him that screamed "sex." It said "look at me, you know you want me, ladies." And I did. I wanted him and then I had him.

As for myself, known by my friends as Katy F., as there were seven other Katies, Kate's and even a Kat in my class, I was less self-aware, almost apologetic about my looks, but they weren't half bad. Long red hair, freckles, white skin, thin. Pink lips, flat-chested, but I carried myself well. I had a small smile and big, round, vulnerable eyes which made me look half myself and half Disney princess. I was innocent, but when I felt his hand in mine, when I felt that smooth skin slide over my rougher, skinny fingers, I tingled. Then he would look at me with his trademark look and I felt like

I could conquer the world. I felt alive. When he touched me I knew that this was it. We were meant to be and nothing could stop us. When he held my hand, I soared. I stood up straighter than my four feet eight inches.

I was seven years old.

He was eight.

His name was Greg. He was the cool, hip and unabashedly good-looking second-grade jock that every girl wanted. He was rich, too: as the heir of the country's largest meat-packing distributor, he had money to spend. And I was…well, I was me. Star of the first-grade school play, music nerd and spelling bee runner-up. Heir of only all of the money my lawyer father and music teacher mother had, which was a figure not even comparable to that of packaged meat royalty. But Greg picked me. No matter I was bad at math and couldn't grasp the concept of a fraction. No matter that I was a little too outspoken at times and gangly and awkward always. No matter that I had recently lost my first tooth and it was my right front one and it left a huge gap in the middle of my face when I smiled, which was almost constantly because Greg was my man. He had looked past all of that and chosen me. He liked me for me, but he was especially impressed by my sense of style.

The first time Greg noticed me was in the hallway as the first and second graders passed each other on their way to recess. He looked down and caught sight of the shoes I was wearing that day. They were pink saddle shoes. I had begged and begged my mom for these shoes for weeks and she had finally caved in and bought them for me the day before. I wanted them because saddle shoes were popular with the seven year-old contingent at the time, but everyone seemed to want plain, boring black and white saddle shoes. But not me. Oh no, I needed pink. I wanted to be different. I wanted to stand out. And I stood out. White leather interrupted by a crisp, smart, neon pink strip in the center, a pink that went slashing through your brain when you looked at it. A pink that widened your eyes and made you sit up and take notice. And Greg noticed. He took one look at those shoes and fell in love with me. His head snapped up and his luscious blond hair swished to the side. He smiled his delicious smile and his ice blue eyes locked into mine. He all but licked his lips. Then he opened his mouth and said: "I like your shoes."

I was stunned into paralyzation. Was that Greg, the sexy second grader, really talking to me? Was I being addressed by the most popular and sought after eight-year-old in all of Kalamazoo, Michigan? I had had my eye on him for a while now, but so had every other living, breathing girl in the vicinity. Really, me? This couldn't be happening to me. Yet, it was. It was happening. And so I responded in the most appropriate way I could think of. I said "Thanks."

And so began our torrid affair. Our interactions consisted mostly of Greg passing by me in the hallway at the specified time, staring at my shoes longingly and then looking up and gracing me with that blinding smile of his. Then I would turn red as a beet, smile back and quickly look down. Twice, he grabbed my hand unexpectedly and said "hi." I was in heaven. I was the luckiest girl in the world. I had a dashing, rich, handsome older boyfriend and I was the envy of all the elementary school girls. I wore those shoes for a solid week and reveled in their power. I owned those shoes. I walked, talked, lived and breathed those shoes. I made those shoes my bitch. I knew I had needed them. They had brought me love, fame and notoriety. They were the best shoes ever.

And then, after eight solid days of rocking them, I did not wear the pink saddle shoes because they did not go with my outfit. This would turn out to be an irreparable mistake, one of the worst in my life. When the time came for the first and second graders to switch for math class, Greg ambled down the hallway as usual, eyes glued to the ground to get his daily fix of the pink saddle shoes, but to no avail. All he saw were the ratty old tennis shoes I had thrown on that morning. The brown, clunky, beat-up, stupid shoes that I had so carelessly tossed on my feet only hours before. His head snapped up much like in our first encounter a week ago, but there was no light in his eyes, no dazzling smile upon his face. All that registered was disappointment. As I caught his eye, he quickly looked away with a frown and a sigh. I was confused and mortified. Had our love been based on the pink saddle shoes? I knew they had been a catalyst for our relationship, but was the whole thing dependent upon them? Did Greg not like me anymore? Had we broken up? I decided the only thing to do was to wear the shoes again tomorrow to rectify the whole mess, and quickly scurried away.

So the next day I donned my cutest outfit; deep purple windbreaker pants, a zip-up windbreaker jacket with pink zig-zags (I figured matching my outfit to the shoes couldn't hurt,) put my hair in a sleek side ponytail fastened with a purple cloth scrunchie and laced up the pink saddles. I was looking good. I was feeling good. I was ready to win him back. When the time came to pass Greg in the hallway, I strutted confidently down the carpet, making sure to kick up my heels to showcase the shoes and flash him my best thousand-watt smile. He looked down at my feet, saw the saddle shoes and looked up into my face. Nothing. No smile. Just a slight shake of his head and another look of disappointment. I had worn the shoes again but it didn't matter. It was too late. The magic was gone. We were done. I could feel it. It was my first breakup and I was crushed. I spent the next week continuing to wear the shoes, but in vain. I tried flirting and smiling, I even mouthed a "hi" to him a few days later, but nothing helped. He barely looked at me, and when he did, the pain on his face was almost too much for me to bear. I had let him down and it was over. Time to move on so reluctantly, I did.

Now, it seems that the obvious moral to this story would be that Greg was an incredibly shallow, snobby and materialistic rich kid who only liked me for my stupid pair of shoes because they were eye-catching and different and to him, denoted some sort of elevated status for me as a lowly first-grader. He probably wanted me to be his younger, trophy girlfriend and once he realized I would not live up to his standards in that way, he tossed me to the curb as if I had never even existed, as if we had never shared something truly meaningful and special. I should have thanked my lucky stars that he let me go when he did; should have realized that he was doing me a favor, or else I would have been locked into a thankless, loveless, one-sided relationship with a maniacal, oppressive and overbearing packaged meat heir, probably forever. Or the moral of the story could have been that we were seven and eight years old respectively, and there was no rhyme or reason to the beginning, middle and/or end of our "relationship."

But I took neither of these morals to heart. What this starter "boyfriend" and experience taught me was that I was a horrible man-picker. I was terrible and hopeless at choosing men and this was never to be changed. Technically, Greg had chosen me because he made the first move, but I had my eye on him for a long time before anything came to fruition, and look how he turned out. He turned out to be the worst boyfriend ever. This was the beginning, and my wild misjudgment of Greg's character would haunt me throughout my adult life as I grew up and continued to choose the wrong guys to like…again…and again…and again….

I am a Jerk Magnet.

Not that I wasn't already painfully aware of this fact, but recently I met my sister and her fiance out at the hottest sushi restaurant in Hollywood and it was solidified. I was visiting them a few weeks after they had gotten engaged, and I was finding it hard to keep my cucumber yellowfin tuna hand rolls down. Public displays of affection are one thing, but their behavior was downright and annoyingly inappropriate. My sister, Christy's, hand looked as if it was permanently glued to Steve's knee. Every five seconds he would nuzzle her neck or roll his tongue in little circles all over it and say "I love you, baby, you are my everything, my little lovey pie and you make me the happiest man in the world! I can't wait to marry you!" Then he would plant wet, sloppy, slurpy kisses all over her gorgeous, cherubic face and perfect California blond hair and she would giggle and put her little left hand up to stroke his thick, flaming, ginger-colored mop of hair, making sure to showcase the four carat monstrosity on her ring finger. It sparkled almost as dazzlingly as Christy's smile and then I watched in horror as Steve stabbed his last piece of salmon sashimi and sticky rice expertly with a pair of chopsticks, swung it up near Christy's mouth air-plane style and…

Fed her.

I literally gagged.

"You guys!" I said, throwing my fork down on my plate with a clatter of frustration. "Seriously? Like…can you please…stop it?"

"Stop what?" Christy asked, reluctantly tearing her eyes away from Steve's freckled face and focusing on my own. She almost looked surprised to see me. It was like she had literally forgotten there was anyone else in the entire restaurant, let alone at the table.

"The schmoopiness! It's making me sick. I am trying to enjoy my thirty-two dollar lump of seaweed, here."

"You're just jealous because we are getting MARRIED! Aren't we, baby?" Christy screeched, flipping her hand dismissively in my direction and rocketing her body back toward Steve, who was now lost in a trance, eyes glued to the screen of the Blackberry that was constantly stuck in his hands. When they weren't somewhere on my sister's body, that was.

"Yes my perfect little angel," he said, distractedly, not looking up. "Sorry, babe, duty calls. Colin Farrell just e-mailed. He's coming to the premiere tonight. He may be joining us later."

"Oh, the life of a Hollywood agent!" my sister sighed, placing her chin in her hands and rolling her eyes dreamily upward. "Hey, Katy!" she said, her head suddenly snapping up and her eyes focusing intently on me. "We need to find you a date to our wedding! You don't have a date, yet, right?"

"Uh, no. You know I don't," I said, shooting daggers out of my eyes at my younger sibling. "Maybe Colin Farrell could accompany me, you know, if he has time," I said, sarcastically, swinging my head from side to side.

Christy ignored my comment and said "Why don't you, though?" And before I even had time to respond, she answered her own question: "because you date jerks."

I glared at her and swished the seaweed pile around on my plate in anger. "No, I don't," I lied, trying in vain to defend myself.

"Yes you do! Yes you do!" she singsonged like a five year-old. "You date jerks you know you do! You just dated that one guy…what was his name? He was a jerk."

"Mark? He wasn't a…" I trailed off.

"Yes, he was. And before that, there was that Anthony guy. He was an even bigger jerk. AND," she continued emphasizing the word, "you dated…" she paused for dramatic effect, "Nick," she finished with a grimace. At his name my head snapped up. I stared at her for a second as the look on her face changed from one of victory to one of anger to one of almost sadness. I opened my mouth to counteract her words but nothing came out. I sat there pondering what to say. Something to defend myself. Something to make myself feel better. Something to prove that me dating Nick wasn't the worst idea in the world. Something to make it clear that he wasn't the worst person imaginable. Something to erase the jarring hurt I had just experienced upon hearing his name. But all that came out was "you're right."

Christy seemed surprised at my acquiescence at first but then quickly went back to being a jerk herself. She slammed a tiny hand down on the table and yelled "You are a jerk-dater! Ha! See, I was right!" Christy smiled smugly in my direction.

"Christy, please stop acting like a child," I whined, sounding like a child myself and shaking off her last retort.

Christy placed her hand on Steve's back and the ring seemed to swirl and sparkle in a rainbow of colors. She leaned in toward me. "I'm just saying," she started, conspiratorially. "That I am sooo glad I didn't get the jerk-picking gene from Mom and Dad, you know? It really sucks that you did."

"I don't even have any idea what the jerk-picking gene is," I said, lying again.

"Yes you do, it must have skipped..." Christy singsonged again and then trailed off, a look of sheer terror passing over her face. "Oh my God!" she said, panic rising in her voice. "Baby!" she turned to her fiancé and shook his shoulder roughly. "What if our kids get it too?"

"Get what, babe?" Steve asked, fingers clacking furiously on his little phone keyboard.

"The gene! The jerk-picking gene! Oh, no! This is terrible!" Christy was nearly in hysterics.

Steve finally looked up at me, and something like pity, or maybe it was sadness passed over his face for a split second. He shook his head slightly and quickly looked back down again. "No such thing, babe, you don't need to worry. It's all kosher." He patted her hair reassuringly.

Christy seemed to ponder this for a moment and then sighed deeply. "Well, you might be right, but I don't want to take any chances. It would be horrible if our children ended up being jerk magnets just like aunt Katy."

"Wouldn't it, though? The worst." I said acidly.

Christy's big, green eyes widened in her pretty face. "Yes, it would be," she said extremely seriously, holding my gaze. She then tossed a lock of blond hair off her forehead, slammed her elbows down on the white linen tablecloth with a defiant thump, and intertwined her fingers. The engagement ring the size of a small country twisted a little on her small, tan finger.

"Dear God," she started, closing her eyes, a look of concentration marring her face.

"What in the world are you doing?" I hissed at her, looking around the room in embarrassment.

She opened her eyes with a look that made me feel like the biggest idiot on the planet. "I'm praying," she said, clucking her tongue at me. "Obviously."

"Dear God," she began again. "Please do not let Steve and my children be born with the terrible jerk-picking gene like Katy. I just don't think I could live with myself if that happened. It would be so awful. It would probably be the worst thing in the world. Please let my children be perfect in every way. Perfect and tall. Oh, and please let them be girls. And make them be pretty. Thank-you. Amen."

"That's it," I said, throwing my napkin down on the table. "I can't take this anymore. I'm going to the bathroom. Save my seat, don't let Colin Farrell take it or anything." But Christy and Steve were no longer listening. Our waiter had just arrived at our table with the third one hundred dollar bottle of champagne Steve had ordered. I hung back behind them as the waiter poured the bubbly, amber liquid into each flute. I was just far enough away for them not to see me, but I could still hear every word they said. Christy said, "What should we toast to?"

"To you, my dear. To you not getting the jerk-picking gene. Your sister totally has it. I just wanted to make her feel better by saying she doesn't."

"I know, right?" Christy said, holding her glass above her head. "She totally does. And I don't, thank God! Yay! To me!" she yelled triumphantly. She gazed lovingly into his eyes.

"To you," Steve said, holding his flute up in the air as well.

And I watched as they threw back their heads in laughter and clinked glasses.

So my sister and her fiancé were toasting to Christy's lack of a genetic defect. Which is essentially what I have. Like most inherent flaws, I suppose I was born with this problem. Something must have happened when my DNA strand was formed. A small molecule in my father's sperm must have crashed into another small molecule in my mother's egg to create the "horrible jerk-picking" gene. I am no geneticist, but I can only assume that this, or something similar to it, happened. It sounds perfectly plausible to me. I know I am not the only person to have been cursed with this abhorrent characteristic because I have encountered many women in my lifetime who have seemed to share similar traits. I hesitate to say the "same" traits because even if we share a kindred jerk-picking gene, I have come to realize that mine must be a hell of a lot more potent than all of the others.

So that makes me the President of Jerk Magnets Anonymous. This club is made up of friends of mine, women I know who, much like myself, allow jerks to gravitate toward them at alarming speeds. They all warmly welcome said jerks into their lives with no hesitation, no second thought. This club has two other members, Natasha and Erin. Both are wonderful, special, gorgeous, kind, funny, intelligent women who should have no trouble finding a "good man." But, again, much like me, they struggle with this seemingly simple task.

Natasha, Erin and I graduated from a credible liberal arts college excited, ready and armed with the tools we assumed would help us get good jobs, make something of ourselves and find a good man, not necessarily in that order. Get good jobs we got, that was easy. Make something of ourselves, I would like to think we have. At finding good men, we failed. Flunked. There have been plenty of men, that was never the issue, the problem was that it was a classic case of quantity, not quality throughout the years. I will never forget the night the Jerk Magnet Anonymous club came into existence. It started with a phone call that I received from Natasha at eleven p.m. one night in late July. I was used to these calls from my friends and they were used to the same from me. The eleven pm calls were the ones reserved for complaining about the latest jerk one of us had been seeing. Natasha's had been more frequent lately, as she had been dating a complete jerk, a guy who had no good qualities whatsoever, at least none that I could see.

So when the phone rang, I picked it up and immediately said "What did Charles do now?"

"I hate him!" Natasha screamed in my ear. It was so loud that I had to hold the phone away from it.

"I'm putting the phone on speaker. Your hatred is too intense right now for me to hold the phone against my face."

"No shit my hatred is intense! I hate him with the fire of one thousand suns! I hate him more than I can describe! He is such a moron!"

These outbursts were completely typical. There was nothing she was saying that I hadn't heard a million times before.

"But what did he do?" I asked.

"I'll tell you what he did. I told him over and over and over that I wanted a massage for my birthday. That was it, a massage. I needed one because I have been so stressed out with how much of a stupid asshole idiot he is and it is exhausting dating such a pathetic loser. So I explained this to him and then told him that I wanted a massage."

"You explained to him that you think he is a stupid asshole, idiot, pathetic loser and that is why you are exhausted and need a massage?"

"Yes."

"Go on."

"So my birthday is the other day, you know, and I'm like waiting and waiting all day for my gift certificate or whatever and then we go to dinner which by the way he takes me to Applebees, like gross, how ghetto and cheap is that…?"

"Yeah, lame."

"And as he's shoving this disgusting burger into his mouth with ketchup all over it and I hate ketchup, you know, and it's like making me want to vomit, he hands a card across the table and says 'oh yeah, almost forgot to give this to you for your, like, birthday or whatever…'"

"He said 'like birthday or whatever?'"

"Yes. Verbatim."

"Continue."

"And I open up the card and on it is a picture of a stupid clown and I hate clowns, you know, and what are we, like 5? And guess what is inside the card? Just guess. You'll never guess."

"Uh…nothing?"

"RIGHT! NOTHING! Not a goddamn thing. How did you guess?"

"Because Charles is a jerk. And he's cheap."

"Arrrghhh!" Natasha screamed exasperatedly. "How easy is it to spend forty dollars and get a girl a gift certificate to get a massage for her birthday? What is wrong with these guys? Can we start a hotline for girls who are sick of dating jerks or something?"

"Well, I don't know about that," I said, taking the phone off speaker. "But we can call Erin. Let's get her on three-way. I bet she'll have some advice for you."

"Good idea!" Natasha said. "But wait, what's your advice for me? Any words of wisdom?"

"Stop dating him."

"I had a feeling you were going to say that. Let's see what Erin has to say."

Erin picked up on the second ring. After Natasha explained the situation to her, and Erin's advice turned out to be the same as mine, she asked Natasha where she had met Charles.

"At a bar," Natasha responded, matter-of-factly.

"Well, there's your problem right there!" Erin said. "You can't date guys that you meet at BARS, Natasha! No wonder he's an asshole! There are no guys that go to bars who are acceptable to date. They are all weird. Everyone knows this!"

"Um, I would have to disagree with that statement," I interjected. "I work in a bar and there are plenty of okay guys to meet there. That's kind of generalizing. And it's kind of a blanket statement, don't you think? And hypocritical!" I said, remembering Erin's last boyfriend. "Didn't you meet Spencer at a bar?"

"Oh. Yeah. I did," Erin responded. "He was a jerk. Case in point."

"Yeah," I said. "But the fact that you met him at a bar doesn't make him a jerk."

"Right," Natasha cut in. "Wasn't he a police officer or something?"

"Yes. He was a detective," Erin said, defensively.

"Well no WONDER he was a jerk!" Natasha yelled back. "You can't date a police officer! They are ALL jerks! Everyone knows this. There was your problem right there."

Erin yelled back "well, at least he got me what I wanted for my birthday! And he was a DETECTIVE!"

Natasha yelled back "So what? At least Charles doesn't lie about his job and say that he's a detective when he's really just a regular police officer!"

"GUYS!" I yelled, cutting them both off. "Stop it, okay? Why are we fighting each other over who dates the bigger jerk? Can't we all just agree that they're worthless losers who we should not be dating? Can't we all just console each other when the going gets tough with these guys which is like, all the time?"

There was silence on both ends and then Natasha piped up. "Katy's right. We need to come together and ban against these idiots. No more internal fighting."

"Right," Erin said. "We'll form a club against them. Like fight club except it'll be a support group of sorts. And we'll call it…"

"Jerk Magnets Anonymous?" I offered.

"Exactly. Jerk Magnets Anonymous. I love it."

So that is how the club was formed. It is always nice have people around you who understand, who go through similar trials and tribulations, women with whom one can commiserate. And commiserate we do. We complain, we bemoan, we lament. Basically, we bitch. And this is how we attempt to deal with our jerk situations. We learn from each other and listen to one another. We try to make things better when it all seems hopeless. It's us against the jerks. Forever. Unfortunately, the jerks usually win.

This is because, in answer to our Jerk Magnets Anonymous club, there is also an elite social group called the Jerk Club. This is where our villains come together. The men of this club meet on a monthly basis and drink scotch and smoke cigars. They take excursions to go hunting or play football. They have poker night where they drink beer and eat pork rinds. They fart and burp and cuss and watch porn. They are forever trying to one-up one another on the asshole scale. They brag about how jerky they were to this author and to Erin and Natasha and any other girl who they may have screwed over. And that list is long. But mostly they laugh. They laugh about what jerks they have become. And the laughter is resounding and evil. I can hear it emanating from the deepest crevices of their lungs. And it haunts me.

Here's my advice: as you discover this book, take mental notes. If any of this sounds vaguely familiar or if a friend or someone you are dating did or does any of the things you are about to read, he or she is probably a jerk. There is a good 90% chance that he is. Don't shrug it off like it's nothing and don't make excuses for him. Get rid of him. Be done. Move on. Run. Far away. For God's sake, save yourself. This is my advice to you. Take it. I have encountered more jerks than I care to count. I can spot one coming from a mile away. I have qualifiable experience with them. I am the President of Jerks Magnets Anonymous. You can trust me when I say I know what I'm talking about.

I'm an expert.

Chapter 1

Sam

The fourth meeting of the Jerk Magnets Anonymous club was held at Bar 21, a trendy new Hollywood hangout, where the two west coast members, Erin and I, downed six shots of vodka a piece, two sides of cheese fries, and played the game "hipster or Euro trash?" with almost every single individual who brushed by our table. Natalie was absent during roll call, as she was busy piloting travelers through Chicago. Her flights were almost all Midwest-based, so she lived near O Hare, and couldn't physically attend the drinking and bitching sessions masquerading as meetings in Los Angeles. But Erin and I took care of business just fine.

We were there on a Sunday night because Erin had just finished a stressful day in the maternity unit at Cedars Sinai, where she worked as a nurse, and needed to bitch about her latest possible jerk. I was there because I needed a drink. I never turn down vodka. Erin spent the hour musing about whether or not the hot male nurse in the Emergency ward was interested in her. They had flirted heavily for a few weeks, but he hadn't yet asked her out. She was debating whether to ask him out at this point. I told her not to do it, to wait another week. I was convinced the extra seven days would tell her all she needed to know about his interest or lack thereof. She agreed with me, vowed to wait another week and then asked me about the status of my love life. Any new jerks or jerk prospects?

There weren't. But all of that was about to change. As I downed the last shot, feeling alarmingly sober and proving that I may, indeed, have a hollow leg, I made a vow myself to be on the lookout for possible candidates to fulfill my dating needs. I hadn't been on a single date since moving to LA three months before, and I was feeling the itch for male companionship. It was time to be social, time to get out there. As much as I loved my "dates" with Erin, I needed some romance, sparkle and pizzaz in my life. Or at least a guy to take me to dinner. At this point I would have settled for a few flirtatious moments of my own. Erin encouraged me to do anything I could to make all of this happen, and we reluctantly paid our bill and went home to sleep. We both had work in the morning.

As I entered work the next morning, I noticed a slight pain in my head and found the lights alarmingly bright. Noises sounded incredibly loud. I finally came to the realization that I was slightly hungover, and that perhaps my leg wasn't as hollow as I had once believed it to be. I hoped my co-workers would be able to take my mind off of my malady, and immediately, they did. I poked my head around the door frame of the office and three excited faces smiled back at me. Jason was the first to speak:

"John Stamos is out in the lobby!"

"What?! Shut up! Are you serious?" I asked, dropping my bag to the floor and staring back at him incredulously. "I just came through the lobby and I didn't even see him!"

"Oh, he's there. And girl, he is so hot."

"Obviously."

"And guess who is around the corner in the Young and the Restless office?"

"Who?"

"Lori Laughlin."

"From Full House?"

"Yup. So you know what that means?"

"What?"

"Uncle Jesse and Aunt Becky are reunited! And we are here to witness it!"

"Oh my God, you're right! I gotta go see Uncle Jesse…I mean, John Stamos."

I pivoted on my heel and raced out the door. I flattened my back against the wall and peered around the corner. There he was. Clad in jeans and a black leather jacket, the hair just as coiffed and perfect as it was on the primetime show almost two decades before, John Stamos was hot. I saw him shuffle the papers in his hands, give a bored yawn, then he looked over and his eyes met mine. He flashed me a wink and a sexy smile. I smiled back nervously before ducking back around the corner. I raced back into the office and addressed the three people staring expectantly at me.

"He. Is. Hot!" I exclaimed, panting breathlessly.

"Of course he is," Jason replied.

"EEEEKKKK!!! I'ma go check dis shit out!" Mya shrieked and ran out of the office.

"John Stamos, big deal," Anna sighed turning back to her computer and trying to act nonchalant. "Aren't you used to seeing celebrities by now?"

"Well, yeah," I said, perching on the counter by the wall. "But it's Uncle Jesse!"

"I totally know!" Anna said, springing up. "I wanna see him, too!" And with that, she ran out of the room. Jason and I exchanged knowing glances and burst into laughter.

I was at ABC in the office of the Primetime Casting department in Los Angeles in August of 2006. I had just moved to LA with Erin from New York City. She had gotten the nursing job at the hospital right out of school and begged me to come to the West Coast with her. Sick of the Big Apple and wanting a change, I hadn't needed much convincing, so I up and moved to the City of Angels with my best friend to try my hand in the entertainment industry. No, not stripping. Hollywood: The land of television and movies. I had grown tired of being a waitress in New York, the luster had slowly worn off and it was time for a "real job." I had decided the world of television and movies sounded glamorous and exciting and something I had always liked. I was obsessed with celebrities and their salacious gossip and always picked up the latest copy of People magazine or US Weekly to peruse. I watched everything on TV and saw every movie. I had had an internship in college while in New York City in a casting office and had loved every minute of it, so I decided to pursue that. After hitting the pavement hard for three months, a friend of mine had suggested I go meet with her friend who worked in the Primetime Casting department at ABC, they were in desperate need of a casting assistant. I called them the next day, came in to interview four hours later and was hired on the spot. I started at 10 am the next day and hadn't looked back.

That's how it goes in the entertainment industry. Everything is extremely fast-paced. They didn't seem to care that I didn't have that much experience or that I had barley any time to process starting a new job. They just hired me, had me sign a paper or two and demanded that I show up in the morning. I was thrown to the wolves immediately. But it was working out well, I thought. I didn't mess up very much, and by very much I mean more than twice an hour or so. Many people don't even know what casting is. Basically my job is to assist the Casting Directors whose job it is to choose which actors get the parts in all of the shows airing from 8-11pm every weekday night. So I help my boss pick out a set number of actors to audition in front of him by reading a script for one of the shows. We pick them by knowing actors in "town" and suggesting they come in to read for us, or by picking out actors who fit the part. We do this by looking at headshots. Millions of headshots. Agents "submit" their clients for the parts and then we call them in to audition if we think they might work out. My job also consists of calling said agents to let them know we are interested in their actors. Then I read with the actors in their auditions. Meaning if there is a dialogue, I play the role opposite them. If the actor makes it far enough, he does an audition in front of the head of ABC along with the producers of the show and they decide yes or no. If they like the actor, he or she has a job on an ABC Primetime show.

I love my job. Not only do I work for the top rated national TV network, but I get to do some acting of my own and meet tons of celebrities, famous actors and gorgeous models. I also love the people I work with…for the most part. Anna is another casting director's assistant. One year older than me, she is an ex-actor who fell into casting accidentally and harbors few bitter feelings about her failed career as an actress. But she likes her job and is very good at it. A hard worker, she is meticulous, organized and a little intense at times. She can do anything that is asked of her, and quickly. Which is fortunate, because when our bosses want something done, they want it done five minutes ago. Anna is sarcastic, witty, funny and a lot of fun to joke around with when she isn't being too neurotic. She is Hungarian so she has pale skin, red hair and interesting Eastern European features. Jason is always trying to get Anna to say anything in Hungarian because he thinks it "sounds funny." He then always laughs and calls her "crazy Hungarian bitch."

Jason is the assistant for the second casting director in the office. Jason is another ex-actor who was also a child superstar. Jason starred in commercials, TV shows and had a handful of small roles in blockbuster movies from the time he was 6 months old until he was eight, and then he just washed up. He grew out of his cute boy, innocent childlike look and no casting director would hire him for roles anymore. So after that, he tried the real-world gig, attending middle school and high school, did some modeling after that, decided he was sick of being in front of the camera and called the casting director who had cast him in so many projects over the years, she recommended him to the people at ABC, and suddenly, he had a job behind the camera. And Jason loves being behind the camera just as much as he loved being in front of it. He has a passion for his work. And he has a passion for celebrities as well. Especially good-looking male ones. Jason is charismatic, loud, over-the-top, gorgeous and flamingly gay. I always have so much fun working and gossiping with Jason.

Mya is the fourth assistant in the office. Technically, she's an intern, because she doesn't get paid. Technically Anna, Jason and I get paid, but not much. Mya is twenty-one, Asian and also strikingly pretty. She got the intern job because she wanted to be an actress and thought it would be beneficial to experience the other side: what casting directors did, what they were looking for, etc… It was smart, really, and so is Mya. While acting, Mya is nothing but professional. She speaks well and loudly and confidently and with no accent because she is from Iowa. But when the cameras stopp rolling and she is in real life, Mya talks like a black girl from the ghetto. It's bizarre and hilarious at the same time. Here is this gorgeous, stylish, tiny Korean girl who looks so demure and sweet and proper, and when she opens her mouth it is almost unintelligible because of the slang she uses. She is the nicest girl in the world, but we all make fun of her constantly for speaking in a way that sounds akin to Ebonics. She doesn't see anything wrong or abnormal about this and Jason preys on this fact, making fun of her every chance he gets.

I enjoy my job very much. It's fast-paced, exciting, exhilarating and fun. It's also exhausting at times, but I can handle it. The assistants with whom I work just make it that much better. For the most part, the Casting Directors are nice people. They get stressed, sure, and yell at us on a daily basis. But we know how to take it. Rachel is Anna's boss and she is the head honcho. Rachel is older and has been working as a Casting Director for ABC for upwards of twenty years. She is kind and competent and everyone loves Rachel. Actors, assistants, her co-workers. Rachel keeps her composure at all times; I have never seen her treat anyone with anything but the utmost respect. Even though she is the head casting director for a major network, she runs the business effectively like the pro she is. Mary is Jason's boss and she mostly keeps to herself. Mary can lash out from time to time and be crazy and mean, but mostly she is a calm, normal person even with all of the insanity going on around her.

And my boss is Gary. Gary is young and successful, but he is the low man on the totem pole. They promoted Gary to Casting Director only a few months before and he hadn't had an assistant until me. So I am his first. The guinea pig. Gary had ranted and raved for months until they finally allowed him to hire someone to help him. Ranting and raving is Gary's forte. He did need help, he had needed me

accidentally, and I began to cough. Upon hearing this, Gary spun around, still spraying, and the mist shot straight out, directly into my face. I coughed violently, waving my hand back and forth in front of my mouth, and shutting my eyes tightly. "Whaaa?" I sputtered, still coughing and rubbing my eyes, as the Lysol burned my face. I opened one eye and watched Gary lunge toward his desk, set down the can and pick up a bottle of antibacterial wipes. He plucked out one white, moist towelette and began furiously scrubbing his desktop and back of his leather chair.

"Katy!" he barked again, obviously oblivious to the fact that I was coughing up a lung and was now blind. Oblivious or apathetic. He continued: "Katy! I need you to go to Duane Reade and pick me up some more Lysol spray!" He stopped scrubbing the leather on the seat of the chair and thought for a moment. "And while you're at it, pick me up some more Lysol towelettes too."

My coughing subsided enough for me to choke out a one word response: "Why?"

"Because this office is a cesspool of germs, that's why!" Gary snapped back. "Mary thinks she has pink eye and she was just in here! We need to de-germ!" Under his breath he muttered "wonder if quarantining would be frowned upon here."

Wow. I knew Gary was crazy, but this crazy? He was definitely a germaphobic, which made sense the more I thought about it. Gary always had to be in control. I couldn't imagine Gary sick or taking a day off work. The world would probably come to an end if he did. But I guessed going to get him some more Lysol wouldn't kill me. At least it was better than getting him Starbucks ten times a day.

"Any specific kind of Lysol?" I asked. "Lemon or Orange?"

"Lemon. And the lemon towelettes too," Gary said, finally ceasing the frantic scrubbing and straightening up. He looked at me and thought for a minute. "Oh, and get some of that antibacterial hand stuff. That little bottle. You can never be too careful, you know. And hurry back. Our session starts in twenty minutes."

"Right. Okay, then," I said, rolling my eyes and backing out of the room. I ran back to the assistant's office and hurriedly grabbed my purse.

Anna looked up from the computer. "More coffee?"

"Nope. Gotta go get Lysol."

"Lysol?" Jason looked confused.

"Yeah, because of your boss. Mary has pink eye?" I asked him.

"What? She does?" He looked baffled. "I didn't know that! But she did say she might go home early today." His eyes got wide as he said, "pick me up some Lysol too! We need to de-germ this office immediately!"

I rolled my eyes again. "You are as bad as Pickles."

"Don't ever compare me to Pickles again."

"Well then stop acting like a little scaredy cat baby, please. I'll be right back. I gotta hurry too, we have a session in like fifteen minutes."

"I put all your headshots in order for you so you're all set. I'll go put them in Session Room A for you," Anna offered.

"Thanks, you're the best. Is the camera all set up in there too?"

"Yep. It should be good to go from my last session. And by the way," Anna waved the headshots in front of my face, "Who is this guy who's coming in first? Sam Lazaro? I've never heard of him. But he's GORGEOUS." When she said "gorgeous" she punctuated every syllable and jabbed her pointer finger at the black and white photo.

I grabbed the photo from her and took a look. Anna was right, he was gorgeous. Tall, wavy black hair, olive skin, piercing blue eyes. (I couldn't tell all of these things from a black and white picture, obviously, but I flipped the photo over where it revealed in the info about him that he was 6'2" and had black hair and blue eyes.) I waved the picture in my hand for a second before handing it back to Anna. "He's a model," I replied. "Mostly runway stuff, and he's done some commercials. Looks like he's pretty green." (Green was an acting term for someone who hadn't done much work before or hadn't had much experience. Someone who was an amateur.) "It says he did a stint on The Young and the Restless as a guest star. Wonder why Gary's seeing him?"

"Probably because he's ridiculously hot," Jason said, snatching the picture away from Anna and fanning himself dramatically with it. "Actually, more likely, Gary's probably seeing him as a favor to Tamara." Tamara was the Casting Director for The Young and the Restless, whose offices were on the same floor as ours. Sometimes, if Tamara saw an up-and-coming actor she liked or cast in one of her episodes, she would suggest that Gary or Rachel or Mary audition him for one of our TV pilots as a favor to her. "Do we think he's gay or straight?" Jason continued.

"You KNOW that boy be STRAIGHT!" Mya interjected, peering over Jason's shoulder to take a look. "He TOO FINE to be likin that dick if you ask me, gurl!"

"Damn." Jason looked crestfallen. "Well, he's your first audition, Katy, so you'll have to let me know if he's playing for my team or yours. Which, speaking of, you better go get Pickles his antibacterial stuff soon. Your audition's in ten minutes!"

"Shit!" I yelled, "and thanks!" And I ran out of the office.

~

Nine minutes later, I bounded back onto the second floor of the ABC building. I didn't even stop in to the assistants' office, I ran straight into the audition room. I did take a quick peek to see if John Stamos was still in the waiting room. He wasn't. Bummer. He certainly wasn't one of my actors I was auditioning today. He was probably going in for a private interview with Rachel.

I ran into the room, and in one fluid motion, dropped all of the Lysol products on the table in front of Gary, spread them out nicely, leaned over, turned on the video camera, picked up my script to read dialogue with the actors, and slid into my chair. I smoothed my hair and smiled up at Gary.

"I'm ready. First up we should have Sam Lazaro. I think he's out in the lobby.

That was a lie. I had no idea if he was out there. I hadn't noticed anything but the fact that John Stamos wasn't.

Gary didn't seem to care. He was too busy squeezing a ridiculously large amount of antibacterial lotion onto his palm and rubbing his hands together in a circular motion. He held the bottle out to me and squeezed half of it onto my palm. "Alright," he said. "Send him in. What pilot are we auditioning anyway?" he said, looking at the schedule of actors I had put in front of him.

He really was out of it. The germaphobia had compromised his brain. "We're auditioning Ugly Betty, for the role of Daniel, the boss."

"Of course, of course," Gary snapped at me. "Bring in Lorenzo Lamas or whatever his name is."

I laughed in spite of Gary's stern face. "It's Sam Lazaro and he…" I trailed off as a man poked his head around the door frame. He was at least 6'2" with wavy black hair and intensely blue eyes. His build was a good size; not too big and not too thin, muscular but not overbearing. He looked practically perfect. I had seen many good-looking actors and models in the months I had been working for ABC: celebrities, regular people, you name it, most of them were hot, but this person was strikingly handsome. It had to be Sam.

"Did someone say my name? I'm Sam Lazaro, the one and only" he said in a deep voice. Then he smiled a sexy, lopsided smile, revealing two rows of perfectly straight white teeth. Wow. This guy was a charmer, I could already tell. Even Gary looked a little starstruck, and Gary never got that way. Reading with him was going to be interesting. I hoped I could keep my composure and be professional. I snapped out of my reverie and smiled back at him. Thank God I had decided to do my makeup today and wear something cute.

"Come on in and have a seat," I said, patting the chair directly across from me. "This is Gary, your casting director and I'm Katy. I'll be reading with you today."

Sam quickly shook Gary's hand. I notice him look down questioningly at his hand after he shook Gary's. It was now covered in the antibacterial goop that had still been on Gary's hand. In one fell swoop, Sam wiped his hand off on his pants and stuck it out again to shake my hand. His eyes locked directly into mine and he said "Katy. Pleasure to meet you." Then he kind of winked. It was cheesy and almost pretentious. He was an actor. Most of them were exactly that way. But I didn't even care because he was probably the hottest man I had ever seen in my life, and I loved the way he had repeated my name and looked directly at me. He sank down into the chair, and his legs were so long that his knees touched mine when he sat forward. I definitely did not mind. He could keep them there for as long as he wanted if it were up to me. "All set?" I asked as Gary flipped a switch on the camera to record the audition.

"Yup," Sam replied. "I've been rehearsing for days now. I'm ready as I'll ever be." So I started my lines and Sam started reading.

He was horrible.

Terrible.

Awful.

Literally one of the worst actors I had ever read, in an audition or otherwise. His comedic timing was non-existent, he didn't stress the right syllables on many words and he made the wrong choices as an actor. He didn't bounce off of me at all, didn't read well with me, but I had a feeling he wouldn't read well with Laurence Olivier or any other amazing actor, he was that bad. He had no spark or life to him, no emotion or empathy, it was like he was just reading the words, and it was obvious he was just reading. It was like he had never seen the material before. It took everything I had not to cringe and I had read with some bad actors before. It was like he was some gorgeous, dumb, male model reading a script. Which was literally the situation, I realized.

When the two minutes were up (two minutes that felt like a lifetime) Sam thanked Gary and shook his hand again. He then turned to me and smiled that dazzling smile again. "And Katy," he said, "thank-you. You are an excellent reader. I hope to be seeing you again soon." With that, he did the cheesy wink again and headed toward the exit. Gary and I watched his back as he turned to leave and followed him with our eyes all the way out the door. When the latch finally clicked into place behind him, Gary threw the pile of headshots he was holding down on the table in frustration.

"Fucking Tamara!" he yelled.

"Was he one of her actors?" I asked, innocently, knowing the answer.

"Yes! I give her chance after fucking chance to send me any of the 'good' ones! One of her 'good' day players! And what does she send me? That?! Fucking sorry excuse for an actor. Fucking model turned wanna-be actor cheeseball! HOW am I supposed to put someone like that on my 8 o clock primetime fucking time slot?! I'd be laughed out of ABC forever!" He finished his rant and said, much more calmly, "too bad he's hot. Did you think he was good-looking?" He turned to me.

"Are you kidding me?" I screeched. "Good-looking?! That's the understatement of the century! He's GORGEOUS. SO HOT! But you're right, worst actor ever," I finished more calmly, leaning back in my chair.

"Thought so. That's what I was afraid of," Gary mused. "Tamara did say he couldn't act for shit but his looks more than made up for it. Okay," he said, opening the door. "Go get him and bring him in for our guest star role in the pilot. The audition we're holding for the role on Wednesday? You know which role I'm talking about right? Pete or whatever? Don't call his agent, he's with Paradigm for TV and I don't want to deal with talking to Marsha about him, just run out in the hall and catch him. You know which role I like him for, right? Pete or whatever? "

"Yep! Paul!" I corrected him, already opening the door handle. I didn't want to miss him before he left. I had to see him again. I bounded down the hall where I saw him waiting for the elevator with his perfect posture and stance. "Sam!" I called, catching up to him. "Gary wants me to tell you to come to the audition for the guest star role for this episode! Next Tuesday at, let's say…1:05? Can you make it then?" I asked breathlessly, losing myself in his blue eyes. I nervously plucked at the hem of my dress as I spoke.

"Well, well, well…Katy," he said my name again. I was melting. "I'm sure I can make that. I would be honored."

Again with the cheesiness, but I barely registered that. "I appreciate it. And what is it you usually do after work in the evenings? I mean, after reading so professionally and poetically with zillions of actors? After your job which you seem like you are very good at? Like say, what is a hot little number like you doing tomorrow after work?" he winked again. Well. If that wasn't the cheesiest, worst pick-up line I had ever heard. But was it a pick-up line? Was I really being picked up by the hottest actor I had ever seen? I certainly hoped so. I was practically jumping up and down with excitement. It took everything I had not to literally jump up and down in front of him. That would be dorky. So I decided to try to play it cool. Just nonchalantly say that I usually had plans or something fabulous to do every Tuesday after work. Very chill.

"NOTHING!" I screamed. "I usually do nothing at all! Absolutely nothing! No plans tomorrow after work! None! No plans at all! Nope! Not me!"

Jesus. So much for nonchalant.

Sam laughed. At least he seemed amused. "Katy, Katy," he said, shaking his head back and forth. He sure enjoyed saying my name, and I liked it. "well, how about this... you and I can go out on Wednesday after you're done with work...if you're not busy? Which...it sounds like you're not," he chuckled again, "and we can grab some drinks and you can give me some pointers on my audition, how does that sound?" The wink again.

Was this a date? Was Sam Lazaro asking me out on a date? Wait until the guys found out about this. They were going to be green with envy. But first I had to say yes.

"Yes!" I said, a little too loudly, again. "I mean, yes," I said in a more controlled voice. "I'd love to go out with you on Wednesday! I'll see you after work."

"Great," Sam said, squeezing my arm. "It's a date then. See you at 6 on Wednesday," and he stepped into the elevator and the doors swallowed him immediately.

I skipped back to the audition room. I would have to wait to tell Anna, Jason and Mya because I was already late for the next actor. I sailed into the room as if on a cloud. I was going on a date with the hottest up-and-coming actor in LA. Okay, maybe he couldn't act, but that didn't matter. He was a model and he was hot, and everyone was going to be so envious. I stole a look at Gary out of the corner of my eye as I glided into my chair for the next audition. He was looking at me out of the corner of his eye. Even he must have been jealous.

Here's the thing about actors: they're weird. Very strange. They are not normal people. I say this because there was a time when I wanted to become an actress as my profession. I never did act professionally, save for a commercial or two, but during the time when I was acting, I met a lot of other actors, obviously, and they were very odd. Great, wonderful, caring, creative, fun, amazing people, but weird as hell. I think it might have something to do with the fact that actors spend their whole lives trying to be other people, or channel other people, so that leaves little time for them to spend on bettering themselves, and little time for them to spend on figuring out who they, themselves are. This is just a little theory of mine, but I'm sticking to it, because every actor I met, and trust me, I met hundreds of them, was like this.

Sam was no exception. I'm not sure why I expected him to be any different than any of the others, but he wasn't. But he was the first actor I really dated. Definitely the first actor/model who actually made his living by doing so. It was for this reason that I decided to give him a chance. That, and the fact that he was the hottest guy I had ever seen, let alone dated.

He wanted to meet me at a bar in West Hollywood called Hydrate. I liked the bar okay, I had been there a few times before, but with my gay friends. West Hollywood was known for its gay and lesbian scene, so I thought the area was a strange choice for a first date, but I had quickly shunned the idea of anything suspicious going on. Jason had helped quell my fears as well. When I found out where Sam wanted to meet, I had called him right away to take advantage of his extremely dependable and reliable gay-dar. Jason had sworn up and down that Sam "definitely isn't gay, girl," and when I still didn't believe him, he assured me that he had even given him some "gay signal" when he saw how hot he was, just to make sure, and he hadn't picked up on it at all. So after knowing that Sam was "100% hetero" as Jason had put it, I chalked up the bar choice to him being a weird actor and met him there.

He was sitting at a table in the back of the bar, with a water in front of him. He was wearing a light blue polo shirt that brought out the color of his eyes and his skin looked tan. His hair looked perfect and he was drumming his fingers on the table nervously and looking around. I could already sense all of the girls and guys' eyes on him. The straight girls, gay girls and gay guys (there were no straight guys there, there never were) all of them were fixated on him, but he didn't seem to notice. As I made my way to the back to sit down at his table, I could sense everyone's eyes on me as well. They looked at me with venom and malice once they realized I was going to join the hottest guy in the place. I heard one buff, gay man actually heave a sigh of exasperation when I took the seat across from Sam, and he realized he was straight. I still didn't understand why he had wanted to come to a gay bar when he was obviously the star attraction, but then again, that was probably just the reason. He was an actor. Actors love any kind of attention, always.

"Hi there," I said, sitting down and smoothing the skirt of my dress. "You look nice."

Sam smiled slowly and took a sip of his water. "Thanks, so do you, Katy." This guy sure loved saying my name. Not that I minded at all.

"Are you drinking water?" I asked, looking around for a server.

"Yeah, trying to keep my boyish figure in check. I can't stay very long anyway, unfortunately. I have to go prepare for an another audition."

My face fell. "That's cool," I said, not doing very well at hiding my annoyance. Sam sensed my disappointment and leaned across the table to nudge my hand. "But I definitely wanted to come and at least buy you a drink. The cutest casting assistant I ever did see." It was probably the cheesiest thing I had ever heard, but because it came out of his perfect mouth, I melted.

"Well, in that case, I'll get a drink," I said, blushing and signaling the waiter who had finally appeared. I ordered and the waiter brought my drink. I had barely taken the first sip when Sam said "So, Katy, how long have you worked at ABC? You like being a casting assistant? Seems like hard work. You could be an actress with how sexy you are. Ever thought about being in front of the camera?"

"I've worked there for a few months. I really love being a casting assistant and yes, it is hard work, but fulfilling and fast-paced which I like. And I used to want to be an actress, but I like working on the other side of the camera more. Thanks for the compliment." I was still melting.

"Cool." Sam seemed disinterested in my answer, as his eyes richoched back and forth across the room. They finally settled on the gay, buff guy, lingered there for a second and then he snapped back to me. "No, that's cool," he repeated.

I cocked my head and said "Can I ask you a question?"

"Sure."

"Why did you choose this bar? I mean, I like this place, but…I should rephrase…why West Hollywood"

Sam looked at me and laughed. "You mean why would I pick a gay bar? Are you wondering if I'm gay? You are, aren't you, Katy?"

"Well, um…I guess so." I was embarrassed.

"I'll tell you why I picked this bar. I'm new to Los Angeles and this place is close to my house. I came here once before with a friend and it's one of the only places I know to go. So that's why I asked you to meet me here. Does that make sense to you?" he asked, a little condescendingly.

"Oh, sure!" I stammered. "I'm sorry, I just wondered, I'm too curious sometimes. This place is great! Not a problem! I didn't mean to be presumptuous or rude," I finished jamming my straw into my mouth and taking a long sip.

"It's alright," Sam said a little defensively with a hard look. Then he softened. "I asked you here because you seemed like a cool girl. And cute too. A proper date with a cool, cute girl."

I found it interesting he considered this a proper date. He was buying me one drink, he wasn't even drinking, and he had to leave in ten minutes. But I stole one quick glance at his gorgeous face and forgave him. If nothing else, he had called me cool and cute so he must have thought so. He was good at flattery, that much was obvious.

"So," he continued, leaning his elbows on the table and staring straight into my eyes, his face inches from mine, "did I blow the audition for Daniel?"

I thought he was making a joke so I threw my head back and laughed.

Sam's face remained completely stern. "In your highly professional opinion, of course," he said, still staring.

Oh. He was serious. This was awkward.

"Um, well," I stammered, slurping the rest of my drink. "Well, okay, obviously you didn't BLOW it. Pickles…I mean Gary, obviously wants to see you for the role of Paul so that's good?" I half stated, half asked, raising my eyebrows.

Sam slammed his hand on the table and pouted. "But that's just a day player role. My agent gave me the script so I know. I totally blew it for Daniel, I know I did!"

I was surprised by his outburst. What did he want me to say to him? "You are a terrible actor, one of the worst in the world, so yes, you obviously blew the audition for the main role, and the only reason you are even getting another chance for a tiny role is because you are probably the most hot guy in the world?" I could have said that to him, but thought that might hurt his feelings. Either that, or it would have boosted his ego. You never knew with actors. So I kept my mouth shut. I felt like I really shouldn't be talking to him about his audition, anyway. There was no hard stated rule against it, but my own moral code told me I probably shouldn't be divulging information or opinions that had been learned or formed at ABC. It was my job and there was a certain understood code of secrecy when it came to the actors and their auditions.

Sam looked at me out of the corner of his eye as I continued to be silent. "Do you think you could put in a good word for me? I could really use this role, even if it is just a day player one. Unless you think you might be able to get me in to see Gary again to read for Daniel?"

Was he kidding? He was either delusional or simply ignorant of how bad of an actor he actually was. And was he actually asking me to do that for him? Did he think this was how it worked? I might be able to put in a good word for him for the role of Paul but I doubted that would even do anything. I was only an assistant, and I really didn't have much pull with anything. It was Gary's project and Gary was definitely opinionated. And if, and that was a big if, he made it past Gary, he would still have to audition in front of the producers and the heads of the network. There was no way his looks were going to get him that far. I also had a feeling that putting in a good word for an actor was way beyond my jurisdiction. Especially an actor who was wining and dining me…with one drink…at a gay bar.

He sensed my hesitation again and said "Look, okay, never mind. How about you and I go out to dinner Friday night? I'll take you to a really nice place and we'll have some drinks and sushi. I really like you, Katy, it's so refreshing to meet a woman in Los Angeles that seems like a cool, down-to-earth girl. And super cute, too." He was starting to sound like a broken record. But I was surprised to find that I didn't mind. He was charming me with those damn good looks of his. Like any other girl, I enjoy being flattered, especially by gorgeous male runway models.

"Okay!" I said, a little too excitedly. "Friday sounds good."

"Great," he said, standing up. "See you Friday then. And," he continued, pinching me on the shoulder, "If you decide you wanna put in that good word for me, I would really appreciate it. You'd be helping out a struggling actor. And not only would you be the coolest, cutest casting assistant around, but I'd love you forever, Katy."

I sighed. "I'll see what I can do," I lied.

"Great! You're the best!" Sam kissed me on the cheek and I felt like jumping for joy. Everyone in the restaurant saw it, even buff gay guy and after Sam kissed me I saw him shoot buff, gay guy a look for one second. Then he turned back around to face me and said "Can't wait for Friday, sexy," and strode out of the room.

I couldn't wait, either.

~

Friday night came and went. Sam met me for dinner like he promised. He looked spectacular and all eyes were on him, as usual. He took me to an expensive sushi restaurant on the Sunset Strip, one that I had been hearing about, but never had the cash to go. We had drinks and dinner and lovely conversation. I could tell that everyone in the place was insanely jealous of me. I love when other people, especially women, are jealous of me and so I pretended Sam was my boyfriend, my famous actor/model boyfriend and he had chosen me to be his girlfriend, above all the other gorgeous actress/model women. It was nice to be in a little dream world, but it also made me oblivious to the fact that Sam was being rude.

It was just little annoying things that I noticed at first, like on the first date. Sam's eyes kept darting around the restaurant, as if he was looking for someone better than me, or as if he was wishing he were with someone other than me. He didn't pay much attention to me, he seemed distracted and kept checking his phone, which I find extremely rude, especially on a first date. And all he wanted to talk about was his audition and how he could improve his acting skills. About which I really did not want to talk. One, because I felt uncomfortable doing so, and two because I truly felt it would be impossible for Sam to improve his acting skills whatsoever.

I had googled him after our first date like the model stalker I had become. I had found some of his small roles on The Young and the Restless and All My Children and a few national commercials he had done. It seemed to me, in my "professional opinion" that he had snagged all of these roles because of his looks. They were ridiculous, silly roles, roles in which he acted way too dramatically and over the top. He had no sense of timing, and he didn't seem to make smart choices, much like in his audition for Daniel in Ugly Betty. So I didn't think there was hope for Sam. But I didn't have the heart to tell him. And I wanted him to like me.

Then, when he realized I was keeping mum about the whole acting situation, he became increasingly agitated. He began begging me to put in a good word for him and to help him out. It was similar to the time at the gay bar, but this time he was more insistent. He seemed kind of drunk and kept whining about how he really needed the role of Daniel to break out of the "daytime soap slump" he was currently in. His begging was unattractive and starting to really bother me so I shut my mouth and concentrated on eating. Sam finally got a clue and dropped it. We sat in awkward silence for what seemed like forever.

Finally, I finished my entrée and Sam smiled at me. He then suggested we get dessert and finish the night off right with a nightcap at his apartment. I liked the sound of that. Maybe I would finally get the chance to hook up with the hottest man I had ever seen. He then persuaded me that he really liked me and would love nothing more than to spend the night with me. He even set up a date with me for Monday night. I reminded him that that was the night before his audition, but he insisted that he wanted to see me again and that he thoroughly enjoyed my company. I pushed all thoughts of his rudeness and tackiness from my mind. I couldn't wait to see him again either, and I definitely couldn't wait to spend the night.

~

Spending the night went…halfheartedly at best. Hooking up for the first time is always awkward and almost never goes well, but this particular hookup was kind of like Sam's acting skills: awful. He was a horrible kisser, and it felt to me like it was a chore for him to make out with me. He fumbled around with my clothes, especially my bra, and I had to take it off myself. We didn't do much: made out and awkwardly groped, and then just as abruptly as Sam had started to make out, he stopped, rolled over and went to sleep. Or pretended to go to sleep. Either he was pretending or he was the fastest person to fall asleep I had ever seen. In the morning, I got up early and slipped out quietly. I had to go to work and Sam was sleeping in. He made it clear that he wanted to sleep in because he told me that if I woke him up he would be very upset. At first, I thought he was kidding, but when I realized he was serious, I decided to just leave and see him on Monday. It was time to talk to my Vice President of the Jerk Magnets Anonymous club.

Erin swooped into the bench seat across from me at Bar 21. We had decided to meet there again, as it was halfway between both of our workplaces.

"Okay, shoot…details!" she said, resting her chin in her hands and blinking her wide, blue eyes at me. Her blond hair swung around her face and she looked excited. "Did you do it? Did you have sex with Sam? Was it amazing?" Her excitement was apparent.

"Um, no," I said slowly.

"Did you give him head?"

"No."

"What? Why not?" she screeched. She flipped her head back as our waitress showed up. "Oh, man, we're going to need tequila for this story, I can just tell. Two shots of Jose Cuervo please. Make that four shots." The waitress scurried away.

"Don't you have to work?" I asked incredulously.

"Later, yes, and don't change the subject! So you just made out? Why didn't you just get down there? He's so hot!" I had showed Erin his headshot a few days ago.

"I know, but, we just didn't get there. We kissed and there was some feeling around. No big deal. It was nice to kind of take it slow you know?"

"Bullshit!" Erin yelled, picking up the first shot that had arrived at our table and pouring it down her throat. "That is such bullshit and you know it! If I know you, and I do, I know that none of what you just said is the truth!"

She did know me well. It was totally not true.

"Okay," I sighed, picking up my own shot and taking it back. "It's not true. It was weird. Really weird. First of all, he's a bad kisser."

"Oh!" Erin waved her hand in the air dismissively. "Then, that's it. Done. You can't be with a bad kisser." I sat there silently so she continued. "Did he touch your boobs?"

"Yes. Barely."

"Barely? Who is this guy? Did he seem into you?"

"To be honest, he seemed kind of not into it at all."

"Wait, did he get hard?"

"Yeah. Sorta."

"Okay, let me get this straight," Erin picked up her second shot and fingered it thoughtfully. "He took you to a gay bar for your first date, and he's definitely using you," she was ticking off the points on each finger. "He's a bad kisser, he barely touched your boobs, he didn't have sex with you, didn't even TRY to have sex with you, didn't seem into it, and didn't get hard. He's a model and an actor and he's gorgeous. He's gay."

I sat back suddenly in the booth in shock. "He's not gay!"

"Katy, he's totally gay."

"No way."

"Have you ever hooked up with a guy in his bed who did not try to have sex with you?"

I thought for a minute. "No," I said, reluctantly.

"I think he's gay. Seriously. But either way, he sounds like a jerk. And he's definitely using you too."

"How is he using me?"

"To get roles at ABC! He's basically admitted it to you. And you're just going along with it. It's fine if you're having fun and he's a cool guy, but he sounds like someone who isn't even into you at all. You deserve better than that."

I thought about defending him. I thought about denying what Erin was saying was true. But I knew she was right. Deep down I knew and I had wanted to talk to her because I knew she would tell me. I didn't want to give up just yet, though. I wanted to go out with him again. I wanted to give him one more chance to redeem himself. I wanted to prove that he wasn't gay, that he wasn't using me. Although, if he was gay it would actually help to explain away the horrible hookup and make me feel better.

I straightened my shoulders and took the second shot. "Okay, well, I'm going out with him Monday night. I'm going to give him one more chance to redeem himself. He may be a jerk, but I don't think he's gay. Besides," I continued, fumbling around for the right words to say. "I really want to go out with him again because…he's gorgeous."

Erin clucked her tongue at me. "He is that," she agreed with me, "But is that reason enough to go out with someone who is using you and is most likely a homosexual? I just don't want to see you get hurt."

"I won't," I said. "This is just casual. I don't really think anything is going to come out of it."

"So why are you doing it?"

"I don't know, okay? I just want to go out with him on Monday!" I was getting extremely defensive at this point.

She looked at me with a look that said a million words, but all she said was "Alright. I just hope you're right. I hope he treats you well on Monday. If not, you're done, okay? Or I'll come and find him and kill his good-looking gay ass."

I laughed. "You have my permission. Can we change the subject now and talk about the nurse you've been flirting with?"

"Sure. Nothing more has really happened with that, though. I'll let you know if it does. But…" she winked at me playfully, "he may be a jerk, but at least he's not gay too."

"Erin," I said "are you sure about that?"

"Well, yeah, why? I mean, why would he be gay?"

"He's a male nurse."

She laughed and shook her head as she signaled the waitress for more drinks. "Touche, my friend. Touche."

~

Sam and I met for coffee on Monday evening. I had wanted to have dinner or drinks, but Sam had persuaded me to do something chill because of his audition the next day. He was in a horrible mood from the minute he sat down with me at a Starbucks in midtown. It was crowded and noisy and I hate coffee, so I was in a horrible mood, too. He didn't even offer to pay for my coffee, just got his triple skim latte and flounced down at a table. I took my seat across from him.

"So, how was your day?" I asked, trying to make the best of the situation.

"Fucking terrible," he said. "Fucking Tamara wouldn't bring me in for the day player role on Young and the Restless. She ALWAYS brings me in," he said as he slammed his coffee cup on the table. A little of the brown liquid sloshed over the side of his cup, and he jammed it up to his mouth to take a sip. "Fuck that's hot!" he exclaimed.

Whoa. Guess horrible mood was an understatement.

"I suppose you wouldn't be able to put in a good word for me with Tamara for Y & R would you?" he asked, swinging his coffee cup around. "Oh, wait," he said, sarcastically and cocking his head to the side, while looking up at the ceiling. "I doubt it. It doesn't seem like you want to help me with my career at all."

I was taken aback by his attitude so I decided to ignore his last comment. "Well..." I started, trying to seem upbeat and positive, "there's always tomorrow. You have your audition for Paul. Have you been rehearsing?" I tickled my fingers over his hand that was resting on the table.

Sam jerked his hand away, glared at me and deadpanned "yeah, I have been just rehearsing and rehearsing for the Emmy-worthy role of Paul on Ugly Betty. Fucking five lines, what a joke. All because someone wouldn't put in a good word for me for the role I SHOULD have nailed." When he said "someone," he glared directly at me. He then grabbed his blackberry and started texting on it.

"Excuse me?" I said, incredulous. Was he really being this rude? Was he really blaming me for his bad day and less-than-stellar acting skills?

"You heard me," he barked back, his normally gorgeous blue eyes flashing acidly, as he continued to text on his phone.

"Did you just yell at me for the fact that you blew your own audition? You're lucky Gary is bringing you in for Paul. Just make the best of it tomorrow!" My heart was beating quickly in my chest, I was so surprised by his outburst.

"Oh yeah, because that role is the only one I'm cut out to play, right? Stupid five line role. Look at me!" he gestured toward himself, blackberry still in hand. "Look at me and tell me that I shouldn't be a lead role in the hottest new TV show. I'm a fucking model! Do you see how much attention I get? They'd be crazy not to put me on a network pilot!"

Oh my God. I couldn't believe my ears. I had never met anyone so vain in my entire life. Him talking was now literally making me sick to my stomach. And his gorgeous face suddenly seemed sickeningly unattractive. His true personality was making him ugly. I was speechless, but that didn't matter because Sam just continued his rant.

"And Katy, I'm so disappointed in you. I take you out to a nice restaurant for an expensive dinner, I buy you drinks, I invite you over to my apartment, I let you sleep in my bed, and I guarantee I'm the hottest guy you've ever made out with, you know that's true, and you STILL refuse to help me get the audition I want. I NEED. Thanks a lot. Really. You've been such a big help to me." He stopped texting and looked at me. "Then the only thing you can say to me is to ask if I have been preparing adequately for the joke of the role of Paul with five lines. You and Gary can take the role of Paul and shove it. Seriously. Thanks for all your help, bitch. You're lucky I even did you a favor to be seen out with you this past week. I gotta take a piss." And with that, he stood up and headed for the bathroom.

I sat there, stunned for twenty seconds, watching his muscular back retreat. Tears stung my eyes and I was on the verge of breakdown. I had never been spoken to in such a way by someone so self-involved. I was hurt and upset, and I couldn't believe I had defended such a jerk. He had been using me. How could I have been so stupid? I had been so blinded by his good looks that I hadn't even realized what a worthless human being he was. I decided to save whatever was left of my self-worth and pride and leave. I had never done that before, but this situation warranted me dashing away without warning. I stood up and smoothed my skirt as the tears began tumbling down my face. I ignored the looks of confusion I received from the other people sitting around me as I banged into their table with my thigh on my way toward the exit. I pushed out the door as my phone started to ring. I ignored it and headed for my car, the tears still falling down my face.

~

"Oh my God, Gary, where are the headshots for the audition?" I asked, frantically searching through the file cabinets at the back of the room. I had looked all over the place, trying to find the stack of headshots that were needed for the Paul audition, the one that started in five minutes.

"What audition?" Gary asked, a little too nonchalantly.

"What do you mean 'what audition?'" I asked, still running around like a chicken with its head cut off. "The Paul audition! The one starting in like two minutes! You need the headshots for the actors!" I was panicking.

"Um, the headshots I asked for this morning?"

"YES! Those headshots!"

"The ones you gave me the minute I asked for them?" Gary gave me a quizzical look. "They're in my hand currently." He waved a sheaf of papers in the air, with a mocking tone in his voice. "See?"

"Oh," I said, finally realizing that they were, in fact, in his hands. I slumped down in the reader's chair. "I'm sorry, Gary, I must be losing my mind."

"Uh, you think?" Gary asked, looking at me like I was dumbest person in the world. "What the hell is wrong with you today? You've gone completely insane."

I sighed. "I know. I'm sorry. I feel like I have gone crazy."

"It's okay. What's going on?" Gary looked at me with a look of semi-interest as he continued setting up the video camera.

I was freaking out. It was the day of the Paul audition and Sam was due to read in ten minutes. I was dreading it. I hadn't spoken to him since I had walked out of the Starbucks days before. He had tried to call me a few times and sent a few texts, but I had ignored them all. They were all apologetic texts, but along with the apologies were lame questions directed at me, making sure I wasn't going to keep him from auditioning for the Paul role. He knew he had screwed up. He seemed to maybe, kind of realize that he had been a jerk, but he was still too worried about his burgeoning career to really see how he had hurt my feelings.

I had realized something over the past few days. I had realized Erin was right. Sam had never liked me. Sure, he probably thought I was cute and cool to some extent, but he had been downright using me. Why he thought that he would get anywhere by taking out a lowly casting assistant and flattering her was beyond me, I had no control over his career whatsoever. But he obviously didn't know that. That was the other thing about certain actors in LA. They were odd, and many of them only cared about what others could do for them. How they could benefit from the situation. They didn't care who they had to step on, or offend, they were going to do it to get ahead. It was a cutthroat profession, one in which many had to kill or be killed. And some of them took that to heart.

And I knew this. I wasn't stupid. I think I had just been swayed by his charm and good looks. His insanely good looks. I had never been out with anyone so hot. But in the end, that didn't matter because Sam turned out to be a jerk. I realized I hadn't really even enjoyed his company. He wasn't funny or witty or interesting. He was actually quite boring and one-dimensional. I had just liked the thought of him. The thought of being seen with someone so handsome. But that got old very quickly, especially after he had said all of those terrible things to me. So I pushed him from my mind. I didn't need him, I didn't need him at all. I had just been caught up in the fun and excitement of dating a model and actor, but a horrible actor at that.

I threw myself a pity party for about a day, and then I got over it. That was all Sam was worth anyway, a pity party for 24 hours. Then I picked myself up, deleted his number from my phone and went on with my life. It's not like we had had some serious relationship; we had had three dates. It was just difficult to remember all of the things he had said to me. But then I erased those from my mind as well, and tried not to give them another thought.

And now I would have to face Sam in about seven minutes. I was dreading it, obviously, and it was making me act like a completely scatterbrained fool. I was so nervous I thought my hands would never stop shaking. I sighed again.

"Gary, can I ask you a question?"

"I suppose," Gary said, distractedly, still fiddling with the video camera.

"Sam Lazaro?" I started.

"The one coming in today? Terrible actor, hot Sam?" Gary asked, still not looking at me.

"Yeah, him."

"What about him?"

"Do you think he's…gay?"

Gary's head snapped up and his hands fell away from the video camera. "Do I think he's gay?" he repeated. Then he threw back his head and guffawed loudly.

"What's so funny?" I asked. "Was that a stupid question?"

Gary stopped laughing long enough to choke out an answer: "Honey, that boy is gayer than I am…and that's pretty gay!" He continued laughing.

"Are you sure?" I asked, startled.

"Am I sure? Yes I'm sure! What kind of question is that? You know I know every twink, fag, fairy and bear from this side of town to Timbuktu! Am I sure?!" he repeated, mocking me. "Yes, I'm fairly sure. He even dated a friend of my ex. Sam. Lazaro. Likes. Boys," he said, stressing every word.

Well, there you had it. He was a jerk, and he was gay. A gay, asshole, actor jerk. I had made out with a gay man. Thank God I hadn't done much more. I was relieved, and knowing that fact somehow made it better. At least I wasn't denied by a heterosexual male. It was going to be easier not to pine over someone who wasn't interested in me, let alone women in general. I would learn from this situation. I had already learned one thing: Jason's gaydar was shit. I should have known he was too hot to be straight.

Just then, Mya burst into the room. "Yo, Pick…I mean, Gary."

"What is it Mya?"

"Jus' wanted to let ya know that Sam Lazaro's agent be callin'. He goin' to pass on the Paul role. He ain't comin' in today, yo. Jus' a heads up. Peace!" Before Mya shut the door, she gave me the thumbs up sign and winked. "Yea, gurl!" she said, before slamming the door.

I felt like a weight had been lifted off my shoulders. What a relief, again. I wouldn't have to see him. He wasn't going to audition. Thank God.

"Fucking Tamara!" Gary yelled, giving the video camera a wimpy punch. "These fucking actors she sends me I swear to God! He's PASSING on the role?! The role wasn't even his to pass on! Who does he think he is? Johnny Depp? I'll tell you what, he is no Johnny Depp! He is LUCKY I even gave him a chance to audition for this role considering he was one of the worst actors I have ever seen. And now he's offending me by PASSING on the audition for a day player role with 5 lines?! Fucking models who think they can act just cause they're hot passing on my projects! He is never to audition for me, Rachel or Mary, EVER AGAIN! KATY!" he said, suddenly switching gears after his rant and addressing me. "I want you to call Sam Lazaro's agent at Paradigm and make it clear that Sam is not welcome to audition at ABC for ANY role, ever. Then I want you to walk down the hall to the Young and Restless office and tell fucking Tamara that Sam Lazaro is a jerk and the worst actor I have ever seen. Literally the worst actor I have ever seen in my entire career."

I looked at him in shock. "You can't be serious-you have got to be kidding. You actually want me to do those things?"

Gary turned and said "Do I look like I'm kidding?"

He did not.

"Okay, then, I'll just go and do that now. Gladly," I added under my breath.

"And hurry up," Gary said, jiggling the video camera. "Now where did I put those headshots?" I heard him mumble as I headed toward the door.

I smiled a secret smile as I walked down the hallway to do Pickles' bidding.

~

"You were right," I said, into the phone as I drove down Pico Boulevard. "You were totally right. Sam is gay." I was leaving work after the audition. I had called Erin right away.

"I knew it!" Erin's voice came at me from the other end of the line. "How did you find out?"

"I asked Gary. He said he was a big hit in the gay community." I sighed. "I don't know why I didn't listen to you, Erin, I'm really sorry."

"No apology necessary," she said. "I'm just sad that it didn't work out. Are you okay?"

"I'm fine, and I'm not sad that it didn't work out. You were right. He was a jerk and he was using me. Why, I don't know, considering he didn't even show up for his audition today." I laughed at the irony of what I was saying.

"He didn't? Well, that's good for you. But seriously, that guy wasn't even worth it. So what he was hot? He also likes dick."

"Nice, Erin."

"Well, he does. And I can't have my best friend involved with some guy who is putting her down and expecting her to get him roles on TV shows. You said the guy couldn't even act, right?"

"Not at all."

"So, good. He sucks, he's gay and that's it. Hey, at least you got to go out with a really gorgeous model. Just think about it that way and move on. We'll find you someone else, don't you worry. Speaking of, let's go for happy hour. Hey! Hydrate has a really good happy hour, wanna meet there?"

"Erin," I said, making a face into the receiver. "No more gay bars. In fact, no more West Hollywood…until I find a boyfriend."

"Oh, right," she said, chuckling. "Sore subject. Let's go to the straightest bar we can think of. How about that one on Wilshire? Wall Street. I heard it's chock full of good-looking, rich men in suits."

"It's actually called Wall Street?"

"Yup."

"I'm in. Brilliant. I will meet you there in twenty minutes."

I hung up the phone and signaled to turn left onto Fairfax which would take me to Wilshire. From there, it was a straight shot.

Chapter 2

John

We all got the text at the same time. All three of us heard our phones ding simultaneously and reached for them automatically. Jason was the first to get to his. He looked down at the message, shook his head and looked at the two of us. He waved his phone in the air and confusedly asked "do either of you know what this means?" I looked at my screen and read the text: it was from Mya and said:

"Ay, waddup homies. On da bus now, Ima b late fo sho tell Picks fo me, yo, luvs yoos."

Anna read it at the same time and started laughing uncontrollably. "Well, she's on the bus now and we're supposed to tell Picks aka Pickles aka Gary that she's going to be late."

Jason shook his head again and sighed. "I know. I mean, I gathered as much after I read it again, but that girl is unbelievable. Why can't she just talk like a normal human being? Why does it have to be all ghetto? And the girl is

Korean, does she even realize this? She's KOREAN, not black!"

"I have no idea," I answered him, "but I'm glad she doesn't talk all normal. Her texts are hilarious. I love reading them and trying to decipher what they actually mean. It takes me a good three times, but I usually figure it out. It gives me some entertainment in an otherwise humdrum world."

"What humdrum world are you living in?" Anna asked, skeptically. "You work at ABC where nothing is ever boring, unfortunately. Don't you have like 5 auditions to run today? And by the way, I'm not going to tell Pickles that Mya is going to be late. This is like her third time this month and he is going to freak. Not it!" she shouted, her hand shooting straight up into the air.

"Not it!" Jason said, putting his hand up as well.

I sighed. "Guess that means I have to tell him."

"Well, you ARE his superstar assistant," Anna pointed out. "That means you have to tell him."

"Ugh," I said. "Pickles is so annoying. And I have to be with him all day long because yes, we have 5 auditions today. So much to do."

Jason, Anna and I were all gathered in the office on Monday morning, waiting for one of the casting directors to come in and yell at us to start doing some work. So far, we had made it almost an hour without that happening. We were gossiping about the weekend, and dreading the week ahead. It was a few months before one of the two TV sweeps weeks of the year, so it was the busiest time for us. All three assistants had to run at least three auditions a day to fill roles in the upcoming episodes of the primetime shows. We spent our days during these busy times running around from the office to the audition rooms, collecting headshots, reading with actors, doing whatever the Casting Directors told us to do, and being on the phone with agents. It seemed like we were constantly on the phone with agents as they begged and pleaded with us to try to convince our bosses to give their clients auditions. This downtime on Monday morning was sacred; the first hour before things really kicked into gear was our time to catch up.

As I was reluctantly heading out the door to tell Gary about his intern being late, I ran smack into Mya. She careened around the corner, smashed into me, and flung her bag on the desk. "Ay! Im here! I made it! Yall didn't tell Picks bout me bein late yet, did ya? Sorry!"

"Nope," I answered her, rubbing my shoulder where she had hit me with her purse "You're safe. I don't think he has any clue that any of us are even here. No one has come in to yell at us yet, and it's almost 10:30. This must be some kind of record."

"It's like, too good to be true," Jason agreed with me, spinning around in his chair. "The phone hasn't even rung yet." Immediately, as he said that, his line rang. "Damnit," he said, stopping his spin and picking up the phone.

"How was yalls weekend?" Mya asked digging through her bag for something. "Do sumthin fun? I met homeboy out at da club. He was hood as heyll! But cute as heyll too no doubt."

"I hung out with the boyfriend," Anna interjected, blushing. "He took me to a fabulous restaurant and then we just stayed in all day yesterday and relaxed."

"Well how nice for both of you," I said, sarcastically. "I'm glad to hear you're off meeting boys in clubs and having amazing dates with your outstanding boyfriends. But not me, oh no, I didn't have a date this weekend. And I don't have a boyfriend. It's just peachy for me."

Anna gave me a sad face and said "we need to set you up with someone. Like a blind date!"

Jason, who had just hung up the phone and heard Anna's comment, shook his head vehemently. "Yes, we do! But I'm not going be any help to you, girl, because all my guy friends are gay. And don't even think about asking that one," he jerked his thumb in Mya's direction, "to set you up with one of her thug friends. You'd end up at some club in Brooklyn drinking 40s and getting stabbed."

"Shut up, Jason!" Mya said, but she smiled in spite of herself.

"Wait!" Anna shouted, waving her hands in front of her. "I have the perfect guy for you!"

"You do?" I asked, skeptically. "Why is he so perfect?"

"Well, I've heard he's perfect! He's my friend's friend and he's single and hot and he's looking for someone to date. He just moved here from Boston to go to med school."

"Wait a minute," I said. "He's your friends' friend? You don't even know him? You're trying to set me up on a blind date with a friend of your friend? Uh uh. I don't think so."

"No!" Anna pleaded with me, clasping her hands together. "I've actually met him…once. And he seemed super cool. His name is John and he's really good looking and seemed normal, which is always good. And he's going to be a doctor! Dating a hot doctor…awesome."

"That is pretty tempting," I mused. "You said you met him? He's cool? And you PROMISE me he's hot?"

"I promise!" Anna squealed. He's your type even… bigger and a cute face. He's exactly your age so that's good too. Oh my God, will you go?! I think you should go!" Anna was getting very worked up.

I laughed. "I'll go, why not? I'm up for anything. He sounds great, actually. Can you set it up for me?"

"I'll text my friend right now and tell her to tell John that I have the perfect girl for him! You guys are going to make the cutest couple! Can I be in the wedding if you guys get married?" Anna finished, reaching for her phone and doing a little dance of happiness.

I laughed again. "I think we're getting a little ahead of ourselves here. I haven't even been out with the guy yet. But I'm excited."

Just then Gary's voice rang out from across the hall "KATY! Did you get those headshots yet? Bring them in here!"

"Better go," I said, grabbing the headshots and dashing out of the room.

~

The date was set up for Sunday night. I thought Sunday was kind of an odd choice for a date but Anna and her friend, Stephanie, assured me that John was very, very busy, what with medical school and all. I told them that the date didn't have to happen, it was okay if he was too busy to go out with me, but they both told me that he was interested in meeting me, and he had seen my picture and thought I looked great. So we decided to meet at a bar called Jake's in Hollywood. Jake's was an ideal bar for a first date because it had good food, a good atmosphere and was conveniently located. I hoped it wouldn't be too crowded, because Jake's had a tendency to get that way, but then I remembered it was Sunday night, and space shouldn't be a problem.

I walked in and spotted him right away. He was the only guy sitting at the bar on the left hand side of the restaurant. He was cute: a little on the short side, but stocky, with wavy brown hair, blue eyes and a smile that crinkled the corners of his mouth and made his eyes sparkle. He had perfect, white teeth and was wearing a blue polo shirt and khakis. He turned around as I walked in and looked me up and down. I was glad I had chosen to wear a new, short sundress that I thought showed off my legs pretty well. He must have

job, I was irritated by the way he said it, by the tone in his voice. It was as if he felt entitled to something, and I can't stand entitlement. I can't stand entitled people.

But I didn't really know this person at all so I decided to try to let it roll off my back. I grimaced and shrugged and said "I guess," and then changed the subject immediately. "So, you're studying to be a doctor? That must be challenging. Do you like med school?" I told the bartender that I wanted a vodka soda, thanked her, and then turned back to John.

"I love med school. It is challenging most of the time, but I like a challenge. I graduate next year and then I'll be good to go."

"Do you know what area you'd like to go into?" I asked, taking a sip of my drink.

"I'm really excited about Plastics."

Of course. I should have known. This was LA and most wanna-be doctors wanted to go into that field. It was lucrative and everywhere you turned. There was always going to be a market for fake boobs and fake noses and botox injections and basically any kind of elective reconstructive surgery one could imagine. It seemed like John wanted to be swept up into the newest craze.

"That sounds interesting. I don't know much about that, but I'm sure that is a good field," I said, smiling.

"Obviously you don't know much about that," he said.

"What does that mean?" I asked. I was confused.

"Well," he began, looking me over as his eyes came to rest on my chest, "you don't seem to have had any work done yourself."

Whoa. Okay. Clearly he was referring to my non-existent boobs. I had always been flat-chested, but this had never posed a problem for me before. I liked my 34 A's. Never been ashamed of them, never thought twice about them. Sure, I had often wondered what it would be like to have big breasts, but it just wasn't for me. I was thin and proportionate. If I had had bigger ones, I would have looked silly. I had never heard complaints from the guys I had dated before, either. I'm sure many of them would have appreciated some bigger boobs. I didn't care. Guys seemed to like me for me, and if they didn't, too bad for them. It was funny how every guy I dated seemed to bring up the fact that they weren't "boob guys" on one of our earlier dates. How they were "ass men," as if they thought I was self-conscious about my lacking chest. I wasn't. I liked the way I looked and assumed that they did, too. If they didn't like the way I looked in some form or another, they wouldn't be out with me on a second or third date in the first place. I usually simply smiled and laughed off their nervous assurances. But this was a first. I had never had a man blatantly refer to my breasts in the context of me having not altered them. I decided to make light of the situation.

"Oh, these?" I said, flippantly, placing one hand over each breast. "These bad boys have been reduced. I used to be a 34 Double D."

John's eyes lit up. "Seriously?"

"No!" I said, taking my hands away from them. "That was a joke!" I said, exasperatedly. "I have never had any kind of elective surgery!"

"Ever thought about it?" he asked, still looking at my chest.

"Nope. Not interested."

"They can do wonders with surgery these days. Most of the implants look incredibly real. You wouldn't even believe it."

"I'm totally okay with the way I look, thank-you very much." My tone of voice was becoming noticeably irritated. I was becoming increasingly offended. Evidently, John wasn't catching on, though, because he continued.

"I'd take you up to about a 34 C," John said, narrowing his eyes to slits and scrutinizing the area below my chestbone. I imagined he was picturing perfectly rounded orbs growing in size, picturing me as a Barbie-esque freak standing naked before him. "Get you some saline implants, you'd look hot." He cranked his elbows, arms outstretched, making a claw-like motion with his hands.

Suddenly, I felt like I was in some pornographic video. I blushed in spite of myself. "I'm good," I mumbled, slurping my drink. "Like, I'm seriously okay."

John gave me one more once over and dropped his hands. "Well, alright then, no skin off my back, or front," he said, winking. "Doctor's joke," he finished and cracking himself up.

Oh God. How cheesy.

"You should be glad you met me, though, if you change your mind. I'm going to be a kick-ass doctor."

"Thanks. I'll let you know," I deadpanned. A "kick-ass" doctor?? Who actually said that, I wondered. I was sure people looked at a doctor's credentials, morality, ethics, bedside manner and experience when choosing a doctor, not whether they were "kick-ass" or not, but I decided not to bring that up at the moment.

I studied John, and while I did, I thought about the date. Currently, it was not going too well. I'd have given it about a 5 on a scale. He was obviously an egomaniac, but I wasn't yet ready to bolt. He was very attractive and at the very least, it was fun to be on a date on a Sunday night with a wanna-be doctor, even if that wanna-be doctor was quite possibly a jerk. Also, I had been set up with him by Anna and her friend so I felt an obligation to see it through. They both would have thought me rude if I didn't finish it. Even if he did want to change everything about me physically. I decided to stick around to see if things got any better.

And they did. He began to act normally again and a lot less offensive towards me. He started asking appropriate questions. We talked about our families and our past relationships. We talked about my job and about Los Angeles and the perks and downfalls of living in the city. We had more drinks and ordered food. We talked for hours and seemed to get along swimmingly. He was even kind of silly; making jokes that weren't as cheesy as before and making me laugh. After awhile, he rested his hand on my knee and rubbed my leg. He then asked me if I wanted to come back to his place for a nightcap. I knew what that was code for, I am not an idiot, and I decided that I wanted to, that my answer was yes. I told him that sounded great, and signaled the bartender for our bill. When it came, John grabbed it away from me and insisted he was going to pay. I was fine with that, I wasn't going to argue with him.

I feel that it is rude to look at the bill if one is not paying for it. I feel it is rude and I always try to look away, try being the operative word. But more often than not, I do. I admit it. I am too curious for my own good. I have to check it out to see how much a guy is spending on me. It's a girl thing. We all do it.

So as that little slip of paper was placed in front of him, determining how much I was worth on a first date, I looked away and then slyly looked back to peer at the total. $78. I watched John put his credit card in the credit card holder at the top of the check presenter, watched the bartender run the card and give it back to him with a pen and a "thanks, guys." And then I pretended to look away again but immediately looked back.

A server or ex-server is always going to look at what other people tip their service professionals. They are going to watch and make sure the tip amount is enough, because we assume that if the person tipping has never been a server himself, that said person will not tip appropriately. So servers do one of two things: A server will thank her date for paying for the meal, but ask or strongly insist that she leaves the tip, and/or if said person does not, in fact, tip appropriately, the server will slyly leave more of a tip on the table for the service professional on the way out. In cash. Because she always carries cash. It's a server thing. We all do it.

I looked back just in time to see John scowl at the tip line and hurriedly scribble in an almost illegible 5.00 on it. $5.00 on $78?! Was he crazy? That wasn't even close to ten percent! Not only had he been rude to our bartender, but now he was getting away with giving her a horrible tip. My face turned red, and I talked myself out of saying something yet again. I wanted to go home with this person and I didn't want to ruin my chances of seeing him again. The jury was definitely still out if he was a jerk or not, but I decided that the first date was too soon to tell. Besides, I liked him and I was attracted to him. I was pretty sure he was attracted to me, too. If I looked past the fact that he wanted to turn my 34 A boobs into 34 C's. So I bit my lip, took his outstretched hand and followed him out the door. But before I left, I threw a $10 bill on the bar to make up for his shitty tip.

John kissed me on the cheek, said he'd had a nice time and that he'd call me soon. I headed for my car in the other direction and immediately whipped out my phone. It was time to call Natasha. Time for a little one-on-one impromptu meeting of Jerk Magnets Anonymous. If nothing else, I needed her advice and wanted her to assure me that it was okay to go out with him again even after what he'd said. I figured Natasha was the best person to call because I knew she would encourage me to go out with him. Natasha's discretion could be almost non-existent when it came to men, hence her being a member of Jerk Magnets Anonymous.

She picked up right away. She had been waiting for my call because she knew I was going on my date.

"What happened? How was it?" she started.

"It was…pretty good."

"Just pretty good?"

"He's cute, and fairly nice."

"And he's a doctor…yummy. What kind of medicine is he going in to?"

"Well, that's just it," I said, climbing into my car, "he's going in to Plastics."

"So? What's the problem"

"He basically told me I needed a boob job."

"He did?" Natasha said, surprised.

"Yeah. And he called the bartender a bitch."

"Well, was she?"

"No. So…what do I do?"

"About what?"

"Do I go out with him again?"

"You said he was cute, right?"

"Yes."

"And did you have fun on the date?"

"Yeah…I did."

"So go out with him again."

"Even though he said those things?"

"Katy," Natasha started, sounding extremely wise and serious. "You went on one date with the guy. You found him to be cute and fairly nice and he paid for your tab. Wait, he did pay for your tab, correct?" Natasha sounded skeptical all of a sudden.

"Yes, he definitely did."

"Okay, good," she continued. "So yeah, go out with him again. I don't see a problem with it. It's not like you're proving anything by NOT going out with him. People get nervous on first dates, especially blind dates, and they say stupid stuff. Stuff they don't mean and stuff they don't necessarily believe. Best case scenario, you get to go on another date with someone who's cute and maybe not actually a jerk. Worst case scenario, he is a jerk and you'll never have to see him again."

"I guess you're right."

"Of course I'm right!" Natasha singsonged. "And don't feel guilty or anything about wanting to see him again. It's okay. Everyone deserves a second chance and if you want to hang out with him again, just do it. And by the way, you knew you were going to go out with him again, you didn't need my advice." I could practically see her smirk on the other end of the phone.

"How did you know?" I asked, sheepishly.

"Because you called me!" she said, laughing. "If you weren't going to go out with him again you would have called Erin. But you called me because you knew I would support a second date. You can't fool me."

She was totally right. I was going out with him again. That is, if he called me.

He did. John took me on a few more dates over the next couple of weeks. He seemed nice enough and we had fun when we went out. He always paid for the meals and we would laugh and joke and have fun and I would go stay at his place afterwards. He was very good-looking and smart so these were all positive things. But John had a lot of negatives, too. He was frequently pointing out women and commenting on what could be changed on their bodies or how, when he became a plastic surgeon, he could improve them. Luckily, he hadn't said anything more specifically to me about my physical imperfections since our first date, but his criticism of other women made me uncomfortable.

He would point out women and remark about how, when he became a doctor, he would increase their breast size, or give them a tummy tuck or give them lyposuction, botox or a nose job. Every woman's breasts could be larger or perkier, nose more sloped, jaw more streamlined, or lips more full. I cringed when he talked about that. I felt bad for them. Is this what was happening? Were men scrutinizing random women on the street or in a restaurant? Were these same men scrutinizing me and disgusted by my cankles or small boobs? They probably were. It was Los Angeles, the city of plastics, fakeness and judgement. If other guys were doing that, fine, I didn't want to think about it, but the fact that the guy with whom I was out, my very own date was doing it, made me sad. And turned off. I hated when John did that and I always tried to steer him away from talking about it, but he always seemed to come right back to the criticizing at hand. Besides it being rude to talk about, it was also a monotonous and uninteresting subject. I was so sick of hearing about other women…on my own dates.

The other thing that was getting monotonous was having to spend my own money to cover the tip that John never gave our servers. I decided that John was a jerk because he was rude to service professionals. Downright rude. I tried to ignore it at first, but every time we went out, it just became more and more obvious. He'd mutter under his breath about them, berate them and mock them. Nothing a waiter or waitress ever did was good enough or fast enough for him. He'd continually give them looks that said "You're here to serve me and I'm better than you." He conveyed all of this with his eyes and body language and actions. He'd be awful all through the meal, he'd send food back, he'd yell and whine, and then he'd leave a ten percent tip (barely) and complain about how bad the service was and ask the rhetorical question of why we, as Americans, had to tip anyway? I would stay quiet and roll my eyes and try to tune out the rude and aggressive behavior when it happened.

I would mouth "I'm sorry" to the server at least twice a meal and always leave a more appropriate tip. It was getting expensive. It was getting frustrating. And most of all, it was getting old.

After our fourth date, I stayed the night at his place and he dropped me off in the morning for work. I liked when he had to go to school in the mornings because he drove to his classes, and he would drop me off in his Land Rover outside the studios. I loved his car, and I loved not having to take the subway even more. I skipped into the office and Anna, Jason and Mya all looked up at me. I guess I was the last one to arrive. That's what usually happened when one of us started seeing someone; we rolled into work later than normal and were more often than not made fun of for it.

"Nice of you to join us," Jason said, not looking up from his computer screen. "Guess now that you have a boyfriend you think that you can just slither right into work whenever you damn well feel like it. Well, sister, I got news for you: this is ain't no picnic in the park, this is TELEVISION! This is important stuff!" he finished, still not looking at me but cracking a smile.

"It's 'walk in the park,'" Anna said, not looking up from her computer either.

"What is?" Jason said.

"The phrase is 'walk in the park,' and Katy is allowed to slither right in here whenever she wants now because morning sex takes precedence over work."

"Yes! Details!" Anna said, stopping her spin and locking eyes with me intently. "You told us you guys had a good first couple of dates, but nothing besides that. Spill!"

"He's…nice," I said, turning away from them and rifling through some headshots that were on the intern desk. "Are these my headshots for the Desperate Housewives screening today, Mya?"

Jason scooted back in his chair and ripped the headshots out of my hand. "No, they're mine and you know they're mine. Girl, stop playing. 'He's nice?'" he said, making quotation marks with his fingers. "That's it? Please. Give me a break. And stop trying to change the subject. What's wrong with him? He's gay isn't he? Just like Sam. I knew it! Set me up with him!"

Anna interjected by saying "he's not gay, okay? He's straight. There's nothing wrong with him, he's cute and nice and smart and funny and he and Katy are going to get married and I'm going to be in the wedding!" Anna took one look at my face and changed her tune. "Okay, maybe he's not perfect," she said. "What exactly is wrong with him, then?"

"He's always talking about other women and about how he will be able to fix their imperfections when he becomes a doctor. He makes me feel self-conscious about my own body and it's so annoying!" I spat. "And…" I paused for dramatic effect, " he's mean to our servers. Like, all the time. It drives me crazy."

"He mean to your servers when you go out, gurl?" Mya asked, her head snapping up from the call sheets she was working on.

"Yes. And I've been a server for like, ever. He's so rude. He's like THAT guy that all of the waiters hate."

"Gurl, you gots ta dump his ass right quick!" Mya was worked up. "I dun a lot of serving jobs in ma day and no trick ass gon' be rude ta me! I be like all SEE YA, asshole!"

"I know," I agreed with her. "It's so embarrassing. I have to apologize to our servers all the time and leave them extra money for a tip."

"He don' be thankan ya people wit a tip, gurl? Uh uh! No way! You do NOT wan' a be dealin wit dat shit. He got you spen in ya own scrilla, gurl? PLEASE! Dump dat broke, triflin' ass! You don' need no scrub, yo!"

Silence ensued. We all just stared at Mya for a second who was shaking her head and wagging her pointer finger in the air. When she realized we were all just looking at her, she dropped her hand and said "Wut?"

Jason said "What do you mean 'wut?' No one has any idea what you just said. No clue. English please."

Mya sighed and looked at me. In a normal tone of voice she enunciated very slowly "get rid of him."

"Now that makes more sense. I agree with homegirl over here. You're done with this loser."

"Now guys! Let's not go crazy all of a sudden," Anna interjected in a pleading tone of voice. "Just because he doesn't tip very well and may be…difficult when they go out, doesn't signify that Katy should get rid of him. I mean, what are we talking here for a tip usually? 18, 15 percent?"

"Try like 10 or less."

"Okay, fuck that."

"I know!" I whined. "It's bad."

Suddenly Gary's voiced rang out from down the hall. "Katy! Did you move the audition from 1 to 4 like I told you to?"

"Yes!" I yelled back, not moving. I didn't want to traipse the 50 feet to his office. I was feeling lazy and depressed because I was slowly realizing the doctor of my dreams was, in fact, a jerk. And the last thing I wanted to do was deal with Pickles at a time like this.

Gary continued shouting, the tone of his voice becoming increasingly annoying and high-pitched: "Then WHY the FUCK is Marla calling me bitching about how Dameon had no idea the audition wasn't until 4 today and he's coming in to the city now?"

I wanted to say "I don't know maybe because Marla is about 1000 years old and has lost her marbles?" but I didn't. I simply shouted back "I don't know!"

"Well pick up goddamn line one and talk to Marla! I don't have time to deal with this shit!" I could hear Pickles banging around in his office.

I rolled my eyes. "Well this day is getting off to a good start," I muttered under my breath.

"Picks is in a terrific mood today!" Jason said, watching me slowly scooch off the desk.

"You get to talk to Marla! Lucky you!" Anna said, laughing at me.

"I'm taking it in the other office," I explained to them, treading toward the door. "Wish me luck. If I'm not back in 2 hours, Marla has talked my ear off and I am dead and you should alert the authorities," I deadpanned.

Marla was one of the agents for the actors. We, as casting assistants dealt one-on-one with agents and managers constantly, all day, every day. One of the most important aspects of our job was to set up screenings with the agents. The casting directors would choose which actors they wanted to come in for auditions and then we were supposed to call their agent to set up the time and give them all the information their actor would need for the role, such as e-mail them the script, sides (the industry name for the lines they were expected to read for the part) and location. The agent would then contact the actor and relay all of this information to them. They were the middle-man, the go-between. Every audition had to be set up through an agent. It was a little stupid and unnecessary, I thought, but it was union rules.

We enjoyed calling some of the agents. Many of them were younger and fun to talk to. We developed a repoire with most of them. It was exciting to talk to them on the phone and we'd joke and laugh throughout the conversation. It was strange getting to know a person on the phone, only, but I felt like some of them were my friends. I was always glad when I got to call the agents I liked to set up auditions with their clients.

And then there were some agents who were awful. Fast-talking, rude, arrogant, narcissistic, annoying types who would try to "push" to you while you were on the phone with them. "Pushing" was the term used for when an agent would try to convince you to talk up a certain unknown actor of theirs to one of the Casting Directors. They were constantly doing this, trying to tell you how great so-and-so was, some actor no one had ever heard of, embarrassingly green (an amateur, new to the business) but raring to go. They would cut you off and yell at you and make your life a living hell for all of ten minutes…on the phone. Marla was one of these agents. 76 years old, she was still working full-time, a chain-smoking, four times divorced old biddy who was married to her job and only cared about money. She was almost exactly like Joey's manager on the show "Friends." All of us hated to talk to Marla. And one of her actors, Dameon, was slated to read for the role we were auditioning later today. Dameon read for us all the time. He was a good actor who worked a lot, and no one understood why he was still represented by Marla. Dameon wouldn't have gotten the time wrong, he was responsible and I know I had told Marla about the time change. It was her fault and now I had to listen to her bitch…and push.

I sighed and picked up the receiver. I pressed line 1 hesitantly. "Hi, Marla," I said, in a monotone voice. "How are you today?"

"What the HELL is going on with the Patrick audition today? 4 pm? What the hell happened to 2 pm?"

"Well, Marla, it was 1 pm to begin with, but now it's at 4. Gary changed it like 2 days ago. We spoke on the phone and I e-mailed you about it? You KNOW this."

"I had no fucking clue! Are you trying to sabotage my actor? He can GET this role! You know it's perfect for him. He was BORN to play Patrick in the pilot!"

I stifled a laugh. It would be pretty sad if Dameon was actually born to play the role of Patrick in our new pilot, considering the role had about 6 lines, maximum. He was most likely going to get offered the role, anyway. He was kind of perfect for it. I tried to quell her fears.

"Marla, he's on his way into the city right now, correct? So, great. He gets here and he just has to wait until 4. Then he'll audition and it'll all be peachy. I'll make sure he's the first actor to be seen, how's that?"

"I will NOT have Dameon waiting in your office for three hours! What do you think he is?? Some green, nobody actor? I'll have you know, missy, that he just booked the Verizon commercial! The NATIONAL Verizon commercial!"

"Good for him."

"Are you mocking me?"

"Not at all." I totally was. "You know we love Dameon in this office. He'll come in early, audition at 4 and he'll kick ass. No problem."

"I'll let it go this time, but no more time changes on us! You tell that Gary to get his shit together."

"Okay, Marla, I'll do that."

"Now that I have you on the line…" she trailed off and I could hear her shuffling papers around on her desk. Oh great, I thought, here comes the push.

"I have this great new actress you just HAVE to see. Oh my God, ABC would just DIE to have her in their new fall lineup. She's GORGEOUS and tiny. Long dark hair, ethnic looking, plays 18-28, GORGEOUS. This girl can act her tits off."

I had already put Marla on speakerphone and was working on my schedule for next week's audition. I was barely paying attention to her. "uh huh," I spoke up, disinterestedly. "What's her name?"

"Whitney Lopez. Spanish beauty. GORGEOUS. I mean, come on! This girl is the golden ticket! You HAVE to see her! I'm going to e-mail you her details. You'd be crazy to pass on this one!"

"I'm sure we would be. Hey, Marla, put Christopher on the phone. Let him push to me. He can e-mail me Whitney's details, too." Christopher was Marla's assistant. I loved talking to him. He was efficient, funny, responsible, adept at his job, and understood the business. He would realize I didn't have time for Marla's bullshit and it was always better to talk to him.

"Oh. Yeah, here's Christopher, honey," Marla responded.

He got on the line. "This is Christopher."

"What's up? It's Katy."

"Katy! Hi. How's America's Broadcasting Company?"

"Same ol, same ol, you know. What happened with Dameon?"

"Fuck if I know. Marla's fucking lost it, that's what happened."

"But he's cool? Like, he's coming in today?"

"Oh, totally. He'll be there. There's no problem."

"Awesome you rock. Oh, and this Spanish girl? What's her name? She really worth it?"

"Yeah. I'll e-mail you her headshot. She's cool. Really pretty. Average actress. Commercial, looks and plays young. You should check her out. You know I wouldn't waste your time."

"I know you wouldn't. E-mail me, I'll pass it on to Gary."

"Will do." I heard Christopher cup his hand over the mouthpiece and yell at his boss. "Marla! Stop smoking! You know what the fire inspector said about smoking in your office! Do you really want us all to get evacuated and fined AGAIN? Jesus." He spoke back into the phone. "Crazy old bitch. Those cigarettes are going to be the death of her."

"She hasn't died yet? I thought she was already dead."

Christopher burst into laughter. "I fucking love you."

"Love you too. I'll call you when Dameon gets the offer."

"Peace," he said and hung up the phone.

~

I had another date scheduled with John for the next evening, but I decided not to tell anyone about it. It was just easier that way if Anna, Mya and Jason didn't know. I didn't want to have to defend myself or explain why I was going out with him to them anymore. In my heart, I knew they were probably all correct in trying to convince me to stop seeing him, but I wanted to give him one more chance. Call me crazy, but I thought things might work out. I thought that by going out just one more time, things might be different, as if by magic. That suddenly, all of John's negative characteristics would go away. That he would become perfect. He was good on paper: handsome, studying to be a doctor, funny, charming and interesting, but his glaring flaws were becoming harder to ignore. If he could show me that he could act like a normal human being, if we could spend one night together without him putting some service professional down, or without him making some inappropriate comment about my or another woman's figure, then, I figured, I could continue to date this person.

I WANTED to date this person. I knew, though, that if he messed up again, that he was out. Three strikes. I was putting a lot of pressure on him for this date. And he didn't even know it.

We were going downtown to an upscale Spanish Tapas restaurant and then to a lounge in Hollywood that had just opened. I wore my new little black dress that hugged every curve (well, what few curves I had, according to John) and my new high heels. I met John at the restaurant a little after 7. He was already at the table and had ordered me a dirty martini, which I thought was very nice of him. He knew what I wanted and had taken the liberty of getting me a drink. This was getting off to a good start already, I thought, happily.

I slid into my chair with a coy smile and placed my clutch on the table in front of me. I smiled at him and said "hi there, thanks for the drink."

He finished the text he was sending and put his phone down. He shrugged and said "you're welcome. Took long enough for the dumbass server to bring it out, though. If I'm paying $14 for a martini, I sure as hell would like it before my food comes, or before the damn restaurant closes for that matter."

Maybe not so great of a start.

He sighed and drummed his fingers on the tablecloth. "You look nice, babe. Have a good day?"

"Yes I did," I replied, opening my menu. I was going to try to look past that first comment. Maybe he'll be okay with the waitress when she comes up to our table, I thought, as our waitress appeared. She was short, with short blond hair, slightly chubby and had a pretty face. She stopped at the edge of the table and introduced herself as "Jenny." She then launched into her opening schpeel:

"Hello, how are you two doing tonight?" she asked.

"Great, how are you?" I answered her. John merely grunted and peered at his menu.

"I'm doing well, thank-you. Welcome to Café Iberico. We are known for our small plates, sangria and tapas-style dining. Are both of you aware of what tapas style is?"

Before I could even respond, John snapped "yes, we're aware of what tapas is, thanks very much," and then under his breath he muttered "I wasn't born in a barn and I wasn't born yesterday, Jesus." I could tell that Jennifer heard this because of the look that crossed her face momentarily, but she quickly hid it.

"Well," she continued, "would you like to hear the chef's specials for the night?"

As I opened my mouth to say yes, John beat me to it again. "No, no specials, we don't want to hear them," he said rudely without ever looking up.

I smoothed my napkin over my lap and looked at Jennifer. "I would like to hear the specials," I assured her, acting like I was giving her my utmost attention. I figured if John was going to be rude, I could at least pretend to care. I wasn't listening to a single word she said, though. I was busy secretly plotting John's death.

When Jennifer finished with the specials, she took a deep breath and said "can I start you out with some of our homemade sangria or a glass of wine, perhaps?" John slammed his menu shut, glared at her and said icily: "no, no wine. We have our cocktails already. Bring two more in 20 minutes. Make sure they're dirty, and make SURE they're Tanqueray. Not any of that other shit. We'll take the calamari, the garlic shrimp, the chorizo with bread and the sea scallops. Bring the calamari and the shrimp first. Make sure they're hot. Last time I was here my dumbass server brought them out not hot and if they're not this time, I swear to God…Check back with us in ten, I might want our martinis earlier, and bring me another fork, this one is dirty," he finished, shoving the fork and his menu in her face and turning back to face me.

I looked back at him, my jaw practically hitting the ground. "What," I asked, incredulously, "was THAT?"

He looked at me with surprise for a few seconds and then a look of recognition came across his face. "you don't like scallops, do you?" he asked. "Sorry babe. We'll get her to change the order. I'm sure she hasn't even put it in yet so don't worry. Those people are always so slow." He looked behind him to signal for Jennifer, but she was long gone. Not like I blamed her. I would have run away as quickly as I could have and started talking shit about John to the other servers immediately, if I were her. I was sure that was what she was doing.

"I'm not worried about the scallops," I hissed at him, "although I do hate them so thanks for not asking me what I wanted to eat. You didn't even ask if I wanted to hear the specials, which I did, or if I wanted any sangria or wine."

"You hate wine," he replied, confused again.

"I know! That's not the point!" I was getting frustrated. "I honestly don't even care that you didn't ask me those things. I cared that you were incredibly rude to our waitress!"

"No, I wasn't."

"What do you mean, you weren't?! You were SO rude! You barely looked at her, you practically yelled at her and you just bossed her around."

"These people need to be bossed around," he defended himself. "If they weren't, no one would ever get any service. Service is terrible here as is."

"HOW is it terrible?" I was raising my voice. "you didn't even give our waitress a chance to be terrible! She could be the best waitress in the world and you would still think she was terrible, wouldn't you? You would STILL be rude to her and treat her like she was nothing."

"Katy," he began, his eyes narrowing "these people don't even know what they're doing. They all suck. Do you know the kind of skill set it takes to be a server or a bartender? No sort of skill set. It takes no talent or knowledge whatsoever to bring drinks and food to a table. It's lame and pathetic. I could do this sort of stuff with my hands tied behind my back and these people still manage to fuck everything up. It's so annoying."

"Do…you…realize," I enunciated every word slowly, "that I was a server for YEARS before I got my job at ABC? YEARS! I was a server last year at this time. Do you think I'm an idiot and have no talent whatsoever? I can't believe you just said those things. We are people, too. Our server is a person. Just like you. And just because you're going to be a doctor in a few years, does NOT mean you are any better or worse than her or her," I said, gesturing around at the waiters around us, "or me." I swept my hand back towards my chest and held it there. I was breathing heavily and was all worked up. "And furthermore," (I was about to break my rule of chastising people for their tipping habits, but I simply didn't care anymore, John was a moron and he deserved it) you tip horribly. You tip the WORST. Ten percent, if that? Come on…these people are trying to make a living, too."

"Yeah, well," he scoffed "she's probably an out of work or wanna-be actress…maybe," he said, cocking his head in her direction "she should think about getting a REAL job or at least fixing those tits of hers so she'd have a shot at SOMETHING. What sort of role is that dumpy girl with no brain ever going to get?"

I was floored. I had never heard anyone say such mean things about another person; another person they didn't even know. I threw my napkin down on the table and yelled quietly (if that's even possible) "how would you know what kind of acting job she's going to get? I'm the one in casting! And WHY do you always talk about other girls' physical flaws? Mine especially? I'm your date. It's so rude to talk about if and how I should get bigger tits or a nose job or a tummy tuck or whatever. I happen to like the way I look, always have, and if you have a problem with it you can just deal with it…ALONE. Here's a tip for our wanna-be, no-brained actress," I threw a $20 bill down on the table, "because I know you won't tip her, and you should probably figure out if you want to sit here and eat by yourself tonight because I'm leaving!" And with that, I stood up and marched toward the door without even a backward glance. I stomped all the way outside and asked the host for a cab. I stood there, arms crossed, fuming, for two minutes until a yellow cab pulled up. I jumped in, scooted across the seat, and was about to tell the cab driver my address when I felt another person slide in beside me, shut the door and tell the cabbie a location, then immediately asked him to tune the radio to 101.7 KISS FM, the top 40 station. It was John. What a strange request, I thought. John listens to Top 40? For the first time all night, I giggled, thinking about John the surgeon singing along to a Britney Spears song as he cut some girls' chest open to give her new boobs. I imagined all of the nurses in the operating room laughing at him, too. Then I remembered I was supposed to be irate so I stifled my smile.

I turned to him as the cab sped away. "What do you think you're doing?" I asked, bewildered. I had no idea why he would have followed me to a cab in the first place. I didn't take him for the kind to follow a girl who had just walked out on him on a date. But then again, he was very prideful.

"I couldn't just let you walk away. I wanted to explain myself."

"Don't worry about it. You're just so rude in so many ways. We have lots of fun together, but I just can't get past some of the things you say, so let's just call it quits. No big deal. I can't date someone who puts down a profession I once had. Any profession, really. Like, who do you think you are? What makes you so special?"

"I'm not really like that, I…" John trailed off as he noticed what street we were on. His head whipped around, back and forth, quickly. "Hey, are we on Sunset?" he asked, leaning his elbow against the glass that separated us from the driver. The driver didn't hear him. He tried again, louder this time. "Hey, MOHAMMED! Are you taking Sunset?"

The driver heard him and turned around. "Yes, I take Sunset to Olympic. It fastest way."

"IT not fastest way, dumbass!" John yelled. "Why would you take fucking Sunset to Olympic? Take Pico!"

"Pico not fastest way this time of night. I know." The cab driver answered.

"Well I'm the customer and I say take Pico! What the fuck do you know?" John was yelling at full force by this point.

"Sunset fastest way, you no yell at me, I know."

"Take fucking Pico right now or I swear to God I will report your Muslim ass to the authorities and have you deported! And put the radio on KISS FM right now before I go crazy on your Osama Bin Laden terrorist ass!"

"OKAY! THAT'S IT" I yelled. "Stop the cab right now! Pull over right here!" I said to the driver. He screeched over to the side of the road. I turned to John, said "don't ever call me again" and hopped out of the cab as fast as I could. I adjusted my dress, pulled it down and started walking in the direction of my house. I never looked back as I heard the cab screech away.

~

"Katy! Paradigm talent is on line 1 for you!" Anna yelled to me from across the hall.

"Is it Marla or Christopher?"

"Christopher!"

"You promise? I cannot deal with Marla at this time."

Anna laughed. "I promise. It's Christopher."

I picked up line 1 and bleated "Hello?" into the phone very timidly and suspiciously.

"What's up, sexy?" It was Christopher. Thank God. It was the Monday after the horrendous date.

"How do you know I'm sexy?" I asked, blushing.

"Well, you have a sexy voice. I'm just going to assume you're smoking hot."

"Thanks, I try. Oh, and thanks for calling me back."

"I should be the one thanking you. For giving Dameon the role."

"Don't thank me-thank Gary. I knew he was gonna get it, anyway."

"Well, you, Gary, whatever, thanks for helping us pay the bills."

"No problem. Dameon's good. We like him over here at ABC. I'll send you the contracts after lunch."

"Sounds good. How was your weekend?"

"Awful."

"Uh oh. Boy troubles?"

"You could say that."

"Give me the shortened version."

"The guy I was dating turned out to be this horribly rude, racist guy."

"No bueno."

"You're telling me. Hey, you're a guy. Wouldn't you think if a guy was trying to impress a girl that he would be nice to service professionals and leave more than a 10% tip?"

"You would think so. I would."

"And don't you think that if you liked a girl, you wouldn't criticize every inch of her body or make her feel self-conscious?"

"That guy did that, too? Wow. Sounds like a serious loser. You just need to meet some nice guys and stop wasting your time on douchebags."

"I know. Hey, wanna go out sometime?"

"I'd love to. But honey, you know I'm gay, right?"

I sighed. A straight man in the entertainment business was almost impossible to come by. But it had been worth a shot.

"I figured as much. Why are all the nice men not attracted to girls?"

"Not sure. But…let's meet. Seriously. You seem like an awesome girl, one I'd really love to hang out with. I'll introduce you to some of my nice, handsome, amazing straight guy friends."

"You have straight guy friends??"

"Not at all. Not even one."

"Damn you." I laughed.

"But drinks tonight at Watering Hole on Robertson. Meet me there at 8. Bring the contracts and we'll do a little work and then we'll drink ourselves silly. You deserve it."

"I'd love that. It will be nice to finally put a face with the voice on the phone."

"Ditto. It will be nice to finally meet a new, old friend."

I laughed. "Can't wait. Oh, and Christopher?"

"Yeah?"

"Thanks."

"Don't even mention it girl, see you at eight. Peace."

I hung up the phone. I was going to be just fine. Tonight was going to be fun. I fluffed my hair and re-applied my lipstick as I checked myself out in the mirror and smiled. I had to start getting ready.

I had a date.

Chapter 3

Serena

It was a Thursday at ABC. I was sitting in the assistant's office, catching up on logging in the Casting Director's notes into Excel. By logging in the Casting Director's notes into Excel I mean that I was gossiping with Mya. We were talking shit about the "celebrities" that were being seen that day for the role of a washed-up actress in one of our new pilots. This was fun because they were bringing in true washed-up actresses. We were being ruthless.

Did you SEE Jackie Darcy? The sister from "The Wonder Years?" I asked Mya. "What the hell is wrong with her face?

"Gurl, I don' know! She be a straight foo if she thinking she be lookin aiight fo sum ABC new fancy pilot n' shit! Dayum, she old looking as heyll! You think she be tweakin on that scant?

"I don't even know what that means."

"You think she be ridin' on that white pony?"

"No, I think she drove here in her car."

Mya burst out laughing. "I mean d'ya think she's a spin doctor? A battery bender? You think she be slanging that ice n shit?"

I continued to look at her blankly. I had no idea if she was even speaking English at this point, but this was a typical concern with Mya.

"Do you think she does METH?" Mya enunciated every word.

"Ooooohhh!!" I exclaimed, finally catching on. "Drugs!" I said, loudly, suddenly feeling like a huge dork. "Maybe. She is really skinny and her skin was all weird."

"Gurl, she look like she tweakin' now. I can' believe you was thinking I meant she rode up here on a white pony! Like all thru the streets of LA n' shit to get ta her audition!"

We both cracked up then, imagining Jackie Darcy galloping through the streets of LA on a white steed, script in hand, valiantly trying to get to her audition. We must have been laughing louder than we thought because suddenly, Gary's voice rang out from down the hall: "Shut up you two! Get back to work!" We looked at each other and cupped our hands over our mouths and our eyes got big. We were busted. And that just made us crack up even more. We continued to laugh quietly until Jason poked his head around the doorframe. "Hey," he said, in a loud whisper, "you guys better shut the fuck up. Pickles is pissed."

"When is he not pissed?" I asked, sucking in air and trying to calm myself down.

"Good point," Jason hissed back. "Whatever, I don't care. But the love of your life Reader Dan is here to see you," he said, wiggling his eyebrows up and down and making a kissy face at me. Try not to make a fool out of yourself this time."

"OOOHHH!!! Reader Dan!" Mya squealed. "You LOOOVEE him!"

"Mya! Not so loud!" I shushed her by rolling back in my chair and clamping my own hand over her mouth. "He can probably hear you!"

"So what?" she said, removing my hand from her face. "Good! I hope he can! Ain't he reading witchu fo Grey's Anatomy wit da producers an network taday?"

"Yes, he is," I replied calmy, but on the inside my stomach was doing flip-flops.

We called Reader Dan "Reader Dan" because we used him for freelance work as a reader for auditions, and because we didn't know his last name. Mostly, we assistants read opposite the actors when they auditioned. It was cheaper for ABC that way because they didn't have to pay an outside person, and it was part of our job requirements anyway. But once in awhile, if there was an important audition, usually one in front of the producers of the show and ABC Network bigwigs, we would bring in another actor to read with the ones auditioning for the role. We called these actors "readers." This just gave the audition more of an authentic, professional feel. This helped the actor auditioning for the role as well as benefitting the reader. He or she was able to get more practice at dialogue and get exposure in front of a network. If we used the actor as a reader, he was more likely to be seen by one of the casting directors and get cast in a role himself. Not that we assistants weren't good at reading, we were and we loved it, but typically during these auditions, we were needed to set up, make sure everything was running smoothly and help in other capacities. Usually, if Gary was holding an audition for a main role he would have me call Reader Dan to come in.

And I loved doing this because I was in love with Reader Dan. Okay, maybe I wasn't literally in love with him, I didn't know him enough to be in love with him, but I certainly had a major, intense crush on him. I had had this major crush for a few months now and everyone at ABC knew about it and teased me relentlessly. Even Gary knew about it, I was that in love. I wouldn't have been surprised if Reader Dan knew about my crush. Reader Dan was tall, had a good build, reddish hair, scruffy facial hair and an adorable smile. He was nice, genuine, funny and an excellent actor. He was always on time when he came to ABC to read for us and more often than not he was early, because he liked to come hang out with Jason, Anna, Mya and me. We had carried on a flirty relationship for awhile now and I looked forward to every day that he came into the office. I had wanted to ask him out for some time, but had never mustered up the guts to do it. I wanted him to ask me out, but so far, it hadn't happened.

Mya clucked her tongue disapprovingly as Jason disappeared around the corner, but before leaving he held his fingers up to his mouth and made a vulgar gesture.

"Ew," I said, turning back to my computer and blushing.

"Shit, gurl! Why you be all 'ew-ing? N shit? You KNOW you be crushin' mad hard fo homeboy!"

Just then Reader Dan sauntered in to the office, stood behind my chair and began massaging my neck. "Is this a private party or can I crash?" he asked, kneading his knuckles into my back.

"Oh my god, that feels so awesome," I said, closing my eyes. "Don't ever stop."

"I won't," he said, continuing the back rub. "I heard you need an amazing reader for your audition today. I'm here to save the day."

"Yeah, I know, Gary called you."

"You called me."

"Gary told me to call you. I just do what I'm told."

"I knew it. You're a good girl. I think I would remember a cute, good girl talking to me. Not sure if I would have come in if Gary the narcissistic, psycho, flaming queen slavedriver had called."

I smiled and said "yes, you would have."

"Okay, you're right, I would have," Reader Dan said, giving my back a final slap and rubbing his hands together vigorously. "Well, Katy, show me to the audition room."

"You know where it is," I said, spinning around in my chair and finally coming face to face with him. "Go yourself. I'm working," I said, coyly.

"You are not. You and Mya are gossiping. I know you two. Come on, let's go," he said, taking my hand and yanking me out of the chair. "The audition's in twenty minutes. "Let's go make out in there until it starts." He pulled me out of the room and as he did, I caught Mya pumping her fists in the air in a victory salute.

We walked down the hall and into one of the Network audition rooms. It was extremely nice. There was a stage with a curtain in front of 25 velvety, plush movie theater-style chairs in which sat the heads of the Network, the Casting Directors and the producers. There were two long aisles going down the right and the left side of the room and fancy stage lights that worked on dimmers. Behind the stage and the chairs was an AV room that held the sound mixers, cameras and equipment, and that's where I would stand with the AV guy and watch the auditions. It was pretty cool to stand back there in the dark and watch the actors on stage and through the camera lens and think that one of them would be playing a main character on an ABC primetime show in the next few weeks. It was exhilarating, really, and I was so glad I was able to be a part of it all. I watched the auditions and then I got to hear feedback from the people in the room, the ones who made the decisions. I listened and learned and took it all in. It was magical and wonderful and fun and exciting. The actors would act their hearts out, and the network heads would confer and discuss and decide and then everyone would congratulate everyone else and they would shake hands and smile and then everyone would file out of the room.

And then I got to pick up their trash. It was glamorous.

I had to set up before every audition as well. Every network head, casting director and producer attending the audition got a sheet with the actors' names, the time they were supposed to read and a headshot. Every person got a bottle of Fiji water, too. It was very swanky.

"Nice job setting up," Reader Dan, exclaimed, looking around the room and nodding approvingly. "You are very skilled at doling out bottled waters."

"Hey," I said, punching him playfully on the arm. "It's actually a lot harder than it looks! Not just anyone can do that."

"I bet."

"Anyway, are you ready to read the role of Dr. Shepard?"

"Ready as I'll ever be," Dan said, striding up to the stage and taking a seat on one of the two chairs that was placed there. "You go do your thing. I'm ready."

"Great, thanks. The audition starts in 15 minutes," I said, checking my watch. "I'm going to go in the AV room." As I turned around to climb the step to the back, Gary came dashing in, flamboyantly flabbergasted as usual.

"KATY!" he shouted, flailing his hands in the air. "Did you put the…?"

"Call sheets and headshots out? Yes," I interrupted him, crossing my arms over my chest. We did this exact same routine before every single network audition. Gary would crazily ask me if I had set up everything, which I always had, and I would interrupt him and finish his questions for him, which I always did.

"Well, did you put out the…?"

"Waters? Yes," I answered, grabbing the nearest bottle to me, opening the cap and taking a sip.

"Is the AV…?"

"Equipment set up and ready? Yes. And Tom's back there to run it."

Gary seemed at a loss for anything else about which to ask. But this did not last long because he suddenly and dramatically yelled

"Oh my God! Where's…?"

"Reader Dan? He's right there," I answered, sweeping my arm toward the stage. Reader Dan waved.

"Hummph," Gary said, slumping down in a chair. "Well, let's hurry this up. I have more work to do!" He pulled out his blackberry and furiously began typing on it. I took that as my cue to leave.

The audition went very smoothly. All of the actors did well, but the part went to one of our regular character actors. He nailed it. When it was over, Reader Dan helped me pick up the empty Fiji bottles and other trash that had been strewn about during the audition. For only fifteen people attending this audition for a total of 20 minutes, they sure made a mess. They always did. As we exited the audition room and made our way down the hall, Reader Dan casually slung his arm over my shoulder. I was in heaven. I was just about to look up at him and say something cute when I stopped dead in my tracks. In front of me, sitting on a chair in the lobby was the last person I expected to see; a blast from my past. I had to do a double take to make sure it was she, but on my second look, I was sure of it. It was my friend Serena from college.

"Serena!" I exclaimed, running up to give her a hug. "What are you doing here?"

"Oh my gosh!" she said, hugging me back after she got over her initial shock of seeing me. "What am I doing here? What are YOU doing here?"

"I work here. I'm a casting assistant."

"You're kidding me! I just got hired on as a new intern for three months!"

"Wow!" I said, stepping back and looking at her. I was still in shock. She looked just the same as she did in college: long blond hair, blue eyes, tall, thin. She was a real California girl and she was gorgeous. Just then, I remembered that she was from LA.

"So, you're back home?" I asked, slapping my thigh with my hand and looking her up and down. "you're from here, right?"

Serena tossed her hair and gave me a dazzling smile. "Yes, unfortunately," she responded, looking down sheepishly and sighing. "I was in San Diego for awhile with my boyfriend, remember Ian?"

"Oh yeah, of course, you guys dated forever!" I saw her face and changed my tone immediately.

"What happened?"

"He broke up with me. Cheated on me with some chick that worked with him at his restaurant. Kicked me out a month ago."

"Oh, no, Serena, I'm sorry."

"It's fine," she said, twirling a lock of her hair and staring off into the distance. "I'm over it. But NOW," she said, emphatically, "I have to live at home and start all over again. I thought I was going to spend the rest of my life with him." She looked like she was about to cry.

I felt a stirring beside me and heard someone clear his throat. It was Reader Dan. I had totally forgotten he was standing there. "Oh!" I said, touching Reader Dan on the arm and grabbing Serena's at the same time. "How rude of me! Serena, this is Dan, Dan, Serena." As Dan extended his hand toward Serena, I saw her stand up a little straighter and pay attention. She smiled a sexy smile and practically purred "hi, Dan, sooo nice to meet you. She batted her eyelashes and twirled another lock of hair. I thought it was a touch dramatic, definitely overkill, but Dan did not seem to mind. He blushed and took a step toward her. "Pleasure is all mine," he stated, never taking his eyes off of her. I looked back and forth between them, anger rising inside me. Now it was my turn to clear my throat. "Uh, excuse me, don't let me interrupt anything."

"Sorry!" Serena said, flashing her perfect white teeth and reluctantly letting go of his hand. Finally she turned to me and said "so, you're an assistant here? Looks like we're going to be co-workers! This is so exciting!"

"Yeah," I said, "this is pretty crazy it's such a small world. Gary didn't even tell me we were hiring another intern."

"Well, you weren't," Serena said, giggling girlishly. "I'll let you in on a little secret. I kind of weasled my way in here," her voice dropped to a conspiratorial whisper and she leaned in toward Dan and me. I saw Dan lean in so close to her face I thought he was going to fall over. It seemed pathetic to me how wrapped up in her he was. She was beautiful, there was no denying that, but I didn't get it. I was probably just jealous. "My mom is really good friends with Rachel, the head casting director here. My mom was making me get out of the house and get a REAL job," when Serena said "real job," she rolled her eyes and made quotation marks with her hands in the air, "so she called Rachel for me. She said she didn't have any assistant positions open right now, but that I could definitely come on as an intern and learn the ropes. So, here I am!" she finished, throwing her hands up in the air. "So…what exactly IS casting, anyway?" she gave an innocent, puppy dog look. I thought it was stupid. Dan evidently thought it was really, really great and cute because he started laughing hysterically.

"Well, you'll learn!" I said, taking her by the arm and walking her toward the assistant's office. "I'll teach you everything you need to know. But first, you need to meet the cast of characters. This is going to be fun!"

Serena looked back as I steered her toward the office. "Seems like I've already met the most important guy of all," she retorted, staring at Reader Dan who was just standing there against the wall, watching us leave. "He's so hot!" I stopped walking and she must have seen the look of concern on my face because then she said, "Oh my God, Katy, is that your boyfriend?"

"No," I said, looking back at Dan as well. "he's not, but I've had the biggest crush on him for months. I can't seem to get him to ask me out, though," I continued, wistfully. "But you guys seem to have had some chemistry back there just now?" I offered disdainfully, hoping she would discredit my statement immediately. She didn't. She said "yeah, he's super hot. It's like I've been on this rampage since Ian dumped me. I'm like constantly dating all of these guys and am really loving just being single and meeting all these new people. Like hot Dan." She stopped talking when she realized I was looking at her, still. My face must have been registering jealousy because that's certainly what I was feeling. Insane, honest-to-goodness, good old-fashioned jealousy. I am a jealous person by nature but this was taking the cake. I certainly did not need another girl, a friend from my past no less, waltzing in here and swooping up the guy I had had a crush on for forever. I was having enough trouble getting him to ask me out without any competition.

Serena looked back at me and for one second, I believed I saw the spark of a challenge in her eye. And then, just as quickly it vanished, and her voice was syrupy sweet. "Oh, wow! I'm sorry! Man, off limits, right?! My bad! Girl code, girl rule 101…he's all yours! We have got to get you to get with Dan! This is going to be my newest project!" She jumped up and down with excitement and then rubbed my shoulders. "I am an excellent matchmaker, so don't you worry!" she assured me. "I am going to get you to go out with Dan if it's the last thing I do! And trust me, I can do it. There can't be that much work to do around here as an intern anyway, right?" She winked at me.

I was dubious regarding her intentions at first. I hadn't seen her in awhile and she and Dan had seemed very flirty. But I tried to get a little more optimistic and smiled at her. I could use her help. I could use anyone's help at this point. I figured a little matchmaking would do me good. Especially if she was going to work here with me now. She could get the inside scoop. But first, I wanted to make it clear that she would have to be helping me and not trying to take him for herself.

"I would love if you could help me out with Dan! Any help would be appreciated. I think I'm striking out and I know he's single. I think he thinks of me as a buddy, you know? But, yeah…" I hesitated, not quite sure how to say what I wanted to, "I'm really pretty into him. Like, yeah… he's great," I said, blushing. That obviously didn't come across how I wanted it to, but I assumed she got the idea. It was girl code. We knew to stay away from the guys our friends were into.

"Girl, I totally get it. You really like him I can tell. We'll make this happen. Now, let's go meet everyone and get this day over with so we can go out and drink and catch up! It's been too long!"

~

And catch up we did. And drink we did. Serena had been my friend and sorority sister in college. We were actually roommates in our sorority house for a semester our senior year. We were the type of friends who became really close when we were in proximity to one another and then just drifted apart after we graduated. Serena had always had a boyfriend so she spent a lot of time with him during school, but we were constantly talking, laughing, having slumber parties, going out and eating meals together at the sorority house.

Serena loved to party. She was the life of the party. Everyone wanted to hang out with Serena. She was beautiful and her personality was contagious. I had always felt somewhat surprised that she had "chosen" me to be her sidekick that semester. But I always listened to her and that is what Serena needed. A constant sounding board. Someone to complain to. Serena was gorgeous, fun, outgoing and smart but she was also complicated. She was a handful, dramatic, vain, a princess, a diva, and above all, extremely selfish. She was always talking about herself and when she wasn't talking about herself, she was thinking about herself. Her problems were always worse than anyone else's. Her time was always more important. Guys loved Serena because they wanted to date her. Girls either loved Serena because they wanted to emulate her or they hated her because they felt threatened by her.

I never wanted to emulate her and I certainly wasn't ever threatened by her. I just enjoyed her company and joie de vivre. Most of the time I could look past the selfishness and find a genuine person inside. Most of the time I could tune out her profound insecurities that presented themselves in the most annoying and frustrating of ways and recognize the interesting, if not troubled girl she was. So I was happy to welcome her back into my life again.

It was like we had never lost touch and had been friends forever. After that first day, we went out that night, drank ourselves silly and talked until four in the morning. We went out to the hottest clubs on the weekend, went shopping, went to the beach, and became almost inseperable. She worked two days a week as an intern, Monday and Fridays, so every Monday and every Friday after work we would go out, too. Anna, Jason and Mya seemed to tolerate her. I could tell they were a little jealous of my relationship with her, especially Mya. Serena's presence as an intern had disrupted the flow of the office somewhat. We had all become so accustomed to the day-to-day grind with one intern. With Serena there, there was less space physically and emotionally. Serena had the tendency to take over when she was around. She took over space, conversations and demanded everyone's attention all the time. Mya and I used to gab on and on all day long, and now, when Serena was in the office, Mya felt like she couldn't get a word in edgewise. Serena basically ignored Mya when we were all together. Serena also liked to talk about our inside jokes at ABC, leaving Jason and Anna out of our own little private world. She acted like she didn't want to share me with anyone else and Jason and Anna weren't used to sharing me at all. Anna had mentioned to me that she didn't trust her. When I asked her why, she told me she couldn't put her finger on it, she just didn't have a good feeling about Serena.

Erin didn't either. She hung out with us sometimes, but she had been very busy with work lately. Her nursing rounds started around 5 am and she typically had twelve hour shifts. When she wasn't working, she was sleeping, or if she came out, she usually headed home early. Erin was never too much of a party girl and I think she was wary of Serena because of that very fact. She and Serena had never been very good friends in college, Erin wasn't in a sorority and they never ran in the same circles. I would always invite Erin out with us but she more often than not would decline. She voiced to me on more than one occasion that she didn't trust Serena. I had a few people in my life coming at me from all sides saying Serena wasn't trustworthy, but when I asked them to elaborate they couldn't put their fingers on it. I chalked it up to the fact that they were jealous of her and didn't think too much of it.

As mentioned, Serena was beautiful. She got a lot of attention from men, and she reveled in it. All the guys hit on her when we went out. We would enter the club and all eyes would be on her. That was how it was in college, too, except the difference was, Serena had had a serious boyfriend back then. Now that she was single, Serena took the men up on their offers. She was constantly going out with guys and going on a different date practically every night. She told me she was loving being single and loving being free to do as she pleased. She was the life of the party and I was the tag along friend, but I didn't care. I liked going out with her to the swanky clubs and the fancy parties, so I didn't mind playing the role of the less pretty friend. I wasn't interested in dating a ton of men, either. I was interested in dating Reader Dan.

Which wasn't exactly coming along as nicely as I hoped it would have been. Reader Dan hadn't been around recently in the office and Serena didn't seem to have much desire to talk about him, even when I brought him up. If I brought him up, she'd usually just change the subject to talk about the newest guy she was banging. But today, Reader Dan was coming in to the office, so we kind of had to talk about him. It was a Friday and Anna was running a big network audition so Dan had been hired to read. I was nervous about him coming in, but I had made sure to look extra cute today and do my makeup and hair flawlessly.

"So Reader Dan today, huh Katy? You finally going to ask him out?" Serena and I were helping Anna set up the audition room for his network and producer session for "Lost." Serena took a break from setting down headshots on every chair to look up and say loudly: "Oh yeah! I totally forgot he was coming in today! That's perfect for you. We need to amp up our efforts to get you to go out with him. It's like, nothing has even happened yet."

I was about to point out the fact that "our efforts" in getting me to go out with Reader Dan were basically non-existent, and that nothing had happened because Serena wouldn't even talk about any ways for me to "get him," but as soon as I opened my mouth to say anything, Anna spoke up.

"Well, what's your game plan, Serena?" The tone of her voice was laced with sarcasm and malice. "I'm sure Katy can take care of herself and ask out Reader Dan on her own if she wants. What are you going to do? Roofie Reader Dan to make him hook up with her?"

I was just about to point out that I obviously did need some help in getting up the courage to ask Reader Dan out obviously, because I hadn't been able to for months, and that I would hope that he wouldn't need to be roofied to have sex with me, but before I could say anything, Serena spoke up.

"I know what we'll do!" she exclaimed, clapping her hands together. If she had caught on to Anna's sarcasm and malice, she didn't let on. She probably was ignoring her or hadn't even heard her. When Serena got a plan going, there was no stopping her or distracting her. I could see the wheels turning in her head. "My friend is in charge of a new club downtown and their grand opening is tonight." She turned to me. "You're coming."

"I am?" I asked.

"Yes. And so is Reader Dan. I'm going to invite him to the party and voila! You guys get together! BAM!"

"Great plan." Anna's voice was dripping with sarcasm.

Again, Serena was oblivious to Jason's obvious contempt for her brilliant scheme. "Thanks!" she replied sunnily, continuing to pass out the headshots. "This is going to be perfect! You can thank me later," she said to me, turning around.

"How about she thanks you when it happens?" Anna was becoming more and more annoyed. She shot me a look that plainly said "get her out of here."

I picked up on the fact that Anna wanted to talk to me alone so I said "Hey, Serena, can you go help Mya file those old headshots, please? There are like, a ton of them."

"Sure," Serena said, breezing past us out of the room. "I'm going to ask Reader Dan right when he comes in, don't you worry. I am so smart and awesome sometimes!"

When she was finally out of earshot and the door had closed behind her, Anna turned to me and said "I don't like this situation."

"Why? What's wrong?" I asked. "Oh, and I'm sorry, did you want to come tonight?"

"No, thanks," she replied. "She didn't invite me, but it was nice of you to. I wouldn't come anyway even if she had."

"You really don't like her, do you?" I asked, setting down my papers and taking a seat in one of the producers chairs.

"No, I don't," she said, sitting down next to me. "I just don't trust her."

"Is that because she's pretty?" I asked.

"No, it's not that, although she is. It's that she doesn't seem to care about you, only about herself." She stopped and chewed on her lip. "And Serena is a bitchy name. All Serenas are always bitches.

"She does care. She's helping me with Reader Dan. But I agree with you on the name comment. The name Serena is kind of a bitch's name."

"You don't need help. You should just ask him out. Serena's just so…vapid. She only talks about herself and I'm assuming she only cares about herself, as well. She's never been particularly nice to me or Mya or Jason and you're such a nice girl and I just don't see why you are such good friends with her…" she trailed off and sighed. "Look, I'm sorry. It's really none of my business, and you guys were friends in college and you obviously know her better than I do and I'm sure I'm wrong…" she trailed off again. "I'm sorry. Never mind."

"It's okay," I said, giving Anna's shoulder a little nudge. "No need to be sorry. I understand what you mean. I know she's not the most…considerate person but it's been fun, you know, rekindling the old frienship. I'm sure her intentions are just fine. I trust her."

"I hope so," Anna said. "Anyway, it's no big deal, I'll shut up now. I hope you have an awesome time tonight and finally get to hook up with Reader Dan! I want to hear all about it!"

"Thanks! I said. "You will definitely be the first to know."

~

"So you're sure he's coming right?" I asked Serena for the millionth time. We were at Club Underground, the newest, hottest club in LA. Serena's friend had come through with the tickets to the Grand Opening and I was nervously holding Reader Dan's ticket in a violently shaking hand. I looked around at the scene before me. The club was beautiful, with lit candelabras, plush, velvety banquettes with tables to dance on, and two bars on either side of the room. The music was loud and bumping and the ambiance was dark. It was like any other club in LA except it was underground, hence the name.

"He's coming! Will you calm down?" Serena yelled back to me. "I asked him to come and he said he'd be here, so chill out please. This is like the millionth time you've asked me that. No one likes a pathetic worrier so put your best face on, okay? Speaking of," she said, scrutinizing my face, "You need some more lipstick. Here, take mine, it's a better color," she said, handing me a tube of hot pink.

I thought her tone and her delivery was kind of rude, not to mention what she had literally said to me, but I was too nervous about seeing with Reader Dan to argue with her, so I brought the tube of lipstick up to my lips and liberally but shakily, applied. All of a sudden, Mya bounded up to us. "What up, yo?!" she said, linking one of each arm through one each of Serena's and mine. "You bitches be lookin bangin, wut wut!" She was dancing around to the beat, swinging our arms. She seemed drunk already.

Serena yanked her arm from Mya's and said disdainfully, "what are YOU doing here?"

Mya stopped dancing and said, "Ma homeboy Trey got invited thru work axed me. He be all up in da club ta-nite!"

"Why do you talk like that?" Serena asked meanly, glaring at Mya. "You're Chinese, not black, in case you hadn't noticed."

Mya glared back at Serena and said acidly, "I'm Korean, not Chinese."

"Whatever, same thing," Serena said, looking away distractedly. "Come on, Katy," she said, pulling me toward the door. "I think I see Reader Dan. Let's go!"

"Sorry, Mya," I said, over my shoulder. "I'm really glad you're here! I'll meet up with you later!"

"I'm glad Reader Dan is here!" she yelled back. "Git it, gurl!"

I was glad Reader Dan was there, as well. He showed up looking incredibly sexy, in a crisp blue shirt. Serena ran up to him right away and threw her arms around his neck. "Dan!" she omitted an excited scream. "I'm sooo glad you could make it tonight!" She tossed her hair and put her hands on her hips, thrusting her chest out, showing the little line of perfect cleavage through her white dress, and smiling a blindingly white smile. I thought the whole act was a little flirty of her, especially since I was supposed to be the one flirting with him. So I decided to start.

"It's great to see you!" I said, hugging him too. I didn't have any cleavage lines to showcase, so I just smiled and started swaying my hips to the music. We all stood around awkwardly for some time until Serena shoved me aggressively into Reader Dan's stomach. "I love this song, don't you guys? You should go dance!"

"Sounds good to me," Reader Dan said, walking toward the bar. "But first, can I buy you both a drink?"

Serena nudged me very obviously and gave me the thumbs-up sign. She winked and mouthed "Awesome! Go get him!" as we headed for the bar at the back of the club. Then to Reader Dan she said, "Why yes, you can, Dan, we'd love a drink, wouldn't we, Katy?"

"Sure," I said, and happily followed behind.

We danced and drank all night. We all had a great time. Dan and I got a chance to talk for awhile when Serena went off with an older guy who insisted on buying her a drink.

From the looks she was sending me from across the room, I could tell she wanted me to save her from the guy, but I wasn't about to leave Reader Dan to go help her. She even sent me a text that said "help!" but I ignored it. She had chosen to go off with the creep to get drunk for free. And she was getting drunk. I saw the guy buy her about five drinks and a few shots. Dan was buying me enough drinks as well. I was getting drunk too and it was getting late. I could feel a headache coming on and suddenly, I was tired. I didn't want to leave yet, I was having a great time with Reader Dan, but when I found out it was almost 3 am, I knew it was time to go. I told Dan I was ready and we headed over to Serena to tell her. I could tell she wasn't pleased that I was going home, she drunkenly narrowed her eyes to slits and made fun of me for being a party pooper. I was also getting sick of Serena's bitchy attitude, but I stopped worrying about it when Reader Dan offered to take me home in a cab. I was elated and jumped at the chance. "You kids have fun," she said, turning back to the bar and rolling her eyes toward creepy guy. "I'll see you on Monday. Bye Dan, you're hot," she slurred and waved her hand dismissively at both of us.

I was glad we were leaving. Serena was getting on my last nerve and I wanted to leave with Reader Dan. We said goodbye to Mya who looked even drunker than before and she whispered to me that she wanted details of what happened with Dan. I told her she'd be the first to know and that I would text her tomorrow.

Turns out there wasn't anything exciting to text. Dan hailed a cab for us and had the driver take me home first. He gave me a hug as I got out of the car and told me he'd see me on Monday because he was reading for one of Anna's auditions again. I wanted to invite him up but I chickened out again. I just told him I had a great time and it would be fun to hang out again sometime. Then I ran upstairs into my building before he could answer because I was too scared I would be rejected.

~

Monday morning I came into work excited to see Reader Dan. Serena had texted me that morning saying she wouldn't be coming in to ABC for her internship that day. It was the first I had heard from her since I left The Underground Friday night, which was strange for us, but I decided not to worry about it, because she hadn't contacted me either. I ran into the office at full speed and flung my bag down onto the desk. I was early, but I was surprised to see Mya, Anna and Jason were already there.

"Hey, guys!" I said, happily. "How was everyone's weekend?"

"More importantly, how was YOUR weekend?" Jason asked slyly.

"It was great!" I replied "Hung out with Reader Dan on Friday night!"

"Did you guys hook up?" asked Anna excitedly.

"No, unfortunately," I said, out of breath, "but he was a complete gentleman and took me home in a cab."

"Yeah," Mya spoke up, looking at me confusedly. "Why did Reader Dan come back to the club after you left?"

"What?" I asked, looking at her in shock. I could feel my heart stop beating for a minute. I felt like the wind had been knocked out of me. "What do you mean?"

"Yeah, gurl, he came back. I thought you knew. I saw chillin' wit Serena at the bar and figured that was the plan or sumptin."

"Did they leave together?" Now my heart had started beating again and was racing inside my chest.

"Yeah, gurl, I think so," Mya looked at me with sorrow on her face. When she saw a tear roll down mine, she corrected herself. “But, but… you know,” she stammered, “I coulda bin wrong. I mean, my ass was toe the fuck up!” She tried to smile and make it come out as a joke, but all she managed was a grimace and a nervous cough.

I still couldn’t grasp what she was saying. My mind was racing as I tried to decipher what this could mean. Had Serena really met up with Dan behind my back? Did she really go home with him? As these thoughts tore through my head, another tear rolled down my cheek. I couldn’t think of any other reason why Reader Dan would have gone back except to be with Serena and that would explain her not talking to me for the weekend. I didn’t want to believe it but I could think of no other reason. Anna, Jason and Mya were all looking at me with pity. You could have heard a pin drop in the room.

“Maybe there’s another explanation for all of this?” Anna said, suggestively, getting up to give me a hug.

“Yeah, right,” Jason snorted, shaking his head. “That bitch fucked him and now she’s being a coward and not showing up to work. Some friend she is.”

“Jason!” Anna said, “a little tact, please. Katy’s upset. And we don’t know that that’s what even happened.”

I looked at Anna with my tear-stained face and asked hopefully: “do you really think she did that? She wouldn’t do that to me, would she? She’s one of my best friends. She knows how much I like him.” I sniffled and listened as Anna went on and on trying to reassure me that maybe it wasn’t what I thought, and you never know, and there must be some other explanation and blah blah blah, but after a minute I stopped listening as I came to my own conclusion. Anna could see that my mind was a million miles away and so she gave me another hug, stepped back and held me at arms’ length. “Well,” she said, cocking her head. “There’s only one way to find out.”

~

I slid into a chair at Starbucks across from Serena and watched her wiggle in her chair uncomfortably. It was six pm that same day and I had just gotten off work. I had asked Serena to meet me at the Starbucks across the street from ABC and she had reluctantly agreed. I was going to confront her regarding Reader Dan.

"Haven't heard from you in awhile," I said, adjusting the strap on my shirt. "And you weren't at work today. That was weird."

"I'm sorry, I was busy this weekend and I wasn't feeling great this morning so I couldn't come in to work, that's all," she said, looking back at me from across the table.

I sat in silence just looking at her for a long minute. She looked back as if daring me to say something about Dan, or about anything in general. The look on her face could only be described as a challenge.

"What happened Friday night after I left Club Underground?"

"What do you mean?" Serena's eyes widened and then flashed.

"You know what I mean. With Dan."

"Nothing." Serena was being short with me while her eyes darted around the room.

"He didn't come back to Club Underground and hang out with you?"

"Well…he did."

"Interesting. Did you fuck him?"

"No!" Serena wrung her hands nervously in front of her chest. I kept staring her down, never taking my eyes off her. "I didn't."

"Serena," I started again. "Let's try this again: look me in the face right now and tell me that you did not sleep with

Reader Dan. Just be honest with me and if you are, we can work this out? Okay?" My eyes pleaded with her as I waited for her answer.

"I didn't sleep with him, okay? Jesus, I'm not lying. I wouldn't do that." Serena slumped back against her chair and spun her empty coffee cup around.

I sat back against my chair as well, stunned. "Liar!" I shouted, banging my fist on the table. "You just lied to me, Serena. Reader Dan came back to hang out with you at the club and you went home with him and you two fucked! Why would you do this to me?" I hadn't wanted to cry but I couldn't help myself. I could feel the tears rolling down my face for the second time that day.

"How did you find out?" Serena asked, wringing her hands more vigorously in front of her face. It looked like her eyes were filling up with tears.

"Anna asked Reader Dan if you guys had sex today. And he said you did. Why would he lie about that? Serena, how COULD you?"

"I'm sorry! I don't know!" Serena was crying now. We must have looked ridiculous to the other Starbucks patrons, two girls sitting around over coffee and crying.

"You don't KNOW why you fucked Reader Dan? After you KNEW I liked him so much? After we've been so close these past few months?"

"No! I don't know!" she defended herself. "I guess I was mad at you for not saving me from that old creep at the bar or something. And I was drunk. I was really drunk. I know that's not an excuse, but I was hammered. I'm really sorry."

I was flabbergasted beyond belief. "Let me get this straight, Serena. You were so mad at me for not saving you from some old creep who YOU decided to let buy you drinks at the bar that you FUCKED Reader Dan??! That is so childish and ridiculous! What the hell is wrong with you? And no, you being drunk is not an excuse. Not for that. You knew what you were doing to some extent."

"I'm sorry, okay?" Serena said, sounding like she didn't even mean it. Her crying was short-lived, she had stopped. "I know you really liked him, Katy, I'm sorry, but he just didn't seem that into you. He came back to the bar to see me and we got drunk and one thing led to another…and…it's been really difficult for me since Ian broke up with me…"

"NO!" I yelled at her, crying harder now. "You do NOT get to use that as an excuse, either! You can and do get any guy you want! Any guy! Out of millions and you fuck the ONE guy who should be off-limits to you. ONE GUY that's off-limits! Remember the girl code, Serena? The one where you don't fuck your friends' crushes whether they're into them or not? I would NEVER do that to you. Ever. And friends don't lie to their friends. I even gave you a chance to tell me the truth so we could work through it, but you looked me in the face and lied." I was shaking my head and tears were falling onto the table. I watched them splat every couple of seconds. "You obviously don't care about me at all. You're completely selfish and self-centered and I still can't believe you would do this to me. You're such a bitch." I spat out the last part venomously.

"Okay, look, I was drunk, okay? I'm sorry, it was a mistake. I wish I hadn't done it but I did and there's no way I can take it back." Serena threw her hands up in the air in exasperation and then tossed her hair defiantly. It almost seemed like Serena was getting mad at me instead of the other way around, which was absolutely astounding to me. She didn't seem genuinely sorry at all, either. And then, she checked her watch as if she had somewhere to be and it seemed like such an inappropriate gesture for the situation at hand, that it hit me. Serena didn't really care. She cared that she got caught, but beyond that, she wasn't really bothered by what she did. Her conscience seemed almost non-existent. She had deliberately set out to take Reader Dan for herself. She knew how much I liked him and cast that notion aside. She was an individual who only cared about herself and her own gains. She had an agenda and the fact that I was so into him, probably only exacerbated the fact that she wanted to have sex with him herself. She was certainly not a true friend, a true friend never would have done that. She was just a self-centered bitch. Serena was a jerk.

"You can have Reader Dan for all I care. I don't want your sloppy seconds. He probably has Herpes now, anyway." I was surprised at the way I was retaliating by saying mean things. That's usually not the way I handle things but I had also never been hurt like this before by one of my girl friends.

"Oh, nice, Katy, yeah, that's right. How DARE you say those mean things to me? I'm sorry he just wasn't that into you, okay? I'm sorry he wanted me. You need to get over that and move on. I made a mistake, but it's not a big deal. We can still hang out. I won't fuck him again."

"I need to get over it and move on?!" I repeated, my voice becoming high-pitched and nasal. I sounded like a stuck pig. I calmed myself, took a deep breath and closed my eyes. "There are just so many things wrong with your last statement, Serena, I can't even begin to tell you. The mistake you made was an irreparable one and you don't even seem to care that much, so no, we can't still hang out and we can't be friends. You messed that up big time. And that IS a big deal. To me." I wiped the tears from my cheeks. I sighed again and stood up and slung my bag over my shoulder. "Don't call me again. And fuck him again if you want, you can have him. I seriously don't care. He was someone I'm not even upset about losing because I never had him to begin with. Honestly, the saddest part is that I've lost a really good friend. Or someone I thought was a really good friend. Stupid me."

I left Serena sitting there, looking down at the table. I never heard from her again.

~

"Who here misses Serena? Raise your hand!" Anna singsonged in the assistants' office that next Friday. Jason, Mya and I clamped our hands down by our sides and giggled. "I don't!" Jason said. "Not me!" Mya said. "Definitely not me," I said, grinning happily.

"I still can't believe she would do that to you," Jason said typing on the computer.

"I can," Anna said. "I warned Katy. I didn't trust that girl at all."

"Yeah, she always rubbed me the wrong way, too," Jason said. "I'm glad she never came back to work." Serena hadn't shown up for her internship the whole week. I assumed she was too embarrassed to show her face at work, knowing everyone knew what she did and hated her.

"I just wish she hadn't done that to you," Anna said, turning around and looking at me. "You didn't deserve that. You thought she was your friend."

"Yeah, well, it's okay, I have you guys. You guys are better friends, anyway. She was just so self-involved. I'll miss hanging out with her, she was fun to be with, but she was never a true friend. It's better that I know that now." I sighed. "And I guess I'll just have to find another guy to have a crush on. No more Reader Dan to pine after."

"Yeah, what a jerk," Anna chimed in. "I can't believe he'd have sex with Serena.

"I can," I said. "It wasn't really his fault. He didn't know I was into him and Serena all but seduced him. He was just being a guy. Serena was the one who maliciously did it. I don't blame him."

"Well, that's nice of you," Jason said, not looking up from the keyboard. "And speaking of readers, you'll be glad to know that my reader today is NOT Reader Dan. It's Mark. So you're safe."

I laughed. "Maybe I'll develop a crush on Mark, then. He's kind of cute."

Jason shook his head. "Oh, boy, God help us." He turned to Mya. "You've been quiet over there, ghetto fabulous. What do you say about all this?"

Mya was silently stacking papers, listening to our conversation. "Weyll…Ay think…she be a triflin' playa playa messed up in da head crazy lady. She be straight wack, yo. You needs tag it yo shit straight wid out sum cheatin' ass gurl. You don't needs ta be steppin' out wid sum biyotch."

We all stared at Mya in silence until Jason commanded, "Mya. Translation."

She laughed and smiled at me. "She sucks and you're better off without her anyway. Besides, Serena is a bitch's name. Every Serena is just a bitch. Everyone knows that."

Mya was right. Serena was a bitch. It was great to talk with my ABC friends at work to keep my mind off of what had just happened but the minute I walked out the door, the sadness hit me again. I needed a friend and I needed a true one. I hadn't had a chance to tell Erin what had happened yet and I suddenly felt the need to cry to my best friend. I also suddenly felt like I had not been a very good friend recently. I hadn't listened to the people who knew me best. I am a very trusting person and I had taken for granted the fact that Serena would be a loyal friend. True, Serena was gorgeous and fun and the life of the party. She and I had had a great time. But it hadn't been worth it for what she ended up doing to me. I wanted to go back to my old life, back to having friends who cared about me and loved me and would never dream of hurting me. I thought about this as I dialed Erin's number. I hoped she wouldn't be mad at me.

She picked up quickly and I could hear the smile in her voice as she said "hi, bestie, I was just thinking about you." Upon hearing that warm and welcoming greeting, I burst into tears. Erin's voice immediately changed.

"Oh no! What is it? What's wrong? Are you okay?" Erin asked, worry apparent in her voice.

"I'm okay…Serena…such a bitch…had sex with Dan… you were totally right…should have listened to you…I'm sorry…don't be mad at me…miss you…love you…" my words came out in a rush. I was crying and blubbering and didn't even know if Erin could understand a word I was saying. But she got it right away. And instead of being mad or condescending or jealous or saying "I told you so," she simply said,

"I'm so sorry, Katy, that's awful. I'm so sorry. What can I do?"

I had stopped blubbering and was now simply sniffling. "You're, you're not mad at me?" I stuttered.

"Why on earth would I be mad at you?" The surprise in Erin's voice was evident. "I feel so bad for you. No one does that to my best friend."

"But…do you know what happened? I haven't even told you yet."

"Katy, I know."

"How?"

"I can just tell. I'm not surprised, either."

"Yeah. I should have known. I should have listened to you."

"You couldn't have known. It's not your fault. It's hers. She's just a selfish, vapid, insecure person. I've always thought that. But don't blame yourself for hanging out with her. She was your friend and you guys had fun. Now, you need to move on."

"You're right," I agreed, climbing into my car. "Thank-you for not saying 'I told you so.'"

"I would never say that!" Erin exclaimed. Then she paused. "Okay," she exclaimed suddenly, "I really really want to, though!"

I burst into laughter. "You can say it, please do, actually!"

"I told you so!" she yelled.

"Thanks, I deserved that. Thanks for being the best friend ever, by the way."

"No problem. Thanks for being my best friend."

"Not much of one lately."

"Yes you have been. I've been busy too. I haven't been available myself much. But listen, this is getting really schmoopy. What do you say we hang out and drink and watch romantic comedies tonight? A girls' night. Just like when we were roommates."

"I would love that," I said, making a right hand turn. "Thanks." I was about to hang up when I remembered a question I had for her. "Hey, Erin?"

"What's up?"

"Do you think Serena is a bitch's name?"

There was silence for a minute and then Erin spoke up, "Serena is the ultimate bitch's name. Every Serena is just a bitch. And, come on, everyone knows that."

Chapter 4

Rob

The entertainment business, like Los Angeles itself, is flaky. One minute, you're in, the next minute you're out. After a year of working at ABC, Pickles was offered the job of head casting director for a show on the Lifetime Network. He took me with him. So I worked with him on that for a few months, then all of a sudden, one day, the show was cancelled. I applied for casting assistant jobs at other networks and on other shows, but my timing was off because sweeps month had just ended. No one was hiring for at least another six months, so I decided to go back to waitressing to make ends meet.

And I decided to do that in Chicago. I was sick of LA. While I had loved working in the industry and getting to live with my best friend, I knew it was time to move on. I was tired of the flakiness of LA, the backstabbing, the fake people, I was even tired of the monotonous weather, however "perfect" most considered it to be. If I was going to have to have a serving job again, I wanted to get one in a different city. A city full of culture and fun and cold weather and snow. A city closer to home. I wanted to meet new people. I wanted to meet new jerks to date. Midwestern jerks.

Natasha lived in Chicago already and was looking for a roommate. The situation would be perfect because, as a pilot, she would be gone most of the time. I was ready for a change, I was ready for adventure. I packed my bags, said a tearful goodbye to Erin, who promised to come visit us all the time and make the Jerk Magnets Anonymous Club complete again, and headed for the Windy City.

I got a job right away working at the Tilted Kilt, a new downtown restaurant. It was kind of like the Scottish Hooters. For work, I wore a plaid miniskirt and bra, a white shrug that exposed my midriff, white knee socks and Mary Jane shoes. My mother and father were none too pleased about what I wore to work, but I actually liked the costume. I thought it was fun. And that's what I had wanted to have coming to Chicago: fun. The girls I worked with were a blast, I made new friends right away. I loved going in to work every day, serving customers, laughing with the girls, and then leaving with tons of cash in my pocket. I didn't have a care in the world with that job. I was living life to the fullest and was almost sublimely happy. All that was missing in my life was a guy. I was in a new place and I wanted someone to show me around the city, take me out on dates, experience everything Chicago had to offer with me. I loved hanging out with my girlfriends, but it wasn't the same. My jerk magnet gene was rearing its ugly head.

And so was Natasha's. Big time. She was dating a guy when I moved in. His name was Alex and he took "jerk" to a whole new level. Natasha had really surpassed Erin and me by way of picking the jerkiest guy she could find. He was a pilot as well, so neither one was around much, which was good because I couldn't stand him. Natasha really couldn't stand him either which was a bit ironic.

When they were together, they were fighting and saying mean things to one another. When they weren't together, Natasha was constantly complaining to me about what an asshole he was. I didn't get their relationship at all, but who was I to judge? So mostly I just kept my mouth shut and did a lot of eye-rolling if I was with the two of them.

Which I was today. Natasha had miraculously received a few days off so we decided to go to the beach. I was excited until Natasha told me that Alex would be joining us. Not only was a he a jerk and a loser who still lived in his parents basement, but he was also cheap and a mooch. He always came around when he thought Natasha might pay for his food. Which she had not five minutes ago, at the terribly overpriced beach burger shack where we had ordered ice teas and chicken tenders. When the bill came, it was wildly more than any of us had expected, and I knew a fight was going to erupt between my lunch companions. Which it did. As the waitress placed the bill on our table, Alex sat back with a smug look, crossed his arms and looked pointedly at Natasha. I glared at him, gave Natasha my best "he's doing this AGAIN?" look, tossed $20 on the table and told them I would meet them back at the towels. I did not want to stick around to watch Alex not reach for his wallet or hear the screaming match that was about to ensue.

So I headed back to our spot on the beach alone, taking inventory of my surroundings as I neared our location. To my right were two fathers with their young girls, "weekend dads" taking their daughters to the beach. Twenty feet in front of me were three boys playing Frisbee. One of them was tall, dark and handsome, the other was smaller and cute, also with dark hair. But the one who caught my eye was bigger and on the short side, with sandy blond hair and blue eyes. They all looked to be in their mid-twenties, and were yelling to each other and laughing as they tossed the

Frisbee back and forth. I noticed the blond one steal a look in my direction and his gaze lingered on me for a minute as I approached my towel and shook the sand off of it. I plopped down on my towel and opened my book, glancing one more time at the blond boy before I delved back in to my reading.

All of a sudden I heard a "heads up!" and I barely had time to react before a frisbee came barreling at me as if out of nowhere. I watched it spin toward me out of the sky at an alarming pace, and cringed as it dove into the sand, burrowing itself only inches from my right leg. I gingerly picked it up with my thumb and forefinger and lowered my sunglasses. I saw the blond guy running toward me with a sheepish look on his face.

"Is this yours?" I yelled

"Yeah, sorry," he replied, coming to a halt in front of me. I raised my hand to shield my eyes from the sun but he was blocking it so I was able to get a better look at him. He was cute in a boyish sort of way. Chubby and stocky, but I prefer my men that way. He had colorful tattoos decorating his biceps, and when he smiled I noticed he had straight, even, white teeth. His smile was the cutest part about him because it made his eyes crinkle and sparkle.

"You almost decapitated me," I said, with a smile of my own. I held up the Frisbee and waved it at him to imitate scolding.

"I am really sorry-my friend is an idiot and has no aim whatsoever-I'm Rob," he finished, extending his hand and grabbing the Frisbee.

"I'm Katy," I said, standing up while pushing my sunglasses back on my nose, "and I'm exaggerating a little. You didn't really almost decapitate me. It was my leg you almost took off."

"Well, good thing you still got it, cause you're gonna need it when you come and throw the Frisbee with us. Let's go!" Rob grabbed my hand and yanked me toward his friends. As I stumbled along after him, tripping in the sand, I looked over my shoulder and saw Natasha and Alex approaching the towels. From the way Natasha was waving her hands back and forth and Alex was stomping along behind her, pouting, I could tell they were still immersed in one of their knock-down, drag-out fights. I pried my hand from Rob's grip and waved it in the air to summon them over.

"Natasha! Alex! Come here! Come meet Rob!" I was thankful for the distraction. I am not very athletic and while I can catch a Frisbee, I struggle to throw one well. I really didn't want to play, anyway.

"This is Rob," I said, sweeping my arm in his direction. "And these are…?" I trailed off as I pointed to his friends, realizing I didn't know their names.

Rob spoke up: "That's Chester," he pointed to the tall, dark and handsome one, "and that's my brother, Kurt." Chester just kind of stood there looking bored, and Kurt smiled and nodded and said "hey."

"Well this is my friend Natasha and this is…Alex," I said, finishing the introductions. I wanted to say "this is Natasha's no-good, loser, parasitic, pathetic excuse for a boyfriend, Alex," but I figured Natasha would not be too thrilled with me if I had. Neither would Alex, but I didn't care.

Alex looked around at the guys, and his eyes finally landed on Chester. "Chester the molester," he said finally, with no expression on his face whatsoever. As we all stood in awkward silence, shifting our feet uncomfortably, Natasha's eyes widened in horror and she smacked Alex on the arm.

"What the hell is wrong with you?" she screeched, whacking him again. "You just meet this person five seconds ago and all you can say is 'Chester the Molester?' You are an asshole. A cheap one at that, you can't even pay for a goddamn iced tea, you cheap son of a bitch…you are so embarrassing." She shot him one last death glare then turned to face us again. "I must apologize for my stupid non-boyfriend's idiotic behavior. He is obviously a moron and he was just leaving, actually." Natasha looked pointedly at Alex.

Alex looked as if he wanted to protest, but then thought better of it and turned on his heel. "Yeah, I was just leaving. Peace. Natasha, I'll call you."

"Don't bother, asshole!" Natasha threw his beach bag at him.

"Whatever, psycho bitch. I'm out."

We all watched Alex walk away in an incredulous silence. Natasha stormed off to her towel in a huff. Finally, I turned back to the group and cheerily said "Well! That was interesting huh?"

"Wow, are they always like that? They act like they hate each other." Rob replied.

"They do."

"So…why do they hang out then?"

"They don't, really. Alex shows up when he can get a free meal or ride out of the situation. Other than that, he's MIA. Which is fine with me. I can't stand that guy."

"Yeah, what a prick."

"That doesn't even begin to describe him."

"So…" Rob said with a mischevious glint in his eye, "what do you think I do?"

"What do you mean?"

"For work. What do you think I do?"

"I'm not sure."

"Guess."

I was confused. I'm not very good at guessing games and I don't enjoy them, so for a guy I had just met to ask me what I thought he did for a living seemed a little strange, but I could tell that whatever it was, he wanted to brag about it. So I decided to mess with him.

"You…are a tattoo artist?"

"No." Rob looked a little put off that I hadn't guessed correctly, but puffed up his chest and arms to show off his tattoos proudly.

"You…are a lifeguard at the beach?"

"No." Rob looked a little more put off.

"You…play frisbee professionally?"

Now Rob looked downright annoyed. "No!" he exclaimed exasperatedly, "I don't!"

"Well, that's good because I would think that taking an innocent beachgoer's leg off with a Frisbee would probably be grounds for expulsion from the team."

Rob said "Guess again!"

"Nah, I'm good. What is it you do?"

"I'm a fireman!" As he said this, he puffed out his arms and chest again like some sort of male peacock strutting around and showing off for his female conquest.

"Well, I can tell that's very exciting for you, Rob."

There was an awkward silence as Rob looked at me as if he was expecting me to start jumping up and down with joy, or bow at his feet for being America's finest heroes or whatever the fireman's slogan was. The few, the proud….? Oh, no. That was the marines. Finally, I repeated myself as I played with a string of hair that had come loose from my ponytail.

"Yeah, so….that sounds really exciting. And dangerous."

"It is!" Rob exclaimed a little too excitedly.

I still got the feeling that Rob wanted to talk more about being a fireman, but I really had nothing else to say and no more questions to ask. I have never been the type of girl who got all starry-eyed when it came to firemen or policemen or even men in uniform, for that matter. I had the utmost respect for the men and women who performed those jobs, and never looked down upon them, but the most important thing to me was that the person enjoy what he or she did. It wasn't about merit or status. It was about enjoying one's job whether it be a janitor or the CEO of a company.

I continued to stand there awkwardly, watching Rob continue to puff out his chest. It was distracting, to say the least. I decided to switch the subject to me for a minute.

"What do you think I do?" I asked, still twirling the lock of hair. "I'll give you a hint: I'm not a supermodel, although that's the first guess for most people," I said, winking at him and striking a pose.

Rob didn't get it. He looked at me blankly. "I have no idea," he said, seemingly surprised that I didn't want to talk about being a fireman anymore.

"Well, I'm a waitress."

"Oh, that's cool, right on," Rob said. "Where do you work? Some nice steakhouse downtown?"

"Nope. Actually kind of the opposite." I laughed. "I just got a job at The Tilted Kilt. Ever heard of it?"

Rob's face first registered recognition, then darkened slightly. "You mean that restaurant that's like Hooters?"

"Yeah, it's kind of like Hooters, I guess, but we're better than that. We have a sexier costume. It's more modern and fun."

Rob only looked away and said "I hate Hooters. I hate their wings. I don't know why everyone loves them so much."

Okkkaaayyy. I didn't work at Hooters. Jesus. I decided to try again. "you should come in sometime to The Tilted Kilt. You'd like our wings better."

Rob looked at me sideways and chewed on his lip. His face was still dark. Exasperatedly he spat out "but don't you feel like a piece of meat working there? Like guys hitting on you all the time, and isn't it degrading to women?"

Well. This was interesting. I wasn't sure what to tell him. I didn't think so personally, but that was just me. So I said exactly that.

"Well. This is interesting. I'm not sure what to tell you. I don't think so personally, but that's just me."

Rob wouldn't look at me. It was definitely getting more awkward by the minute so I wracked my brain for a way to change the subject. Luckily, I didn't have to wrack too hard, because Rob ended up doing it for me.

"Bet you've never dated a fireman before!" he said, chest puffing out for the eighth time in five minutes.

Huh. I hadn't realized we were dating. But at least the uncomfortable conversation was over.

"I didn't realize we were dating."

"We're not. But we will be."

"And what makes you think that?"

"Well, you and Natasha are going to come meet me and my friends out tonight. We're going to Stanley's. It's the fireman's bar in Lincoln Park. Then I'm going to bring you back to my apartment and show you the view. It's going to be the best view of the city you've ever seen. I'm going to show you a good time and you're going to have fun and you're going to love the view from my pad and then we're going to start dating."

Well. Rob sure was confident. What made him think that Natasha and I wanted to meet him and his friends out at some stupid fireman bar? What made him think I wanted to see his incredible apartment and the "amazing" view of the city? And above all, what made him think that we were going to start dating because of one night out? What made him think I was so easy that I would just go right up to some (cute) stranger's apartment and be so impressed by the view and the "pad" that I would hook up with him that night and then we would just enter into some relationship? This guy had it all wrong.

Well. Natasha and I went to the fireman bar and met Rob's friends and had a blast. We drank a lot of alcohol and laughed and laughed. Asshole Alex came and behaved himself. It almost seemed like he was on the verge of smiling once or twice. I went up to Rob's apartment at the end of the night to see the view and it was amazing. Incredible. It was the best view of the city I'd ever seen. We hooked up. I had fun. And then we started dating. I was a walking cliché.

Rob was the person I was looking for to have fun with in Chicago. At first. It was the end of summer so he hosted a lot of barbeques and grilled out on the deck of his apartment with the beautiful view in Lincoln Park. I met a lot of his friends and they were fun, friendly people. He took me out on dates and showed me the city. We took rides on his motorcycle to the North Shore of Illinois, a grouping of small, ritzy towns best known for rich people, beautiful mansions, and landmarks where John Hughes shot many of his most beloved films. Rob showed me the Home Alone house and the football field where Judd Nelson famously fist pumped at the end of The Breakfast Club. I had only been on a motorcycle once before, and I looked like a nerd in my pink sweatshirt, clutching on to Rob for dear life, and wearing a helmet, because I had insisted.

He took me to a biker bar where we sat outside in the sun and drank coronas and listened to bands play. When we got back on his bike, he convinced me to take off my sweatshirt (he said because it was warm outside, but I knew it was because he thought I looked like a dork) and to ride for awhile without the helmet on. I was hesitant. I knew my father would have killed me if he knew I was on a motorcycle, let alone without a helmet on, but I did it, and it was thrilling. I loved the feeling of the wind rushing through my hair and the view of the scenery all around me. I loosened my grip on Rob and sat up straighter in order to take in everything. It was like being on a roller coaster but without the twists and turns, and better because I was able to hold on to the cute boy in front of me.

I also made many trips to the firehouse to visit him. I would go for hours and hang out with all the boys. They would always feed me, even if I said I wasn't hungry. They were insistent and so proud of the food they had prepared. They were crazy, fun guys and I would be the only girl there so I would get lots of attention, which I loved. Rob was a firefighter and an EMT so sometimes while I would be visiting, he would get called out for runs and it would be just me with some of the other men, watching movies and shooting the shit. They never made me feel uncomfortable or weird, they were always accommodating and the utmost of gentlemen. The atmosphere in the firehouse was mostly lighthearted and silly. The guys did a very serious job, and were extremely committed to their work, but when they didn't have to go on runs, they were comical and laid-back.

One thing we never did was talk about my work. He never wanted to come in to the Tilted Kilt to see it, or to see me. Whenever I would talk about my day or something funny that one of the girls did, Rob would get a grim look. He didn't like what I wore to work. He didn't like that men were looking at me wearing what I wore. Even though I tried to convince him that I wasn't interested in anyone who came in to eat there, and I assured him that I always denied their advances, that never placated Rob. On one hand I was flattered that he cared enough to be concerned, but at times, his concern bordered on being dominant and controlling. And I didn't like the fact that all he ever wanted to talk about was *his* job and *his* day at work. It was frustrating and I felt like he didn't care about something that was important to me. Being a server at The Tilted Kilt may not have been as important as being a fireman, and wearing what I wore at work may not have been the most morally commendable thing, but I had no qualms about it. I was having fun and making lots of money. As time went on and we became closer, I became increasingly frustrated with these particular misgivings.

A couple of weeks after we started dating, Rob invited me to be his date to his friend's wedding. I thought it was a little soon into our relationship, but he insisted that he wanted me to come and we would have a good time. I liked Rob, but I didn't know where things were going or where I wanted them to go. I had only been in Chicago for two months and on one hand, I felt like dating him exclusively was keeping me from meeting other people. I didn't know if I wanted to be tied down to him so soon. On the other hand, I liked having someone to care about and who cared about me. I didn't want to lead him on, so I wasn't sure if going to a wedding with him was the best idea, but I agreed that it would be fun.

It was time for some advice from my girls at the restaurant.

They were funny and beautiful and intelligent and interesting and I got along with everyone and had made some fast, close friends. The group of them had become a good surrogate Jerk Magnets Anonymous Club themselves. No girls would ever replace Erin and Natasha, of course, but

Erin was still in LA and busy with work most of the time, and Natasha was busy with work and with stupid Alex.

And I was beginning to realize that TK girls gave great boy and relationship advice. I determined that the best girls from whom to get sympathy, empathy and advice are girls who are comfortable wearing a tartan bra and miniskirt to work. They all had different experiences and opinions and were completely open when discussing love and relationships and sex. Especially sex. Nothing any of us could ever say was too crazy or graphic or embarrassing or weird. Most likely, one of the other girls had been through something similar or would be more than willing to listen for hours and sympathize or empathize. These girls were the most non-judgmental women I had ever met. It was like we were all in a sorority together. A Tilted Kilt sorority; us in our miniskirts against the world.

So I walked in to work on a Monday morning ready for a barrage of brilliant words of wisdom from my tartan-clad co-workers. I entered the restaurant to find the usual suspects. I'm always early, so I'm usually the first one to work wherever that may be, but at TK, Kelly and Jessica always beat me to the punch.

Kelly was our floor manager. She was 26 years old, down-to-earth and extremely qualified for her job. She was also an ex TK girl. She was a server with all of us for a couple of weeks until the floor manager left suddenly and the owners needed someone to replace her immediately. Kelly was sick of serving and wanted a position in management so she convinced the owners to promote her. Because she was so young, and because she used to be "one of us," she understood our job and was sympathetic towards the servers especially. She was also our friend. Kelly and I had been close when we served together, and now that she was my manager, nothing had changed. I was grateful to be such good friends with my boss. It made the workday more fun, and I usually got whatever shifts I wanted and special privileges. Kelly was cute with freckles and short brown hair, a beautiful smile and dark, chocolately eyes.

Jessica was a fellow server, and while she was caring and kind, she was also inherently neurotic and anal. Jessica and I had become fast friends after day one of training when she and I were the only two trainees to know what was on the California Burger. I knew the answer because it was not a difficult one and pretty self-explanatory: Swiss cheese, red onion and guacamole, but Jessica knew the answer because she was an over-achiever who liked to make money. Jessica loved money. If anything got in the way of her and her money, you would hear all about it. And that was why Jessica was always there before anyone else. She would come in and set up the restaurant a good hour before we all were expected to be there, just so she could be guaranteed a good section every day with the most money-making potential. She was one of those girls who had to be reminded to loosen up and have fun every once in awhile. Jessica was short and super skinny with big boobs and long brown hair that was always immaculately done.

So I waltzed in and swung my bag down on the chair next to Jessica. She raised her eyes from her crossword puzzle and said "what's up?" but the spoon with her oatmeal on it was still hanging out of her mouth so it sounded more like "whauz uuuu….?" Kelly, who was making the floor chart at the hostess stand said "you seem frazzled today, what's the deal?" without looking up from her board.

"Rob asked me to go to a wedding with him and I'm not sure if I should go."

Kelly, eyes still glued to the server board said "Fireman?"

We at TK had nicknames for all of the men we dated. No significant other was ever referred to by his real name. We always came up with some pet name that denoted him. No guy was safe from our nicknames.

"Yeah, fireman," I said.

"Oh, I forgot he was a fireman!" Jessica said. "Stop dating him immediately. All firemen are jerks. I'm serious."

"Your dad is a fireman!" Kelly said with disbelief in her voice.

"Exactly. My dad is a jerk."

"Don't talk that way about your dad!"

"I'll talk however I want about my dad!"

"I'm sure he's not a jerk."

"Oh, he is."

"Anyway," I interrupted. "We're getting off topic here. Should I go to this wedding or not?"

"Well, what's the problem?" Kelly asked, finally putting down her crayon and turning to face our table. "You guys are dating, right? Weddings are fun. You get to get dressed up and eat for free and drink free booze and…have sex in a hotel room afterward. I don't see the problem here."

Jessica scraped the last of her oatmeal out of the cup and said "she's worried about the ramifications of going to the wedding with him. Like, what kind of message will that send? If you go to a wedding with someone that means it's getting serious and I don't think Katy is sure she wants that. Am I right?"

I nodded my head. "You are dead on."

Kelly said "Oh, I gotcha. You don't want to lead him on."

"Yeah, I don't. I feel like we're in a relationship, though. We spend all of our time together and I really like him, but I feel like I may be limiting myself by just dating him. We met literally a month ago, and right away it was like I had a boyfriend immediately. I wanted to meet and date someone, definitely, but I think it's more about having fun and being casual for me at this point. I mean, but we do have fun. I like hanging out with him a lot because our schedules are similar and weird…" I trailed off.

"Also," Jessica shifted her eyes to me as she opened a package of gummy bears and shoved half the bag in her mouth, "isn't he a TK hater?"

"A TK hater?" I repeated.

"Ohhhh….he's one of THOSE" Kelly said, shaking her head, sadly.

"Yeah," Jessica piped back in. "You told me he never wants to talk about your work, he hates the uniform, thinks it's degrading, never wants to come in here and thinks all dudes that come in here are pigs, and are hitting on you, blah, blah, blah…right?"

"That's pretty much exactly it."

"Well, let me tell you something right now," Jessica continued. "Dump him immediately. Right now. I dated a guy like that when I worked at Hooters. It got soooo annoying to the point where he would come in there, and just sit at the bar and scowl and yell at me and any dude who tried to talk to me. Including my customers. He got kicked out like 6 times. It was bad."

"I can't see Rob doing that."

"Doesn't matter. Get rid of him."

"Yup," Kelly chimed in. "He's a classic Madonna/Whore case."

"Madonna/Whore?" I repeated, perplexed.

"Yeah, you know…where the guy wants his girlfriend to be the Madonna, and looks at all other women as whores. So Rob wants you to be his girlfriend, and by fulfilling that role, you would have to be sweet, demure and virginal. NOT some girl who works at the Tilted Kilt. Rob's okay with other girls working at places like that, he sees them as whores and that's okay for them, but for his girlfriend? No way. She's gotta be classy and conservative if he's gonna call her his. A guy who has Madonna/Whore complex would never be okay with his girlfriend wearing a slutty skirt and bra to work. I've known plenty of dudes like that. I agree with Jess. Lose him." Jessica nodded vigorously.

I kept quiet as I pondered this new information. It did sound exactly like Rob, and that wasn't good. I decided to mull it over a little more, while the only sound in the restaurant was Jessica's chewing.

Kelly looked disapprovingly at Jessica as she shoved six more gummy bears in her mouth. "You are the most unhealthy eater I have ever known in my entire life. I don't know how you stay so skinny. I seriously don't."

"It's because of the stupid vegan boyfriend!" Jessica shouted, slamming the bag of gummy bears down on the table. A green one flew out and hit her on the nose. "He's been making me ingest weird-ass foods with bizarre names! Like bean tofu soy grass burgers and almond soy lactaid curdled farm-grown almond milk and shit like that! It's disgusting! I would sell my soul for a regular, normal cheeseburger at this point. He says I need to eat healthier and it's better for me but I'm STARVING!"

I stole a glance at Kelly who was already looking at me out of the corner of her eye.

"Okay, the weirdest part of that statement wasn't even the soy, farm-grown milk tofu part, although that's pretty weird, it was the fact that you called Vegan your boyfriend."

Jessica had been dating Chad (we called him Vegan) for about three weeks now, and this was the first time any of us had ever heard her refer to him as her boyfriend.

"Yeah, I guess he's my boyfriend," Jessica said waving her hand and blushing. "Whatever. BUT!" she said, throwing her empty package of gummy bears away, "what does it mean that I went through his gym bag when he went to work the other day and found condoms in it? Like, why would he have condoms in his gym bag? We don't even use condoms!"

"Okay, first of all," Kelly said, "why were you going through his gym bag in the first place? Gross."

"It was the next thing for me to snoop through after his closet and his drawers. Obviously."

"Alright," I said, "there is an easy explanation for this. Guys have condoms. As they should, and they put them in random places and then forget about them because guys are dumb. You two haven't been dating for that long, so I guarantee you he put those in his gym bag for whatever reason BEFORE you started dating, and has since forgotten about them. There's nothing to worry about. It's not like he intentionally put condoms in his bag just in case he gets the opportunity to suddenly bang some chick at his gym. Not the case."

"Oh, good." Jessica sighed with relief. "That's what I kinda figured, but I wasn't sure. I got paranoid there for a second. It's just why did I have to find condoms of all things?"

"What about condoms?" a loud voice reverberated through the restaurant. The voice belonged to Keri, who was practically sprinting up the escalator and careening toward us, quickly. Keri did everything fast: walked fast, talked fast, thought fast. She was loud and brash and incredibly crazy and fun. She was the oldest of us servers but was one of the most fit. She was also the most promiscuous girl in the restaurant. She was probably one of the most promiscuous people I had ever met in my life, male or female, but the great thing about Keri was that she made no excuses for that fact and was never hesitant to admit it. She owned her sexuality and was proud of it. She screeched to a halt in front of us. "What about condoms?" she demanded again.

Kelly spoke up "Jessica found condoms in Vegan's gym bag and is paranoid about that, but Katy reassured her that he's just a guy and probably put those condoms in there a million years ago and forgot about them so there's nothing to worry about."

Keri looked thoughtful for a moment and cocked her head to the left. "Nah," she finally said, "probably wants to bang some chick at his gym."

Kelly and I started to laugh, but Jessica looked crestfallen, so I piped up: "Jess, she's kidding, it's Keri, don't listen to her, she only thinks with her dick, you know that. But I need an answer now...do I go to the wedding with Fireman or not?"

"A wedding?" Keri said, her face lighting up "A wedding as in free food and alcohol and sex all night in a hotel room? Is there even a question?"

"Yessss...but...." Jessica chimed in, "Fireman has Madonna/Whore complex. Big time."

"Ooohhh," Keri said. "That's really bad. I changed my mind. No wedding. No anything, as a matter of fact. Dump him."

"I say no," Kelly called over her shoulder as she made her way toward the back.

"And I definitely say no," Jessica said, polishing off her bag of gummy bears. "A resounding no, as a matter of fact. Don't do it. Don't go."

~

So I went to the wedding. I shouldn't have done it. I should have listened to my girls. Attending turned out to be a big mistake, and it was a night filled with drama. Rob was in the wedding, so right off the bat it was a difficult situation for me. I didn't know any of the people at the wedding, and would have to be on my own for much of the reception. I could deal with this, I was a big girl and was fine holding my own in social situations. I liked meeting new people and weddings are always fun, but I was wary of how much fun this wedding would be from the start. My plan was to drink a lot.

Evidently, that was Rob's plan as well. I sat by myself in the pew during the ceremony, while he was standing up with the groom. I didn't get a chance to see him before it started because I made it just on time, and snuck in and took a seat in the back, so as not to cause a commotion. We didn't go together, because he had to be in the suburbs all day with the groom, so I drove separately. He had gotten a ride with his friend and I was supposed to take us home in the morning. It was a miracle I made it, because I got lost on four separate occasions. But now, the wedding was over and I could finally meet up with Rob outside of the reception hall. I couldn't wait to see him, so I could start feeling a little less awkward.

But as soon as I made my way toward him at the entrance to the hall, I could tell he was drunk. His eyes looked glazed over and he seemed to be laughing with his friend just a little too loudly. I had a sinking feeling in my stomach that this was not going to be a good night. If he was drunk and I was feeling uncomfortable and on edge, we were going to battle, I just knew it. But I decided to think positively. I squared my shoulders, took a deep breath, ambled up to Rob and tapped him on the shoulder.

"Hey handsome," I said, shrugging off my sweater, revealing my sexy black dress underneath. I struck a little pose so he and his friend could get a good look at me. Rob turned to me and a look of disinterested recognition crossed his face.

"Oh, hey, when did you get here?"

"I was here for the wedding, remember? I waved to you when you came down the aisle from the pew in the back."

"Oh, right. Cool."

An awkward silence ensued. Rob acted like he neither wanted to converse with me more, or introduce me to his friend. So I took it upon myself to get to know him. I stuck out my hand toward the friend and said very loudly:

"Hi, I'm Katy."

The friend stuck his hand out and shook mine. "Hey, I'm Connor. Nice to meet you." Then he turned to Rob and said the words no girl wants to hear from a friend of her boyfriend's: "Hey, dude, this your girlfriend?"

I turned to Rob slowly, waiting for his explanation. Rob kind of swayed on his feet and looked off into the distance. Then he looked at me, almost as if waiting for me to say something, thought better of it and turned back to Connor. "Yeah, dude. Meet my girlfriend, Katy," and he kind of waved his hand in the air as if to indicate that we should shake hands…again.

"Yeah, we've met," I retorted, still glaring at him. Rob didn't seem to catch on. He kind of looked back at me and stood there. Another silence ensued. I didn't know how I felt about the "girlfriend" title. I wasn't too happy about it, actually, considering Rob was being kind of a jerk. But I quickly brushed it off and attempted to break the ice… again.

"So, Connor, what is it you do"

"I'm in marketing for a fast food chain. What is it you do?"

All of a sudden Rob jumped in to the conversation and answered Connor's question. He said "She used to work at

ABC in LA" at the same time I said "I'm a waitress." Connor looked extremely confused, and I gave Rob a weird look then turned back to Connor. "I USED to work at ABC in LA, yes, but NOW I work in a restaurant."

"Which one?" Connor asked me.

I could feel Rob bristle next to me. He started chewing on his lip which was what he always did when he was nervous. I ignored him and replied "The Tilted Kilt downtown. Ever heard of it?"

Connor smiled and said "yeah, of course I've heard of it. I've actually been to that one. You guys wear those outfits like Hooters, right?" When he said "Hooters," he looked me up and down.

"Yes, we do. But we're much better than Hooters," I said, wagging my finger playfully at him. "That's cool that you've been there. I can't even get this one," I said, squeezing Rob's arm "to come in and visit me."

"Dude, you have to go," Connor said, "those girls are super hot there."

Rob rolled his eyes and shook my hand off of his arm. He looked almost angry as he said: "I'm not going there. Why would I want to go eat somewhere where the girls dress like whores?" The silence that followed was the longest and most awkward of my life, and I stared at him in stunned disbelief. Did he really just say that? I thought. I was used to hearing that from plenty of people, but those people were strangers and I always brushed off their comments as ignorance. Now the guy I was dating had basically called me a whore in front of his friend. I was livid, but I didn't want to act as rude as he had been so I took a deep breath and tried to calm down. I said "Excuse me, I'm going to get a drink, I'll be right back," and practically ran away from the guys.

I went over to the bar and asked for a Grey Goose on the rocks. This night was calling for some serious drinking.

I could tell that Rob was already wasted, so why shouldn't I drink a lot, too? And after what he had said, I could tell I was going to need some liquid help to calm down. As the bartender handed me my drink, I could see the guests streaming in to the dining hall to sit down for dinner. I actually considered setting down my drink, running out to my car and driving home, I was so angry at Rob for his comment, but I decided that wouldn't be the right thing to do. So I decided against that and psyched up for the long night ahead as I walked in to find my table.

Dinner was uneventful, mostly because I spent the whole time trying to ignore Rob. He kept drinking and so did I. He didn't introduce me to one single person the whole dinner, not even the others at our table. I had to do it myself. He barely tried to talk to me. I was getting angrier by the minute, and the alcohol was only perpetuating an already tense situation. As dinner ended, dessert was served and the band began setting up. The first song they played was one of my favorites and people started streaming out onto the dance floor, so I decided to try and be civil with the jerk who I called my boyfriend. I cocked my head toward him and, very sweetly asked if he wanted to dance with me.

He flicked his eyes over to the dance floor and saw all of his friends dancing and having fun. Our table was empty because everyone had decided to go dance. It seemed like he thought about it for a second and then turned to me and said, very meanly, "I don't dance."

"But all of your friends are out there. It would be fun. Come on! I love to dance, come dance with me."

Rob just shook his head and downed his vodka on the rocks in one gulp. "I don't dance," he repeated, "it's dumb."

"Fine!" I said, as I threw my napkin down on the table and gulped the rest of my vodka as well. "Don't dance with me even though I came all the way out to this wedding to be your date and I love to dance! Don't worry about it! Just continue to ignore me and not dance with me. Sounds good! I'm going to the bathroom." And with that, I stormed away from the table, leaving Rob in a shocked stupor. I had been pretty loud.

I slammed my way into the bathroom and put my hands down on the sink and looked up into the mirror. I was surprised to find that a few tears were rolling down my cheeks. I was so upset. I had no idea why Rob was being such a jerk to me and I was having an awful time. For the second time that night, I wanted to run away, but I wiped the tears away instead and sent a mass text to Kelly, Keri and Jessica instead. Maybe they would be sympathetic to my plight even though I had chosen to ignore their advice about the wedding. The text said: "At the wedding…having a horrible time. Rob is being a total dickhead," and then I included a sad face for dramatic measure. I set my phone down on the counter and waited for the texts filled with sympathy and understanding to start pouring in. After a few minutes, the texts did come. There were three of them; one from each girl. Kelly's said: "Omg! What did you wear?" Keri's said: "I guess all firemen are jerks…too bad they look so hot with their shirts off in those firemen calendars," and Jessica's simply said: "Told you so."

So much for sympathy and understanding. Guess I was on my own.

I put my phone away and banged out of the bathroom, making a conscious effort to continue to be nice and sweet, to keep my mouth shut and make sure not to cry. If Rob wouldn't dance with me, I would just sit with him and drink and try to have a better time. As I got to the door of the dining hall, I peeked around the corner and looked toward our table. It was empty. Thinking Rob must be up talking to the bride and groom or over by the bar, I checked both places, but still saw no sign of him. As I peered through the crowd, my eyes settled on the dance floor and I saw a sight that made me literally do a double take. As my eyes adjusted to all of the movement, I saw that it was, in fact, what I thought. I had found Rob.

He was dancing.

Drunkenly, stupidly, sloppily dancing. A blond girl was very close to him, and as I kept looking, I saw him put his hand out to take her hand and spin her around in a circle. There was no doubt that he was, in fact, out on the dance floor. With another girl. My heart was racing and I saw stars. I stormed over to him, across the dance floor, my heels clacking on the wood. I pushed past the blond girl, stuck out my arm, took his hand and yanked him toward the door. He stumbled after me, trying to process what was happening. I barely gave him another minute to think, though, as I pushed through the door and out into the hallway. I put my hands on my hips and screamed

"What the FUCK do you think you're doing?"

So much for nice and sweet and keeping my mouth shut.

Rob looked at me as if he had no idea to what I was referring. Then he shrugged and looked away. "I have no idea what you're talking about," he said, not very convincingly.

"You know EXACTLY what I'm talking about you stupid dickhead! You were on the dance floor…dancing!"

"Yeah? So?"

"YEAH? SO?" I repeated, trying to keep my voice down and trying to keep from crying. I was reaching my breaking point. "I just asked you to dance twice and you said no, you don't dance, I go to the bathroom for 10 minutes, I come back out and you are dancing with another girl! How do you think that makes me feel?"

Rob wasn't looking at me. He was trying to keep up his appearances of not caring, but I could tell he was embarrassed. He stayed silent and looked down at the floor. Then he spoke up and said "I wasn't dancing with her, I was just…dancing."

I exploded. "It sure LOOKED like you were dancing with her! You put your hand on her waist and twirled her around. I'd say that was dancing with someone else. Besides, it doesn't even matter, it's the principle of it, and furthermore, I can't BELIEVE you called me a whore in front of your friend. You don't even introduce me to him, you act so rude and then you call me a whore."

Rob finally looked up and met my eyes. "I didn't call you a whore. I said I didn't want to go eat at a place where the girls were dressed like whores. And my girlfriend just happens to work at a place like that. It's awesome," he said, sarcastically.

I took a step back and crossed my arms over my chest. "First of all, I'm not your girlfriend and you might as well have called me a whore. That was awful to hear and you really hurt my feelings. I expect that from ignorant strangers about my work but from you…" I trailed off and felt another tear roll down my cheek. So much for not crying. It was full force now.

Rob rolled his eyes again. He didn't even seem to care that I was upset. "I don't like that you work at The Tilted Kilt, okay?" he hissed with venom in his voice. "I'm a fireman and I have an important job that means something and people in the community look up to me. It's embarrassing that my girlfriend wears a bra and a miniskirt to work. It makes me look bad. Why can't you just make money some other way or work at another restaurant? Jesus, don't you have any self-respect?"

I was beyond shocked. I had stopped crying because I was so surprised at what he said. I took a step back in amazement. I could not believe what a jerk he was. I had always figured that he wasn't the biggest fan of my job, but this was absolutely unbelievable. I steadied myself and looked him straight in the eye. "I had no idea you felt this way," I began, trying to keep my voice from trembling. "And stop calling me your girlfriend."

"Yeah, well, I do," he said, raising his voice. "It really bothers me, okay? I need a girl who is just sweet and respects me and the work I do. Not some chick who is out flirting with every cock that comes into her restaurant so she can get a big tip. Not some chick who is a tease and who thinks she is hot shit and who sells her soul by using sex to her advantage. Just some girl with a NORMAL job."

When he stopped talking, I took a moment to just look at him and think. His face was all red and he was in a defensive stance; feet spread apart and arms crossed over his chest. Rob had been hiding these feelings and they had been building up inside of him. He wanted a girl who got off because he was a fireman. He was most likely used to girls falling all over him just for that fact. But I never had. I respected his work, but it never impressed me. And as far as my job was concerned, I realized why he never came in to the restaurant or gave me the credit I deserved for my work. He was ashamed of me and my work. Kelly was right: he had a classic case of Madonna/Whore complex. He wanted me and wanted me to be his girlfriend, but he was definitely not okay with the fact that I had a sexy job in which I wore sexy clothing. He wanted me to do something more "respectful" and I was not okay with him being ashamed of me and my work. Which, essentially, he was. If I were to be his girlfriend, he would label me and put me into a box with strict guidelines of how I should act and how I should look, and that sounded nothing like the kind of person I actually was. I knew this relationship would never work if he really viewed me as the type of person who would put up with or be okay with that. I guess he really couldn't see that I wasn't that sort of person. It was like he never knew me at all. And I couldn't stay with anyone who didn't know me for me. So I ripped into him:

"First of all, who are YOU to say this to me? SO WHAT you're a fireman? No one cares. You're not heroic, or brave or cool. You guys are just lame. You sit around all day and eat. And watch TV. It's so stupid. I may not have the most important job in the world but at least I'm not a loser who thinks he's more important than he is." I was yelling. People would pass us in the hallway and stop to stare, but I didn't even care. I was on a roll. "And furthermore," I continued, swinging my arms in the air, "while you're EMBARRASSED that someone you're dating is hot and can work at a restaurant where she can make money wearing revealing clothes, I know plenty of guys who would KILL for a girl like that. If you think I "sold my soul" why are you still with me anyway? Why would you be with anyone who doesn't have a soul?"

Rob opened up then and said: "I don't really think you don't have a soul, I was just saying that I don't..."

I interrupted him with "well then don't SAY that I've sold my soul because I haven't!" I was crying harder now. "I really like my job. It pays me and I have fun and I love the girls I work with. And that's more than a lot of people can say about their jobs. And that's enough for me right now. It has to be. And you know what doesn't help? Not the dicks that come into my restaurant and tip me because I look good in a miniskirt. No, they actually HELP me. It's YOU who doesn't help. Dicks like you, who find my Achilles heel and try to make me feel bad about myself. But you're going to have to try harder because I don't feel bad about myself, I only feel bad for YOU because you are such a moron!" I paused and realized I was shaking. I was almost done but I had one more thing to say.

"And as far as me having no self-respect is concerned," I stopped for a minute to suck in a deep breath, "that is the biggest load of bullshit I have ever heard because I have never had more self respect in my life than right now because I can't wait to get in my car and drive away and leave your stupid drunk ass here."

Rob's head snapped up and his eyes flashed. "You wouldn't dare," he said, a challenge in his eyes. "You're supposed to drive me back tomorrow. How am I going to get home?

"Oh, I wouldn't?" I snapped back. "I would. Watch me. And I couldn't care less how you get home tomorrow. But it's not gonna be with me. Wouldn't want you to be too embarrassed to be riding around with a whore like me. Figure it out. Bye." And with that, I threw on my sweater, fished my keys out of my clutch and headed for the exit. "Asshole," I called over my shoulder. I pushed the door open, ran to my car, started the engine and drove away..

Rob just stood there, alone in the hallway, swaying a little, incredulous, watching me leave.

~

"You're so lucky you're a lesbian."

"Why's that, girl?"

"Because you don't have to deal with guys and their stupid bullshit."

"Oh, there's still bullshit. Trust me. But it's bullshit laced with estrogen, and that's worse."

"I suppose so. But still, I hate guys."

"Hey, can you put a lemon on that iced tea for me?"

"Sure thing."

It was the Monday after the wedding. I was in the back pantry at Tilted Kilt during a lunch shift with my friend Heather, the lesbian. Whenever one of us girls would have guy problems, we'd always complain and moan about them to each other, and then eventually end up finding Heather and declaring that we "hated men" or we "wanted to become lesbians" or that Heather "had it so lucky cause she dated girls." It was always one of those untrue statements or some variation on them that came about because of anger and hurt and frustration, and Heather would always listen and counter with some words of wisdom that convinced us that "no, we did not want to become lesbians, truly," or "girls are just as much drama and can be just as big of asshole as guys are." She was usually right. We needed Heather to say these things to us. Every single time.

"I heard about that fireman guy who turned out to be a real jerk. That was him, right? I'm really sorry, girl. Sounds like a loser."

I sighed. "Yeah, that was him. He is a loser. I just can't believe he said all those things to me."

"Have you talked to him?"

"Not since I left his ass in the suburbs."

"Nice work. That's what you should have done."

"Yeah, but it's weird. Like, I don't even want to call him. I was that mad."

"You should have been, girl. He obviously didn't know you or care to get to know you. He just thought he was awesome cause he was a fireman. Like, please."

Suddenly, Jessica bounded into the back pantry, twirling her hair nervously. "Did someone say firemen? All jerks. All of them. Did you see the guy at table 51? So hot."

"Isn't your dad a fireman?" Heather asked, picking up her iced tea. "He's not a jerk. Oh, and don't care."

"He is a jerk! Why doesn't anyone believe me?" Jessica squealed. "And you don't care about what?"

"How hot the guy is at table 51. Unless he has a nice set of tits, couldn't care less." Heather walked away.

Jessica slumped over the soda machine and blew a strand of hair out of her face. "Heather is so lucky to be a lesbian. She doesn't have to deal with all of this bullshit."

"Yes she does," I said, slumping beside her. "It's just estrogen-filled bullshit."

"What?"

"Never mind."

"Anyway," Jessica continued, reaching for a cup and filling it with diet coke. "I really am sorry about Rob. I know I seemed insensitive, and I'm not. I just saw it coming. And I want someone better for you. Just think of it this way: you were hesitant being with him in the first place. He wanted to tie you down, and you're not ready for that right now, maybe. Definitely not with him. You want to go out and have fun and date casually and now you're going to have the opportunity to do just that. I love you and you're awesome and you work in this awesome restaurant with awesome girls like me." Every time she said "awesome" she made quotation marks in the air with her fingers. Then she laughed. "I'm just kidding. But seriously, we might complain about working here and it might suck sometimes, but we all do love working with each other. I love working with you. You're a great, smart girl. You're nice, you're fun, you're hot, and he didn't realize how lucky he was to have you. And it's certainly not your problem that he had a serious Madonna/ Whore complex. To him I say 'good luck with that!'" She raised a plastic cup in a mock toast and then reached out and squeezed my arm.

"Thanks, Jess," I said, straightening up. "That's really nice. I was telling Heather that I don't really even want to call him. And he hasn't called me. I'm sure I'll miss him, but it's definitely better off this way. Especially after what he said."

"Yup," Jessica said, picking up her diet coke and flinging a straw into it. "You're gonna be just fine. You should not have to deal with Madonna/whore complex guys. They need to figure it out. They never will, but that's not your problem."

Suddenly, Heather came running into the back pantry again and leaned against the wall. "Katy," she said, with an apologetic look on her face. "You just got sat." She grimaced. "It's a 5 top."

"So?" I said. "Thanks! Why do you look so weird about it? I could really use the money."

"Well, um," Heather said, looking at the floor. "You probably don't want this table."

"Why not?" I asked, peering around her shoulder. "Is it creepers? Women?"

"Worse."

"Well, what?"

"They're firemen."

"You're KIDDING me! That has to be a joke."

"Oh, my God, I'm sorry girl, I wish it was."

"Jesus Christ," I said, slamming a menu on the counter. "Is this bad karma or what?"

"I'll take em," Jessica said, pushing me out of the way. "You've been through enough."

"Are you sure?" I asked, shooting her a thankful look. "But you hate firemen too!" I said, laughing.

"Positive. I DO hate firemen, but I know how to deal with them. Been dealing with them my whole life."

"Thanks a lot," I said, smiling at her.

"It's the least I can do," Jessica said, smiling back. "But I still stand by the fact that all firemen are jerks. All of them!"

And with that, Jessica gave my hand a squeeze and headed toward her table.

Chapter 5

Kyle

Natasha and I were out to dinner on a Friday night. She was in town for a few nights so we decided to go out and celebrate. We were also celebrating the fact that she had officially dumped Alex, the asshole.

"How does it feel?" I asked her, twirling stringy pad thai noodles around my chopsticks and sticking the whole thing in my mouth.

"To be rid of dumbass Alex?" Natasha asked, slurping her wonton soup. "It feels fucking great is what it feels."

"He was such a jerk. I hated him."

"You and me both. I don't know why I even got together with him in the first place."

"Yeah, that was really weird," I said.

"I need a man who can be supportive of me. Not some 32 year old loser who still lives with his parents. And he was such a cheapskate! I swear to God he never paid for anything!"

"Yeah," I agreed with her, nodding my head vigorously. "How come you put up with that? I mean, he NEVER paid. You need a guy to buy you dinner at least."

"But you know what, Katy?" Natasha said, suddenly setting down her fork and becoming very serious. "Finding a guy to buy you dinner is like, impossible to come by nowadays. They're a dime a dozen."

"They are?" I asked, genuinely surprised. "Is chivalry dead?"

"I don't know about chivalry, per se," Natasha responded, picking up her fork again. "But the dudes who pay for our dinners all seem to have died. I'm all for equality and going dutch and and pro feminism and all that shit, but a guy still needs to pay for stuff like seventy-five percent of the time. I think." She twirled her fork with a flourish.

"I would agree with that statement," I said, mulling over her words. "I'm the same way. I make my own money, I'm proud of that fact, but guys need to step up to the plate these days. They need to prove that they're still the breadwinners and still men. You don't have to pay for everything for me, but it's always nice to be treated to dinners and gifts."

"So here's to us finding guys who will pay for stuff!"

"Here's to us!" I said, raising my glass. "May we find non-cheapskates!"

"Non-cheapasses," Natasha said, raising her glass as well.

"We will. I'm sure we will," I said, full of hope and optimism. We clinked glasses.

~

It was ironic that we had that conversation when we did. Because a week later, I met a guy. What was even more ironic was that he turned out to be the biggest cheapskate I could have met. I met him at work. It was the very beginning of

January and The Tilted Kilt was packed with businessmen as usual. But these days it was packed with even more businessmen because it was fantasy baseball time. I am not a fan of the game of baseball. It's slow, it's boring and I can never pay much attention to it. Football is the only sport I truly enjoy. And understand. But one thing I don't understand is fantasy football. Fantasy any sport, really. I do not understand grown men sitting around, picking out made up football teams like their lives depended on it. What happened before fantasy sports happened? Oh, that's right, guys just watched the ACTUAL teams play. But evidently, that's boring and not enough now.

So because the Tilted Kilt was a sports bar and fantasy team-picking had to do with sports, men would come in to the restaurant to have "Fantasy baseball parties." They would call a month in advance to book tables at the restaurant, and they usually requested the separate party room we had in the back. Fantasy baseball was serious business to these men. There was no joking around about this. They would come in with their computers and their sheets of paper, and sit all hunched over and type away on their computers and shuffle their papers and barely look up for the 4 hours that they would be there. And some would order a beer or two, but mostly it was water and a few appetizers for the table; usually 20 or more guys. So we servers hated serving them. They took up our precious tables for hours and didn't order nearly enough beer or food to make it worth our time. We always wondered why they didn't just stay home to pick their teams. They were at a restaurant with 25 beers on tap, greasy pub food and servers who wore miniskirts and bras. If they didn't drink, barely ordered food, and never looked up to appreciate their hot girl server, what exactly was the point of being there?

So it was a Friday and of course I had a table of fantasy douchebags. I was in charge of the section in the party room and my only table was 15 computer typists and paper shufflers. They had waltzed in like they owned the place, hurriedly set up all of their belongings, complete with a chart on an easel, denoting what I imagined to be some very important fantasy baseball pie graphs and charts, and immediately buried their faces in their made-up baseball team picking worlds. I had bounded into the room, cheerily said my name and asked them how they were, and my introduction was met with three scant nods and four quick glances. I thought I heard one of the men mumble a "hi" back, but I couldn't be sure. The rest of the guys made no indication that they realized I was even there. It was about 2pm on a Friday, so these businessmen, dressed in their suits and ties fresh from the office had obviously taken the rest of the day off of work…to participate in fantasy baseball. Lame. So lame.

In order to get their drink orders, I had to physically walk around the table to each one of them specifically and touch them on the shoulder. Touching never hurts, it makes the guest feel special and like he is getting personal service, especially working in a restaurant where the girls wear skimpy clothing, but in this case, it was necessary. None of the guys would have ordered anything or looked up at me if I hadn't. But I got it out of them. Three guys wanted a beer, two of them diet cokes, the rest waters. They had gotten three orders of nachos for the table, two orders of wings and two burgers. That was it.

I headed over to the computer and punched in the small order. Their bill was going to be about $70. For 15 people. This was annoying. I sighed.

"What wrong wiii you, you saaaa? Pawrine no waaann you be saaaa." I turned to my right and saw Pauline, one of the servers, standing next to me and smiling broadly. Pauline was Chinese and one of the best servers in the restaurant. She always made fun of the fact that she was Asian and of her slight accent. We weren't exactly politically correct at TK, but no one minded. We constantly laughed with each other at one another. It made for a fun, lighthearted working environment.

"I have the stupid fantasy douchebags in the party room. 15 of them, their bill's like seventy bucks. So not worth it. Stupid fantasy parties."

Pauline's face took on a surprised look. "Fantasy party? For what? Football?"

I put my hands on my hips. "Yes. I have a fantasy football party. These guys are picking teams for football when the season is already over and the Superbowl is in like three weeks. No, Pauline! Baseball! Fantasy BASEBALL!"

Pauline huffed and puffed. "Well, someone's in a bad mood! Sorry, not my fault you got that dumbass party. Sucks to be you."

"Thanks, that's nice. You're so sweet."

"I know, I am." Pauline flipped her long black hair behind her and tapped her fingers on the wooden counter behind her. "Come on, I'll help you carry your food over. I wanna fuck with the fantasy douchebags."

"Okay." I followed Pauline around the corner where we encountered the typical Friday kitchen scene at The Tilted Kilt. Tickets covered the top of the expo line; there must have been at least 30. Sandra was working at expo, yelling to the cooks in Spanish. Sandra was a server with us on most days, but when the kitchen got crazy on busy days, she would expedite. Sandra was Mexican and beautiful, and the nicest person in the world. She hardly ever swore and she almost never had a bad thing to say about anyone. And when she did, we were all shocked and appalled. Keri spent most of her time trying to "bring Sandra over to the dark side," as she always put it.

Darla was our kitchen manager. Darla was fat, had dyed red hair, glasses, was around 60 years old and pure evil. If Sandra never had one mean thing to say about anyone, Darla never had one good thing. She was the bigger, uglier Cruella Deville of the restaurant world. We had all tried to get along with Darla or at least to put up with her, but to no avail. She was constantly yelling random obscenities at us in her gravelly smoker's voice, and today was no exception. Nothing anyone ever did was correct. If you were behind the expo line trying to run food, she'd yell at you to get out. If you were not at the expo line trying to run food, she'd yell at you to get back there and help. Then she'd shove a basket of food in your hand, slam her fist down on whatever hard surface was in front of her, and threaten to have you fired. If you messed up an order, or even if the guest wanted something different and something had to be changed, it would be as if World War III was happening in the kitchen. This occurred with every single server roughly two or three times a day. No one was safe from Darla's wrath. Most of us tried to stay away from her most of the time, but when she was behind the line, today for example, that was next to impossible.

Pauline and I rounded the corner as Sandra spun around with wide eyes. "Katy!" she squealed, "can you take your food please? Darla is going crazy!"

"What else is new?" Pauline said as she grabbed my two burgers while I picked up my nachos and wings. I could see Kelly and Jessica standing at the edge of the line yelling at Darla, who was yelling right back. "I don't fucking CARE if the guest wanted no bacon on the chopped SALAD!!" Darla roared, glaring at both of them. "I said NO SUBSTITUTIONS today AT ALL!" She grabbed at the salad in Jessica's hand and threw it behind her, bowl and all. Lettuce and dressing went flying and landed on Jorge, one of the cooks. Another cook, Valentin, ducked just in time, narrowly escaping being decapitated by the bowl.

"Let's get out of here," I said, motioning for Pauline to follow me. I scurried away and slid to a stop in front of my douchebags where I placed their huge plate of nachos in front of them. No one noticed. Pauline lifted her arms above her head, auctioning off the burgers that two of the guys had ordered.

"Who got the barbecue bacon cheeseburger?" she yelled.

No one looked up.

"Let's try this again!" Pauline yelled even louder, raising her arms higher. "Who got the Barbeque bacon cheeseburger, anyone??"

Silence. Computer typing, paper shuffling and face burying.

Pauline set down the baskets of food, stuck out her tongue, crossed her eyes and put both of her middle fingers up. Then she started doing a crazy dance; tossing her hair, shaking her hips and turning around in a circle. I joined her. We must have looked like two totally insane girls, dancing four feet away from a table of businessmen. Our manager, Danny, walked by, stopped in his tracks, took one looks at us, opened his mouth to say something, thought better of it, shook his head, and walked the other way. Pauline and I stopped dancing and burst into laughter.

Not one fantasy douche ever looked up.

So Pauline picked up the baskets of food again, took a deep breath and screamed at the top of her lungs: "YOU DO FANTAAASSEEE BASEBAAAAWWW YOU ORDAA NUMBAA FOORRTEEEN, FLIEDD LIIICCCE ANNN

EGGRAAALLL??? YOU WAAANNN WONTON WIII THAAAA??"

Finally, everyone looked up, confused.

"That's better!" Pauline smiled sweetly. "Now that I have your attention, who got the burger?" she asked in a quiet, singsong voice.

I cracked up as Pauline set down their food in front of them and ran off to tend to her tables. The men were back in their own worlds. At least I could leave them alone and wouldn't have to worry about their needs. They had all obviously forgotten they were even in a public place.

I watched the hostess seat me with a table of 7. Excellent. At least I could put gratuity on this table. They all looked fairly normal and sat down in a normal sort of way. This was a good sign already. I walked up to the edge of the table and introduced myself with a small wave.

"Are you guys planning on ordering a normal amount of food and drinks for a table of seven?" I asked with a wink. "I have a bunch of fantasy baseball douchebags at my other table who ordered like, nothing, and I don't think I could handle that again with you guys…wait! You guys aren't having a fantasy baseball douchebag party too, are you? Because if you are, I'm going to have to get you another server. I'm at the end of my rope, here." I put my hand on my hip and banged my pen against my thigh. I tried my best to look exasperated, but a little smile made its way onto my face.

Most of them just looked at me with confused looks. Only one guy laughed. He was sitting to the left of me at the head of the table. I looked down and caught his eye. The first thing I noticed about him was that he was extremely good-looking. Reddish hair, brown eyes, good build. He was looking up at me with a nice smile.

"That was funny," he said. "No, we're not fantasy baseball douchebags, we got off work early so we thought we'd come in and have some drinks. I'm Kyle," he said, extending his hand. I shook his hand and his eyes reluctantly left mine. "So, guys," he said, addressing his companions, "what does everyone want to drink?" Everyone ordered a beer, as did Kyle, and then he added "and a shot of Patron for me, and one for you, too."

Awesome. Kyle was my kind of guy.

I smiled at him again and said, "you read my mind. Let me just go ask my manager."

"You do that," Kyle said, giving me the once over.

I ran over to Kelly who was at the host stand, doing something at the computer. She looked distracted and probably didn't want to be bothered, but I needed my shot from hot guy.

"Hey, Kelly, see that cute guy over there at 24? He wants to buy me a shot. Can I have one, please? I think he likes me. He's super hot."

Kelly craned her neck around to take a look. "Yeah, he is pretty hot." She looked back at me and clucked her tongue. "I don't know. It's only like 2:30, a little early for shots." She took another look at my pleading face and said "Okay! One shot! Got it? Uno shot! Only one!"

"Got it! Thanks!" I said, skipping away. "I'll only take one, I promise!"

Four shots later, I had forgotten my troubles with the fantasy douchebags and had a date with Kyle for later that night.

~

Kyle really did seem perfect, at first. He was funny, sweet, cute, fun and had his shit together. He seemed more perfect than any guy I had dated since college, actually. It had been years since I had felt like I could feel a certain way about someone again. I didn't feel it yet, it was way too early to know that much, but I felt like this person and I may be a really great match for one another. I didn't want to screw it up.

The one big thing that bothered me about him, though, was that he seemed kind of cheap. Again, it was too early to tell, but it was a feeling I got about him, the "cheapskate guy vibe." That vibe is never good. Just as Natasha and I discussed, we women understand that, these days, things are changing. We want to be treated as men's equals, and, with that desire comes equality in everything, money included. We know this, we do. And while this is something we believe in, we still expect chivalry not to be dead. We don't mind paying for our share, or treating the man every once in awhile, or even frequently in some circumstances. We have our own lives and make our own money and we're not ashamed of that fact, nor should we be. BUT we do expect to be taken care of to some extent. We expect and appreciate being treated to nice things and being shown that we are worth it in that way. Not ALL THE TIME but as frequently as any man would like to do so. Basically, we like guys to pay for shit.

So for me to get the vibe from Kyle was not good. He paid for the bill on our "first date." It had been that night after we met at the TK, and I had brought Kelly along with me as my wingman. That actually worked out, because Kyle had told me his friend Jake would be tagging along as well. So it was a kind of double date. In the loosest sense of the word. We had had fun and barhopped to three different bars over the course of about eight hours. And, in doing so, had racked up three significant bar tabs along the way. Kelly and I, being the strong, independent females we are, offered to give the boys money every time the check came at each bar. Basically, we didn't expect them to actually take us up on it, but we were just trying to do what we were "supposed to do." And every time the check came, the boys waved our money away, assuring us that they "had it," and it was "their treat" and not to "worry about it." Basically, they were doing what they were supposed to do as well. That, and they weren't idiots and they knew that if they didn't shell out, we wouldn't put out. So they did. And we did. Everything seemed to be going well.

Except one little thing that I noticed. When Kyle was handed the bill for the first bar, and he and Jake were reaching for their wallets, his face took on look of contempt. It was a look that said "this bill is really high and the night is just getting started and I am upset that I have to spend my money on this girl." And when Kelly and I asked if we could chip in, and we said it sincerely, or seemingly enough, Kyle refused, but a look of utter resentment then crossed his face. It was a look that said, "I'm going to say no to your request to help pay for this, but I don't mean it. I am going to pay for this because I am supposed to, but I resent you for asking that question when you know very well I cannot take you up on it."

I realize that those statements may sound completely ridiculous. They sound dramatic and silly and possibly untrue. But that is what I saw in those looks on his face for a fleeting second. Call me crazy, but I knew I saw those things and that is why I got the vibe from Kyle immediately. I brushed them off, though, because I had just met this person. What the hell did I know about what his looks looked like or meant? Nothing. And I liked him already. He was "perfect," so I overlooked the looks.

I caught Natasha on the phone at Dulles airport on her two-hour layover to discuss the most recent Kyle developments and to get her opinion. She hadn't been home in three weeks so I hadn't spoken to her much. She knew about my first date and I had very hurriedly tried to explain to her what a great time we had had. But today on the phone she sounded like she was rushing through the airport. I could hear the loudspeaker announcing flights to LaGuardia and LAX and Hartsfield-Jackson International airports. Natasha was huffing and puffing and I heard her speaking to another employee in a hushed tone.

"Is this a bad time?" I asked her.

"No, no, sorry. I was just talking to this flight attendant. Her flight got delayed and she was asking me about my flight. It's like no one speaks to you unless you have your phone up against your ear. Then they automatically bother you. It's like, fuck off, I'm on the phone, duh."

"I know. That's so annoying. So is your flight delayed?"

"Oh, probably. So, what's up? Kyle? He's perfect, right?"

"Almost. He may be…a cheapskate."

"A cheapass?!" Natasha squealed. "How is this possible? How do you even find this guy who seems so great and he turns out to have the one bad trait that we are both specifically trying to avoid at this juncture on our respective jerk-meeting journeys?"

I sighed. "I don't know. But I just get the feeling."

"The feeling is not good. Intuition is usually dead on. At least our jerk intuition is dead on. Has been for years."

"Yeah, but I'm not sure he's a jerk. I think he's a nice guy and really great. And I really like him!" I was almost whining now, trying to push all thoughts of him being cheap from my mind and focus on his positive attributes.

"But does he pay for your shit?"

"He paid for our first date. But I got this weird vibe from him when he did it and he seemed really put out by doing it. He gave me the 'I can't believe I'm paying for all your drinks and food' look. Is that even such a thing, though? I'm not sure that's a thing. Maybe I'm just crazy. Tell me I'm crazy."

Suddenly I heard the airport loudspeaker announce boarding for a flight to Des Moines. There was a pause on Natasha's end of the phone until the squawky voice became silent. Then she said "You're not crazy. I know the look. Alex used to give me that look all the time. And we know how much he ended up paying for my stuff. Never."

"Damn. And here I was hoping I made that look up."

"Nope, you didn't. The look on the first date is definitely not a good sign. But it's very, very early. Don't freak out. There's hope that he's not a cheapass yet."

"When do I get to start freaking out, then?"

"Not sure. But you'll know. And you better recognize it when it comes."

"And what if I don't?"

"Then you're stuck with the cheapass for all eternity."

"Okay. We'll see what happens."

"Keep me updated. And hey," Natasha continued "I know your birthday's coming up but I'm so sorry I'm not going to be able to make it to your party. I'll be in Canada then for about four days. I suck, I know, I'm the worst friend ever. I'm never around and I'm not going to get to meet your perfect, but cheap boyfriend."

I laughed out loud. "It's okay. You have to work, I understand. We'll miss you, though. Let's hope you get to meet the soon-to-be boyfriend. And more importantly, let's pray he doesn't turn out to be cheap."

"Here's hoping. Talk to you later, girl." And with that, Natasha clicked off the phone.

~

Two weeks later, I was leaving my local bar, McGinny's. The girls and I got together there every Monday night to sometimes drink, sometimes not, but always to wind down from the day and just hang out. We were usually the only people in there on Monday nights, and we liked it that way. We had the run of the place. We went to see our friend, Tim, our favorite bartender, and to just chill. Tim was the best. He was our go-to guy for guy advice. We were constantly asking Tim about what to say to these guys we dated, and what to do. If a guy texted us and said something cryptic, we'd run it by Tim to find out what he really meant in "guy speak." Tim probably thought we were absolute crazy girls, insecure and pathetic (which we probably were) but I believe he also actually enjoyed it. He was always willing to help us and was such a good sport about it. McGinny's was our Cheers, our home away from home, and Tim was our Sam.

I had just stepped out the door after waving goodbye to Kelly and was heading to my car, when I received a text message. I yanked my phone out of my purse and looked down. It was from Kyle and it said:

Hey whats up

My first thought was "Yay! A text from Kyle!" I hadn't heard from him for two days. We had hung out at his place three days before. He had made me dinner and watched a movie, and I had stayed over. He had made dinner for me twice before. He liked to cook and was good at it. I found it very nice and romantic that he would want to cook dinner for me at his place. Most guys I had dated before had not cooked for me, although I do enjoy a dinner out over a home cooked meal any day of the week. But again, Kyle was "perfect," so I was over the moon about it. My second thought was "I'm so glad I waited two days to text him and he was the first one to break! He must miss me desperately and is thinking about me!" My third thought was "but wait, there's no punctuation in this text message and that's a bad sign," and my giddy feeling began to wane.

I am an overanalyzer of text messages. I think girls by definition, are, but I think I take it to the very extreme. I obsess over them, I think about what they mean, what they could mean, and what they might possibly perhaps mean. Text messages are serious business to me. They are not something to be taken lightly, so for Kyle not to put any punctuation in the aforementioned text, was very telling to me. It was indicative of him not caring, or of him about to launch into something more serious than asking me what was up. So, without wasting any more time, I texted him back and wrote: *Not too much what's up with you.* With no punctuation, obviously. Because I didn't care either. And I kept walking, and I waited for his response. And then it came, one minute later, and it was long so it was broken up into two parts. And this is what it said:

> *Was going through some of my receipts and found the one from TK on the day we met and the ones from all the bars we went to afterwards. I spent so much money on you. Fuck, you're expensive.*

Complete with perfect punctuation.

EXCUSE ME??

WHAT THE FUCK??

What was this? Was this a joke? Was he kidding? He had to be kidding. I stopped walking and re-read the text. As I read it a third time, I decided it was the rudest text I had ever received in my life, joke or no joke. I looked up, hoping, PRAYING that it was some sort of sarcastic joke he was playing on me and pondered what to do next. As I looked around, I remembered McGinny's and Tim. I was only one block away. Perfect! I would wait to respond and go hear what the wise Tim had to say. He would know what he meant. He would know what to tell me to say. I ran back to the bar.

Thankfully, Tim was still the only person in there. "Back so soon?" he asked, swinging his legs off the bar stool in front of him and jumping behind the bar. "Did you miss me? Red bull, vodka?"

"Let's make it a straight vodka."

"Oh, shit. What happened?"

"Kyle."

"The marine?"

"Yes, Tim! The Marine!" I yelled exasperatedly. "The guy we were just talking about for the past 2 hours! The guy who I was trying to determine with you if he likes me or not?!"

"Katy, you have a different guy every WEEK who you are trying to determine if he likes you or not. The only way you'd ever really be convinced if some guy liked you would be if he got 'I like Katy' tattooed on his forehead." Tim poured my drink and set it in front of me. He looked at me with a look of pity and said "even then, I'm not sure you'd believe it, actually."

"Shut up, Tim." He was totally right. "ANYWAY," I continued, taking a sip of my drink, "Kyle just texted me and I'm not sure what to make of it. Maybe you can figure it out. Let me show you." I held my phone up in front of Tim's face and his brow furrowed as he read it. When he finally comprehended it, he took a step back and whistled low under his breath. "Oh, man," he said.

"OH, MAN?!" I screeched. "Oh, man is bad, right? That's really bad. Why are you saying oh, man?!" I was close to hysterical. I was not handling this well. I needed this to be okay. I needed Kyle to continue to be perfect. I needed that text to not have been sent to me.

"Katy, calm down," Tim said, laughing at me. "It's not good, okay? I mean, come on, you don't need me to tell you that. You're a smart girl. It's kind of rude. In fact, it's really rude. It obviously didn't make you feel very good, either, so yeah, 'oh, man.'"

"Yeah, I know," I said. "So what do I do now? What do I say back to him?"

Tim looked thoughtful for a minute. "You say… *expensive huh? What makes you think that?* Coy, but curious enough. It actually requires a response."

"Tim, you're a genius." I typed it in and waited for his text back, tapping my fingers nervously on the bar. Right away, it came back. This one was long as well, so it was broken up into three separate texts. It said:

> *8 shots of Patron: $70, pepperoni pizza: $10, 3 vodka red bulls: $30, 4 shots of Jameson: $40. That's a lot of money. Again, expensive*

EXCUSE ME??

WHAT THE FUCK??

I scooted my chair back in shock. If I had thought his first text was the rudest one I had ever received in my life, I was wrong; this one was. I put my forehead in my hand and with the other, held the phone up for Tim to see. I heard him whistle again and looked up just in time to see him shaking his head. "He bullet-pointed you."

"He what?"

"He bullet-pointed you. He listed out all of those things for you to see. That's..."

"Bad," I finished for him, making a pouty face.

"Bad. Exactly. He seems like an asshole. Who does that?" Tim asked, looking thoughtful.

"No! But he's perfect!" I said in a whiny voice, realizing as I said it how annoying and ridiculous I sounded. And how untrue it was.

"Katy, um, he's not. Obviously," Tim said, leaning back against the bar. "First of all, who does that, like I said, who sends a text to a girl he's just started seeing, BULLET-POINTING all of the drinks she ordered on their first date, rubbing it in her face and making her feel bad about it? It's rude and he sounds like a loser. Second of all, who goes through their receipts anyway? That's just really weird."

"I know," I sighed. "But I really like him. I really do. I think he's a cheapskate, but maybe I can look beyond that. Maybe this is just a misunderstanding?" I mused, trying to convince myself of the statement as much as Tim.

Tim looked at me sympathetically. Or more accurately, with pity. "You're so much better than that, Katy. Seriously. Just let it go." He looked at me pointedly but to no avail. He could tell by my face that I was not going to let it go, at least not yet, and he knew me better than that.

"Okay," he sighed and continued, "I can tell by your face that you're not going to let it go right now and I know you better than that. So here's what you text him back..." Tim trailed off and leaned against the bar.

"What?! What?!" I screeched, putting my elbows on the bar in anticipation.

"You text back 'well, I may be expensive but at least I'm not some ex-Marine loser douchebag who goes through his receipts and then texts hot chicks I'm banging about my lack of finances which makes me look even more loser-y and douche-y."

"I text him that?"

"No."

"Wait, you think I'm hot?"

"I do. You are."

"Thanks Tim!"

"No problem."

"Wait, we're getting off track! What do I really text him for real?"

"Nothing. You don't text him back. Ever. You drop the loser and move on with your life."

"So…I don't text him back? At all?"

"Nope."

"Ever?"

"Correct."

I pretended to consider this novel idea for half of a second and then I sprung open my phone and started typing.

"What are you doing?" Tim asked.

"Texting him back."

"Jesus Christ, Katy, why?"

"Because I don't want to mess anything up with this!"

"YOU don't want to mess anything up with this? Seems like he's already the one who messed things up with his rude comments. What is it about this guy?"

"He's perfect!" Even as I said it, I realized how ridiculous it sounded. Was I really this girl now?

"How is he perfect?" Tim challenged me.

"Because he has a good job and he has his own place and he's cute…" I trailed off.

"That's why he's perfect for you? You could find a million guys with those things going for them. Ones who don't have money issues."

"But it doesn't seem like he has money issues!"

"Regardless if he does or if he doesn't, he's a cheap ass. Seriously cheap. Obviously."

I pondered this for a moment. Tim was most likely correct. But what did he know? I had found a really cool guy and there was no way I was messing this one up. I would text him back but I would wait until I got home. In the meantime, I would make Tim think that I wasn't going to.

"Fine!" I said, snapping my phone shut. "I won't text him back!"

Tim looked at me again with the pity face and filled my glass with vodka. "Yes, you will. You're just waiting until you get home so I don't yell at you anymore."

Damn, he was good.

~

I went over to his house twice in the next week. We watched movies and he made dinner for me both times. As we were sitting at the table at the end of the meal on the second night, I reminded him my birthday was coming up. I had told him the week before, but wanted to keep reminding him so it was impossible for him to forget. I was really looking forward to it. I couldn't wait for him to come. He had met some of my friends, but not officially and it was going to be nice for me to actually have a date to my own birthday party. It had been awhile since I had, and I had told everyone that he would be coming.

"Yeah, so," I started, setting my fork down. "Next Friday is my birthday, you excited?" I asked him, looking at him hopefully.

"Sure, that'll be fun," he said, not so excitedly. "What's the plan again?"

"Well, McGinny's, and dinner before at Topo Gigio, that amazing Italian restaurant downtown."

He stopped while clearing the dishes from the table and looked at me accusingly. "Isn't that place pretty expensive?"

"Um, sort of," I said, glaring at him. "I mean, I guess so. But it's my birthday, and it's really good food." What was his deal? He was always talking about how expensive everything was. It was really becoming a turnoff.

"Well, that's cool, but I don't know if I'll be able to make dinner, babe." He turned his back on me and headed into the kitchen.

"What?" I yelled, a little too loudly. "What do you mean? I thought you said you could come?" My voice was wavering slightly and I was trying to keep the panic and surprise out of it.

"Yeah, well, I forgot I have to go to a function on the north side right after work. I would skip it, but I totally have to go. It's for, like, work. I'll definitely be able to make it to McGinny's afterward, though. Wouldn't miss it. Can't wait," he finished, giving my arm a pinch.

Okay. This sucked. It sounded extremely shady. I weighed my options. I could either tell him how upset I was, start an altercation, and have him possibly bail on coming to McGinny's too, or I could keep my mouth shut and ignore it. I chose the latter, smiled, told him it was okay as long as he came to the bar, and suggested we start the movie. I thought that was the right thing to do. And I thought, it must have been, because I felt happy and like I had made the right choice. Sort of. Somewhat. Possibly. Perhaps.

~

I didn't see Kyle for the rest of the week. He was busy with work stuff and I wanted to put a little space between us so when we saw each other at my birthday party, it would be that much better. I wanted the night to be perfect. Already it wasn't going to be, because Kyle wasn't going to be able to make it to dinner, but I had perfected the art of telling myself things were perfect when they really weren't, so I decided to just have a nice dinner with my friends and then meet up with him later. I had more friends coming to McGinny's as well, and I told Kyle he could bring Jake, too.

I showed up to my birthday dinner in a little black dress and heels. I wanted to look exceptionally hot so Kyle would immediately regret missing dinner and regret being a cheapskate. Jessica, Kelly, Keri, Pauline and Sandra all squealed when I showed up to the restaurant, and Heather said "you look hot, girl."

"Thanks, guys," I said, sliding into my seat. "Gotta look good for when Kyle shows up later."

"He IS showing up later, correct?" Kelly said with venom in her words. "Because, if not, I will murder him. I'm serious. He will die." Then she softened almost immediately and a smile graced her face. "Hey, is Natasha coming tonight?"

"No, Natasha can't make it. She's working. But Kyle is coming to McGinny's later. So no need for murder."

"Okaaaay," Kelly said, drawing out the word and looking skeptical. "He better."

"Where is he now anyway?" Sandra asked, chewing on a breadstick.

"He had a work thing up north."

"Like suburbs north?" Jessica asked.

"Yeah, pretty much. The North Shore he said."

"What kind of function would be held at The North Shore?" Jessica was pensive. "All there is there are really ritzy mansions and…like, Whole Foods stores."

"I don't know, okay? Some Marine function thing, I don't know!" I was getting exasperated. "I didn't ask any more questions. He's coming later, that's all we need to know. Let's just eat. And drink. Where's my Grey Goose?"

I signaled for the waiter. I caught the girls all look at one another, but then they all put on smiles.

"Yep! Let's drink!" Sandra exclaimed. "To Katy-Happy Birthday!" We all clinked glasses.

~

Four Grey Gooses later, we were ready to head to McGinny's, all pretty drunk. We exited the restaurant and walked to the corner to try to hail a few cabs to get to the bar. As we stumbled along the street, laughing, Heather looked to her right and caught sight of the bar whose windows were facing the street. "Look at that place" she said, "it's packed! Wonder what that is, is it new?"

Kelly peered through the window and said "no-that's Sidebar-hey Katy, isn't this the bar we came to with Kyle and Jake that first night you guys met?"

"Yeah it is," I said, looking up from fishing through my purse where I was trying to find my I.D. "That's Kyle's favorite bar. He's always talking about how awesome it is."

"Well, is it awesome?" Pauline asked. "It looks busy."

"It was fun," Kelly piped in. "They have really good happy hour specials."

"Do you want to go in?" Pauline asked me. "Get one drink before we head to McGinny's? We have time."

"I saw a really hot guy through the window," Keri said. "I say we go!"

"And I saw a really hot girl," Heather said, throwing the butt of her cigarette across the street. "I'm down."

"Well, let's do it!" I said, following all of them into the bar. "This will be fun."

We all walked in and lined up so the bouncer could check our I.D.'s. Mine was lost in the depths of my purse. I continued to fish through it as my friends filed in one by one. I finally found it and held it out to the bouncer. As he handed it back to me I yelled over the noise to the girls who were already inside the bar. "Hey, I'm glad we came here! Kyle can suck it…he's going to be so jealous that we're at his favorite bar on my birthday meeting hot guys and girls! So jealous!" I singsonged drunkenly.

Kelly stopped short in front of me then, and I ran into her back. She whipped around to face me and said "maybe not so jealous."

"What? What are you talking about?" I asked, confused.

"Kyle might not be so jealous that he's missing out on this…considering he's here."

"What? He can't be! He's at the North Shore, he just texted me saying he was going to leave for the city in an hour…" as I was speaking I was swiveling my head as fast as possible, yammering on to try to convince myself it wasn't true. Kelly took her hand, placed it on my chin, yanked my head forward and pointed in front of her. "Look."

And I looked straight ahead to see a group of guys at the far end of the bar. First I saw Jake, laughing, holding a drink in his hand. And then I saw an auburn-haired man in a suit, holding a drink and laughing, turn around and lean on the service bar.

It was Kyle.

My jaw dropped to the ground. I stood there, flabbergasted, just staring at him. A bunch of thoughts were rolling around in my head, but I couldn't make sense of any of them. How could he be here? He had told me he couldn't make dinner because he had to be at a Marine function in the suburbs, and now he was downtown, at his favorite bar, which was right next to the restaurant where we had been. I looked down at my phone and checked the text message that said he was still in the North Shore and would be heading back to Chicago soon. He had sent me the message

22 minutes ago. Now he was standing in front of me. It was difficult for me to comprehend what was going on.

"What's going on?" I asked Kelly, stupidly, and still a little drunk, although this was killing my buzz significantly.

"What's going on is that Kyle is an ASSHOLE!" she yelled very loudly, standing on her tiptoes and cupping her hands around her mouth, as if Kyle could hear. She came back down on her heels and put her arm around me and said "he lied, Katy. He's a liar and an asshole. He said he couldn't make dinner cause he had something to do but he didn't and now you caught him red-handed."

Even though she was exactly right, I was still having trouble comprehending. I couldn't believe he was standing twenty feet in front of me, laughing with his friends. He just hadn't wanted to come to dinner so he lied to me. What a jerk.

As I stood there, dumbfounded, just staring at him, Kelly brought the other girls in for a huddle and explained to them what was going on. I saw her whisper and point toward the end of the bar, and then five heads whipped around suddenly to glare in his direction. They all snapped back in tandem and five pairs of pity-filled eyes focused on me. I was certainly getting a lot of pity-filled looks lately. I decided right then and there that I was sick of it and it was ending now.

"What are you going to do, girl?" Heather asked me.

"I'm going to take a shot and then I'm going to march over there and confront him. I can't believe he's here," I said, under my breath.

Sandra scurried to the bar to buy me a shot and Heather said "you go, girl, give him hell. Stupid guys, all of them."

"Yeah, what an asshole," Keri said.

"I will murder him, I swear," Kelly said.

"Fuck him," Jessica said, passing over the shot Sandra had brought. I took it down, said "thanks girls, wish me luck" and made my way through the crowd to the other side of the bar. I stood right next to Jake and elbowed him as hard as I could in the ribs. "OW!" he yelled, turning around "what the fuck?" He turned around to see who had elbowed him and his eyes met mine. I smiled sweetly at him and said "oh, geez, I'm sorry! I didn't mean to hurt you. I was just wondering if you could get Kyle's attention for me?" I batted my eyelashes and crossed my arms over my chest.

Jake looked shocked when he realized who I was. "oh, um…shit," he stammered, and then just stood there.

"Never mind, I'll get him myself." I tapped Kyle on the shoulder.

He turned around just as he was putting the straw to his lips and was taking a sip of his drink. When he saw me, he choked on his drink and the straw went flying out of his mouth. Just like in the movies. When he was done coughing, he said nothing but simply looked at me with terror in his eyes. At least it wasn't pity.

"Hi, Kyle," I said. "I'm very surprised to see you here, considering you said you couldn't make my birthday dinner because you were going to be in the suburbs."

"Katy, I'm really sorry," he said and set his drink down on the bar. "Do you want to go outside somewhere to talk?"

"Nope. This is fine. Right here."

"Are you sure? We could go…"

"I SAID right here is fine. And you can buy me a drink as well."

Kyle hesitated and ran his hands through his hair. He looked at Jake.

"I have no idea why you're looking at your dumbass friend when you should be buying me a vodka on the rocks and attempting to convince me that you are not a lying, scumbag jerk." Kyle said nothing but signaled to the bartender. "Vodka on the rocks," he said, holding out a $10.

"Any specific kind of vodka?" the bartender asked.

As Kyle shook his head "no," I told her "Belvedere," never taking my eyes off of Kyle. "Better get some more money out." I continued to glare at him. He took out his wallet, fished out another $10 and handed them to the bartender. She gave me my drink and he tried again: "Katy, I really am sorry."

"You're sorry that you lied to me? You're sorry that you're an asshole? You're sorry that you're a lying asshole? What are you sorry about?" I was getting meaner as I was drinking more.

And Kyle was obviously getting more defensive. He dropped the puppy dog persona and said: "Look, I didn't lie to you, the function got cancelled and I stayed at work late, I just texted you that I was in the North Shore because it was easier than explaining all of that…I was going to tell you it got cancelled when I saw you later." He saw my dubious look and continued, talking very quickly "Jake asked me if I wanted to grab a quick drink before we headed over to your thing and I said yes. We literally just got here. This is my first drink," he said, motioning toward the drink he had set down on the service bar.

"Huh," I said, staring at him. He looked even more terrified and started fidgeting with his shirt. I turned toward the bar and yelled for the bartender. "Ma'am? Can you come here for a minute, please? When you get a second?" I asked very nicely. She came over, poured a drink for another customer and said "what's up?"

"What's your name?"

"Maria."

"Maria, can you please tell me what number drink this is for this gentleman right here?" I pointed to the drink first and then to Kyle, and then I gave her the fellow service industry professional/girl-to-girl look. We who work in the restaurant industry can convey so many things to each other with just a look. We get it. And so can girls. Girls understand each other. So the look I gave her was one that said "I am trying to catch this asshole jerk scumbag in a lie, can you please help me with this by answering the question?" and she got it. Big time. That's the other thing about restaurant industry people; they always know exactly how many drinks you've had, even when you don't.

She looked first to Kyle then to me and smiled a little smile. "This is his fifth drink and his friends' sixth beer," she said, nodding in Jake's direction. "They've had three shots of Jameson apiece, and ordered calamari and hot wings about an hour ago." Then she stuck a piece of lime on the rim of a glass, leaned in and pretended to whisper to me, although it was loud enough for Kyle and Jake to hear and said "and by the way, in case you were wondering, they've been here for three and a half hours." She picked up the glass, straightened up and we both turned our heads to glare at Kyle who was almost cowering in the corner.

Busted.

Kyle grabbed his drink and took a sip and kind of shrugged. "Look, Katy, I'm sorry," he said for what seemed like the millionth time. "I did want to hang out with you on your birthday but dinner was going to be really expensive. That place is a lot of money. I just don't have those kinds of funds right now."

"Dinner was only about $50 a piece!" I yelled at him, exasperated.

"That's a lot for dinner!" he yelled back. "Can't you understand that I can't just be throwing money around?

It must be nice that money grows on trees for you, but I need to save and can't be just spending tons of money on dinner!"

"Maria!" I yelled, slamming my drink down on the bar. "Can you come back over here for a second?"

Maria looked over and practically ran toward me when she saw that I was beckoning to her. I think she was enjoying the excitement and drama of our fight and was happy to be involved. "How can I help you?" she asked, leaning in toward me conspiratorially.

"Can you please tell me how much this gentleman's bill is? Currently?"

She didn't even need to pull it up on her computer screen. She looked toward the ceiling for a second, counted on her fingers and said "currently, it's at $76. $76.54 to be exact." We glared at him for the second time.

Busted again.

"So you're telling me you couldn't, or rather, I'm sorry, didn't WANT to spend $60 not even on ME on my BIRTHDAY dinner, but instead LIED to me and came to a bar with your dumbass friend where you are about to spend AT LEAST $76 dollars?! Is that what happened?" I was screaming now.

"Seventy-six FIFTY-FOUR" Maria chimed in.

Best bartender ever. I loved her.

Maria walked away and Kyle just stood there with nothing to say and then I realized that Kyle had enough money. He had a car and a house and nice things and a good job. He may not have been the richest person ever but he certainly had enough money for everything he needed and wanted. He just didn't have enough money that he wanted to spend on anyone ELSE, me included.

It all made sense now. Kyle was cheap. He was a cheapskate. So much so, that he lied to me to get out of paying for a dinner, even though we were dating and it was my birthday. It explained all of the dinners in, the looks of contempt when he had to pay for anything for me. It explained the bullet-point text. I had known all of this before, but it finally became alarmingly clear. Kyle wasn't perfect. He was fun and cute and fairly nice. But he was totally cheap. Cheap as could be, and he was a jerk about it.

"You know what, Kyle, I think you're a really cool guy," I said, slurping the rest of my drink and placing it down on the bar. "I THOUGHT you were a really cool guy, I should say. But you lying to me about your whereabouts during my birthday celebration is just unacceptable and rude. And you know what else is rude? You texting me to say that I'm expensive, even though I'm not. In fact, I'm the least expensive girl you'll ever meet. I am not high maintenance, I pay my own way, or at least OFFER most of the time, and I have way more of my OWN money than you do, even, guaranteed."

Kyle tried to butt in to speak but I was on a roll. "I have NEVER in my life received a text BULLET-POINTING the drinks and shots you bought for me that you OFFERED to pay for on our FIRST DATE. I should have dropped you right then and there. Good luck finding a girl who doesn't mind being called expensive or receiving a text spelling out how much shots of Patron shots cost." I couldn't stop. I was boiling mad, and Kyle was still cowering and I was having too much fun giving him hell.

"And FURTHERMORE, did you really think it would be effective to spell out what each shot cost on that ridiculous text? I KNOW what a fucking shot of Patron costs, you idiot, I work in the bar where you purchased them and I sold them to you because I was your server! Take my advice, don't EVER do something like that again if you want to date another girl. And don't bother coming in to my restaurant ever again, either. The menu seems a little too pricey for you, and no one likes a cheapskate. Have a great night and don't forget to tip the lovely Maria. And by tip I mean 20% or more, asshole." With that, I spun on my heel and headed back toward the girls who were all standing in a group, suspense on their faces.

"What happened, what happened?" they all cried.

I held up my hand to silence them and said "I will tell you, but first…"

I summoned for Maria who smiled when she saw me and bounded over. "Maria, before we go, all six of us would like a shot of your most expensive tequila, salt and limes." Maria mixed the shots and we all took them down like water, except for Jessica who practically choked drinking hers.

Maria gathered the shot glasses then winked at me. "I'm going to assume these shots go on the gentleman's tab," she said.

I smiled. "They do, as a matter of fact. And here's $20," I said, extending a bill to her. That's the first part of your tip. I then pulled out a pen and wrote Kyle's number on a napkin and handed it to her. "That's the gentleman's number. If he doesn't tip you 20% at least, you have my permission to stalk him over text until he gets his lying ass back in this bar to give you what you deserve. And when you text him, make sure to bullet-point how much each shot, drink and morsel of food he had, costs."

Maria smiled. "I'll do that. Thanks. Oh, and by the way, Happy Birthday."

"Thanks, Maria," I said. And with that, I headed for the exit and the girls followed me.

~

"WHAT?!" I yelled as Tim poured me another shot of tequila. "What did you just say?"

"I asked if you really let him have it like that? Like, you didn't really say all of that stuff to the Marine?"

"I seriously did."

"That's awesome!"

We were shouting to each other over the noise in the bar, which was deafening this Friday night. People were packed into McGinny's, wall-to-wall. Around 10 more girls from the restaurant had showed up for my party, and the rest of the room was filled with random people who were out on Friday night. They must have heard about my extravaganza and wanted to see what all the fuss was about. In the cab on the way to McGinny's I had told the girls what had happened at Sidebar. They were incredulous. And when we got to McGinny's, Tim asked where "my douchebag Marine" was, so we all told him the story, too. Pretty soon, almost everyone in the bar had heard the story. I was getting shots bought for me left and right in celebration, and I was definitely drunk. But I was having fun. It was turning out to be a really good birthday.

"Are you sad he's not here?" Tim asked.

"A little, to be honest, I mean, we had fun. I was really just kind of looking forward to being with a guy on my birthday, you know? As in having a date?"

"I'm a guy," Tim assured me, winking at me. "A cool guy, too, I'll be your date on your birthday. Just don't tell my girlfriend."

"I won't. And thanks. You'd be a good date. You're not a cheapskate."

"I am not. In fact, I'm so not, I'm buying you that last shot."

"You buy us every shot, Tim."

"True. And it's your birthday. Your bill will be zero dollars. Just don't tell my boss."

I laughed. "I won't."

Just then the girls walked up to me. Pauline lurched into me and gave me a hug. She was drunk too. "I'm sorry Kyle was such an asshole. Are you upset? We're here for you."

Kelly said "I will go murder him for you if you want. You know I will."

"Guys!" I said, pushing Pauline away and smiling. "I'm okay! You know, I'm actually so much better than I thought I would be. I'm not really sad. I'm more mad than sad right now."

"That's probably because you're drunk," Jessica said, twirling her hair nervously.

"Could be," I said. "But I realize now that I was putting him on a pedestal for some reason."

"A pedestal he didn't deserve to be on." Heather said.

"Yeah, but he was a cool guy. I liked him. I think the problem was I was so desperate to have someone in my life with all of his qualifications. But the money thing was a glaring problem. I don't need someone who pays for everything for me, like some sugar daddy, far from it, but I do need someone who is willing to spend some money on me and someone who doesn't rudely rub it in my face when he does."

"And someone who doesn't lie to you on your birthday, or ever for that matter," Sandra piped in.

"You're totally right. That was really shitty. I think that's why I'm not that upset. I feel like, if someone could do that to me, I don't need him anymore. I'm sure I'll miss him and probably text him when I get drunk...but then again…maybe not. Maybe I'll find someone else tonight! In this bar! Someone….better."

"I'm sure you will!" Sandra crowed.

"And until then, there's always Tim!" Kelly yelled.

"We always have Tim!" Keri chimed in.

"To Tim!" Heather shouted, raising her glass in the air. We all did the same.

"No, to Katy," Jessica smiled. "Happy Birthday."

"Happy Birthday!" all the girls shouted, and we clinked our glasses together.

Chapter 6

Ricky

I can't remember exactly when I really got to know Ricky. He had been coming in to The Tilted Kilt for months before I actually took notice of him. He usually sat with Jessica or Keri, and he always came in with his friend, Casey. They worked down the street at a news station, so they had to get up very early in the morning to be at work in the wee hours. Because of this, they were usually done early in the day and would come into TK around 2 pm. This was when things were dying down, and we girls would be bored. So when Ricky and Casey would walk in, they provided a nice break from the tourist tables. They were regulars around our age with whom we could talk and visit.

Casey was tall and lanky, and always joked around that he looked like Justin Bieber. He didn't really, but had the same blond hair, blue eyes, and boyish looks and charm. He looked much younger than his 32 years. Ricky was taller and bigger. He was more my type physically and you couldn't help but notice him when he was around. In fact, you couldn't miss him. Not only was he tall, but he had glasses and a beard. And he had a crazy head of hair. Insanely crazy. Dark brown, long, curly, almost kinky hair that he usually wore back in a ponytail. So it was the hair that everyone noticed first. Then it was the height. Then it was the beard. At least, that's the order it went in for me.

And I had noticed them around the restaurant, but never paid much attention to them, because I had never served them before. Until one day I needed Jessica for something and found her talking to them at their table. They always wanted to sit at one of the two-tops at the back of the restaurant by the windows. That was their M.O. I was introduced, and after that, was aware of who they were. They seemed like silly, fun guys. Extremely outspoken, charming and funny. Hilarious, really. We started becoming friendly. Sometimes, after my shift, I would stay and have a drink with Ricky. I was dating Kyle at the time, but things were starting to fall apart. He was starting to become a jerk. I would whine and complain about his jerkiness to Ricky, and he would listen and make fun of him. I thought Ricky might have a little crush on me. It was just a feeling I got. He would look at me and there would be a spark in his eye. We flirted quite a bit. I liked flirting with him. He was good at it. We were good at it. He was very different from me, it didn't seem like we had many of the same interests, but I found him to be intrinsically interesting. He seemed mysterious, secretive and perplexing to me all at the same time. Ricky was complex and exceedingly smart. He was also exceptionally funny. He was one of the funniest people I had ever met. The things he said would be so off-the-wall and witty, and his delivery of them would be perfect. I would sit at the restaurant and laugh and laugh for hours at the things he would say. I would laugh until I cried. It had been a long time since anyone had made me laugh that hard consistently, and I was so appreciative of Ricky for that.

He was undeniably sexy because he made me laugh and he made me happy. As time went on, I would find myself hoping that Ricky and Casey would come in during my shift because they were such a good time. I was developing a crush on him, too.

The day of the blizzard, Ricky and Casey came in. I got off of my shift early and I changed quickly so I could join them for a drink before Kyle picked me up. As I neared their table, I noticed Casey had left.

"What happened to Casey?" I asked Ricky, setting down my bag and my drink.

"Oh, he had to go," Ricky said, looking up from his beer. "Shot? In celebration of the upcoming MurderDeathBlizzami?"

I laughed. "MurderDeathBlizzami huh? Is that what they're calling it? Well, in that case, that sounds pretty bad and definitely calls for a shot." I looked out the window and saw that the snow was starting to come down hard. It was starting to shower sideways and the ground was already coated with a thin layer of flakes. It was beginning to look dark and ominous out, like something out of a movie. I put my hands on my hips and mused aloud: "I hope Kyle gets here soon and doesn't get stuck in this before it gets any worse. I really don't want to have to take the train home."

Ricky leaned back in his chair and crossed his hands behind his head. His eyes surveyed me up and down. I felt a little thrill. I loved him checking me out. "You still dating that loser?"

"Yes, I am."

"Too bad."

"Isn't it? But why do you care?" I asked, a smile playing at the corner of my mouth.

"I don't. But if I did, it would be because I have a proposition for you."

"Well…what's the proposition? Not like I care."

"Let's go ahead and pretend that you care a lot. For simplicity's sake. For some reason, the higher-ups at my very important job believe that it is essential for me to show up to work tomorrow morning bright and early even though the blizzard of the century is upon us. Therefore, they are putting me up at the W hotel for the night." He paused.

"And…your proposition for me is what?"

"Come with me."

"To see your room at the W hotel? And what would we do?"

"Watch MurderDeath snow fall. Drink vodka. Mess around." He winked, leaned back farther in his chair and checked me out again.

"So let me get this straight…you are literally propositioning me, then? You must think I'm some kind of whore who would just go off with some random guy because he has a hotel room downtown and vodka and wants to mess around with me," I shot back, winking at him.

He surveyed me again and chewed on his lip for a minute. Then he cracked a big smile, leaned forward in his chair, looked me straight in the eyes and said, "Do I think you are a whore? No. Am I some random guy? No, again. But do I think you would be a fun, cool, spontaneous, vodka-drinking, horny type of girl who just might do something like accompany an amazingly handsome, debonnaire and intellectually stimulating type of guy back to his downtown hotel room? Absolutely, I do. And that's a compliment. Trust me." With that, he leaned back in his chair again with a look that was nothing except cocky, playful and coy. It was a look that said "I'm totally right, aren't I?"

He was totally right. This was excellent. This was some serious and intense flirting. I could feel my face getting flushed and red, but I was loving every second of it. I really wanted to go back with him to his hotel room. It sounded exciting and fun and I was so curious about this person. But I couldn't. I had to go with Kyle. I had told him I would, and I really wanted to see where things were going to go with the relationship. I was about to respond with a particularly dry comeback to falsely negate what he had just said, but I never got the chance because suddenly, my phone dinged. I fished in my bag for my phone and pulled it out. It was a text from Kyle. He was nearing the restaurant. I shoved my phone back in my bag and looked up at Ricky. "I'm really sorry, I gotta go."

He gave me a quizzical look. "Boyfriend coming? Here to rescue you from the blizzard of the century?"

I looked back at him as I gathered my things. "He's not my boyfriend."

Ricky shifted in his seat, scratched his head and then held up his pointer finger. "You know how I know your 'relationship' with this dude is never going to work?"

"How?" I asked, humoring him, with a very doubtful tone in my voice.

"You were very quick just now to make it very clear to me that he is not your boyfriend, yet, when I called him a 'loser' earlier, you made no move to defend him whatsoever. Not even remotely. This is particularly telling. Oh, and it's never going to work because he actually IS a loser."

"Oh, is he now? Well, I don't know what to tell you."

"Tell me you'll meet me at my hotel room. I'll make it memorable for you."

"Nope, sorry, I have plans with a loser who's not my boyfriend. Rain check on the shot?"

"Rain check for sure. Room 435 if you change your mind."

I smiled slyly at him over my shoulder and headed for the exit. His eyes followed me all the way to the door and down the stairs.

~

It was two Fridays after Kyle, the loser, had ended our non-existent boyfriend/girlfriend relationship by lying to me on my birthday. I was still upset about it, but the pain was starting to wear off much quicker than I had anticipated. I still thought about him frequently, and vascilated between being angry, sad and downright confused, but the girls at TK had been amazing, as usual. They continued to comfort me, console me and rant and rave about what a jerk he was and how he was never allowed in the restaurant again. They made me laugh, and they made me feel better. They were the best friends a girl could have asked for. It was morning and I was at the restaurant early. Jessica had been there for 45 minutes already and she was hard at work cutting lemons. I was hard at work watching her work, and complaining about how horny I was.

"You think you're horny?" Jessica spat at me, brandishing her knife in the air. "I'm horny! Vegan is so lame. He never makes a move to do anything with me anymore!" she pouted as she stabbed her knife into a second lemon.

"First of all," I said, stealing a purple Skittle that was part of one of her notoriously healthy breakfasts, "I don't want to hear it. YOU have a boyfriend. And he is hot. So I don't want to hear any more complaining from you. People with boyfriends do not get to complain around me, ever. About anything."

"What's the second of all?"

I pondered that for a second. "There is not second of all. Just a first of all. That's enough."

"Well, I AM allowed to complain because having a boyfriend who doesn't want to fuck you is WORSE than not having a boyfriend at all.

"I suppose so. What is WRONG with these guys? He's hot, you're hot, you like each other, just get it on."

"Exactly. I'm hot! And he is hot too, I guess. But he's a moron and a pain in my ass. And a goddamn vegan…and a goddamn ASIAN!"

Suddenly a voice echoed throughout the hallway outside the door as a flash of black swooped up the escalator. "Who goddamn Asian? Why you be mean to Asian? You goddamn Caucasian. Fuck you."

"Hey, Pauline," I said, putting my head in my arms on top of the table.

"Hey," she said, swinging her bag onto the table and laughing as she tried to peer at my face. "What's wrong with her?" she asked, turning to Jessica and stealing a Skittle from the bag.

"She's horny."

"Join the club," Pauline said, smacking on her Skittle.

"Uh uh!" I cried, raising my head from my arms. "No way! You especially do not get to complain, Pauline! You have a boyfriend and you guys have sex like 20 times a day! I don't want to hear it."

Pauline smiled and said, "this is true. Sucks for you."

I sighed and placed my head back in my arms. "It does suck for me."

"You and I just need to get laid," Jessica said, putting down her knife and placing the remaining lemons back in their plastic container.

"I just need someone to pay attention to me in a sexual way. I would settle for that."

"We'll find you somebody," Pauline said, stroking my hair. "Don't you worry."

~

That Friday turned out to be busy. We hadn't been that busy in quite some time, so it was kind of a shock to all of us servers. We were running around like chickens with our heads cut off. What made matters worse was the computers kept going down and resetting themselves. Friday lunches were the absolute worst shifts during which the computers could go down, but they frequently did. It was like the Aloha system knew what mayhem it created and did that to spite us; just to make our day that much more frustrating. I was in the 90s, the section with all two-tops by the windows. The section was excellent for moneymaking purposes, but it was also the most stressful section in the restaurant. The two-tops turned quickly, and the guests expected their food quickly and expertly. It was definitely not a calm day for me.

It was nearing one pm and the restaurant wasn't slowing down. We were on a wait and I could see a line out the door. I rushed in to the back pantry and almost ran into Keri who was filling a cup with coke. She tossed her brown, curly hair and wagged her eyebrows at me.

"Crazy day, huh?"

"Yes, it is," I said. "But it's good. We haven't been busy like this in awhile."

"Totally," Keri said. "We're gonna make some money today! Hey, by the way, heard you were super horny."

"How did you?...never mind, why do I even ask how you girls find this stuff out?"

"Uh, yeah, duh, we all know everything all the time. Jessica and I discussed it at length after the meeting."

"You discussed me being horny?"

"At length."

"Interesting."

"It was, actually. Well, you know me, I always think horniness is interesting."

"That's because you're always horny, Keri."

"True! I am!"

"Well, it sucks. At least you can commiserate with me. You don't have a boyfriend."

"Yeah, but honey, I have like 12 boyfriends. You just need to sit on someone's face. Then you'll be fine."

"Oh, Jesus."

Suddenly, Pauline came skidding around the corner. "Move, bitches!" she yelled, throwing the weight of her body into mine and practically sending me flying. "I need the Aloha! I have three four tops and a party of ten! They just ordered and I need to remember it!" Pauline was jabbing at the screen, trying to pull up her table.

Keri finished filling the coke cup and came to stand directly behind Pauline. She placed her chin on Pauline's shoulder and started talking loudly in her ear just to annoy her.

"Um…you didn't write anything down? You know, you're supposed to write your orders down, that's the rule and…" she got cut off in midsentence by Pauline who yelled "Shut up, Keri! I will bring you down! Down to Chinatown!" Her eyes were still trained on the Aloha, but there was a hint of a smile on her face.

Keri cackled an evil laugh and headed for her table, but was stopped dead in her tracks as Kelly came barreling around the corner and came to a halt at the entrance to the pantry. She placed her hand on the wall and doubled over at the waist. She was extremely out of breath as she tried to spit out non-coherent words:

"Computers….reset….*gasp*….had to…Miller Lite…change price…*gasp*…have to wait…don't put any orders in for….sorry…*gasp*…

Keri and I stared at her, trying to make sense of the gibberish that was coming out of her mouth until Pauline's scream pierced the air:

"NOOOOOOOOOOOOOOO!!!!!!!"

I turned my head just in time to see the screen Pauline had been furiously jabbing at, go completely black. Then the Windows logo popped up on the Aloha in a screen of blue.

"STUPID FUCKING PIECE OF SHIT COMPUTER! GODDAMN IT! YOU HAVE GOT TO BE KIDDING ME RIGHT NOW! FUCK ME!" Pauline yelled. I was sure the whole restaurant could hear her.

Kelly straightened up and said "That's what I was trying to tell you! I had to reset the computers to change the price on Miller Lite and not to put any orders in for a minute!"

"Well then learn English, bitch! I was right in the middle of an order for a table of 10!"

"ME learn English?! Why don't you? Don't you speak Mandarin or whatever? And, just order it again when the computers come back up!" Kelly yelled back.

"Gotta love our political correctness," Keri chuckled under her breath.

"I CAN'T just order it again!" Pauline screeched. "I didn't write it down!"

"What?" Kelly asked. "What do you mean you didn't write it down? It's a goddamn ten top, Pauline!"

"I know but I'm usually fine with that many! As you so eloquently pointed out yourself, I'm Asian! We're really smart!"

Kelly just looked at Pauline in disbelief and threw her hands up in the air.

Keri spoke up: "Um, well…she's right, you know. Asians are really smart."

Kelly looked at the three of us, and if looks could kill, we all would have been dead and buried. "Yes, Asians are very smart," she said in a highly controlled voice. "AT MATH AND PLAYING THE VIOLIN, BUT EVIDENTLY NOT AT WRITING DOWN FOOD ORDERS!"

It was time to go. I grabbed Keri's arm and steered her away from the back pantry. When we were out of earshot, we burst into laughter and ran toward our respective tables. As entertaining as it was to watch Kelly and Pauline duke it out, it was time to go greet my next table.

It was two men in their early 40s. I slid up to the table and placed two coasters down in front of them. "Hi, guys, how are you doing? My name's Katy and I'm going to be helping you…"

"You have lemonade?" one of the men interrupted me, keeping his eyes on the menu. Neither man looked up from his menu, or seemed interested in doing so anytime soon.

"Yes we do."

"I'll have a lemonade."

"And for you, sir?" I asked, turning to the other gentleman, crossing my eyes and sticking my tongue out at him slightly. He didn't notice. I could have caught on fire in front of him, and he would have been none the wiser.

He flipped the menu page and asked "do you have lemonade?"

What an idiot. His friend had just ordered one. I did not have time for this.

"Yes. We do." I was clenching my jaw and balling my fists.

"Do you have pink lemonade?"

"No."

"What color is it?"

"What color is what, sir?"

"The lemonade." He finally looked up and glanced at me disinterestedly.

He couldn't be serious.

"The lemonade….is…yellow."

He pondered that for a moment and then asked: "is it sweetened? Sweet lemonade?"

"Yes. It is."

"Okay," he said thoughtfully. "I'll have a lemonade. Yellow lemonade. Sweetened."

"I'll be right back with those, guys," I said, edging away from the table, but I wasn't fast enough. Suddenly: "Miss? Oh, miss?" The first guy was calling me. "Change my order to an iced tea." Then the second guy spoke up: "yes, miss? And can you put some iced tea in my lemonade? Make it an Arnold Palmer. Thanks."

Christ.

I raced to the back of the restaurant to try to help out with running some food while I got the drinks for Mr. Idiotic and Mr. More Idiotic. That turned out to be a huge mistake. The kitchen was pandemonium. Tickets were lined up all across the board. There must have been upwards of 30. There were only four baskets of food actually in the window. That is never a good sign. I saw Sandra at expo, yelling to the cooks in rapid-fire Spanish. She looked stressed to the max. I poured my drinks and was about to sneak away without being noticed until I felt something jab into the small of my back. I turned around slowly, so as not to spill the drinks and looked into Sandra's face. Terror was the only word I could use to describe the look in her eyes.

"(Can you take this) ensalata (to table 42)?" she asked me.

"What?" I asked her, blinking dumbfoundedly. "Did you just speak Spanish to me?"

"Oh my God!" she laughed, shaking her head. "I did! I'm so sorry! I meant, can you please take this salad to table 42? It's so crazy up here I'm losing my mind!"

"No problem," I said, shifting both drinks to one hand. "I will do this for you only because you are the nicest person on the planet and I love you."

"Whatever works. Thanks!" Sandra said, swirling around to the line to yell in Spanish once again.

"De nada," I said, and headed back to my tables.

I delivered the drinks to their table, and took their food order. The first man ordered a burger, medium rare, and the second ordered a cheese quesadilla. I thanked them, took their menus and bounded back to the Aloha. I ordered the burger, then I went to the appetizer screen to order the quesadilla. We offer a chicken quesadilla, but that comes with chicken, peppers and onions, so for our vegetarian guests, we can make it with only cheese. On the Aloha screen I saw the button for the chicken quesadilla, as well as the one for the cheese quesadilla, so I punched the cheese option and exited out of my screen. I served a few more drinks, chatted for a second with my regular, Rocky, and went to check on lemonade table. Heather was just setting down their food. Even with the kitchen being slow today, that was pretty fast.

"How does everything lo…." I trailed off in midsentence as I watched businessman number 2 pick at his quesadilla and make a disgusted face. He shoved the basket toward me and crossed his arms over his chest. "I ordered a cheese quesadilla. This one has chicken and peppers and onions in it."

Sure enough, it did.

"I am so sorry, sir," I said, snatching the basket off his table. I will get a cheese quesadilla right out to you. Give me just a minute."

I ran back to the Aloha, pulled up the table on my screen and found the cheese quesadilla button once again. This time I wrote "no peppers no onions" underneath it and put five exclamation points after it. I pushed "order," and ran back to the kitchen to make sure the cooks understood. I jumped behind the expo line, tried to pass the basket off very discreetly to Sandra, and started to whisper in her ear what I needed. Evidently I wasn't discreet enough. Darla, our kitchen manager, snapped her head up and glared at me with daggers in her eyes. Her dyed red hair looked orange in the lights of the kitchen lamps and her fat face was forever creased with lines from only frowning in her lifetime. She had a gray bandana wrapped around her head, but sweat was still dripping down her face. The cooks called her Rambo when she wore that bandana. She was about as big as Rambo and a hell of a lot meaner. She was waving my ticket in her hand and her eyes flashed down to the basket I was holding.

"WHAT," she yelled, looking back up at me angrily, "is WRONG with that?"

"Um, well," I began. "My table 94 wanted just a cheese quesadilla, no peppers no onions and this came out as a regular chicken quesadilla," I said, indicating the food. "So I re-ordered the cheese quesadilla with no peppers no onions," I finished, out of breath.

Darla leaned over the expo line as far as she could until her large chest was touching the metal. She continued to look at me menacingly and screamed even louder this time "You are SUPPOSED to order it as a CHICKEN quesadilla NO CHICKEN!!!! THAT is how you order a FUCKING cheese quesadilla!!!! WHAT the FUCK is wrong with you servers?"

"But there's a button for a cheese quesadilla under appetizers so I just ordered that." I could feel Sandra beside me nod her head vigorously.

Darla's eyes narrowed and she leaned in closer. "WHAT the FUCK are you doing arguing with me on a Friday lunch?! ALL you fucking servers do is make mistakes! Go find KELLY!"

Sandra motioned her head toward the end of the line and gave me a little push out of the way. Guess I was going to find Kelly. I brought the quesadilla with me as proof that Darla was a complete psychopath. I wasn't sure how I was going to prove that with a quesadilla, but I was certainly going to try.

I found her by the bar.

"Uh, Kelly, can you come with me? Darla wants to talk to you."

Kelly turned around and saw me standing there with a basket of food. "Oh, God. What does she want? What did you do?"

"Nothing," I tried to explain. "The kitchen made my food wrong. I ordered a cheese quesadilla for my table cause there's a button for it in the computer and Darla is trying to tell me I order a cheese quesadilla by ordering a chicken one with no chicken. How does that make any sense if we have a button for the cheese one?"

"It doesn't," Kelly said, hurrying toward the back. "And furthermore, the cheese button is a cheaper price than the chicken. Obviously. I'm not charging my guests the same price for a tortilla with cheese in it and no meat or vegetables."

Well, at least someone had some sense around here.

I followed Kelly to the back where we were met once again with utter chaos and Darla screaming. When she saw Kelly, she let loose.

"WHAT the FUCK is WRONG with your SERVERS? Can't they order their shit right?"

Kelly lashed back. "She DID order it right, Darla! There is a BUTTON in the Aloha for a cheese quesadilla which is

CHEAPER than the chicken one. Tell your guys to make it right!"

"If you hadn't noticed, we are SLAMMED back here! I can't be making all of these goddamn specialty orders! No SUBSTITUTIONS on FRIDAY LUNCHES!"

"Darla, that's stupid! It's not even a specialty order! Her guest is a VEGETARIAN! Do you know what that even means? He can't eat MEAT. So you need to make him a CHEESE quesadilla and NOW!"

As Kelly and Darla were arguing, Sandra handed me a new quesadilla. I looked down. This one had no meat.

But it did have peppers.

And onions.

Shit.

I looked up at Sandra and she immediately knew. I shook my head slightly and pointed it in the direction of Kelly and Darla, who looked like they were about to start punching each other in the face. There was no way I was going to interrupt either of them to point out the fact that the kitchen had messed up again. I would probably have gotten murdered right there on the line.

"Sandra," I hissed, very quietly, "I need one with only cheese. Right. NOW."

"I got it," she whispered back. Then, in one fluid motion, she expertly leaned over the line to speak to Valentin, our head cook. Darla was too busy yelling at Kelly to notice. Sandra said a string of words in Spanish, winked and leaned back with a satisfactory look on her face. "Thirty seconds," she said to me.

30 seconds later, I had the correct order in my hand.

"How did you do that?" I asked her, looking down at the basket incredulously. "What did you say to him?"

"I told him that if he got me a cheese quesadilla in under 60 seconds, I'd show him my underwear!" Sandra laughed and blushed.

"Oh, my God! Sandra! I love you! That is hilarious! Are you going to do it?"

"Of course not!" Sandra said, blushing even more. "Just go give that to your table. And don't tell anyone I did that for you!" she finished. "I have a sweet, innocent reputation to uphold!" she winked at me and turned back to the line.

The day continued in much the same way. Heather got into a screaming match with Darla over a pizza, and Pauline's order for one of her four tops got messed up when the computer restarted again. I could hear her swearing from all the way across the restaurant. It was a remarkably stressful day, but eventually, things began to wind down. Around 3 pm, Jessica found me in the back, talking to Keri.

"Hey, Katy," she said. "It's your lucky day. Your boyfriend's here. He's at table 86."

"Who? What boyfriend?"

"Ricky."

"Oh." I perked up a little. I was really glad to hear that after the day I had had. But I couldn't let them know that. "He's not my boyfriend."

Jessica ignored me and kept talking.

"Yeah, I told him you were super horny. You're welcome."

"You did not!" I could feel my face turning red. "Jessica!"

"What?" she said, a sly smile crossing her face. "You are. And he loves you. I'm sure he'd take one for the team and uh…assist you." Jessica was cracking up. Keri gave her a high five.

"Go sit on his face!" Keri screamed.

"Keri, be quiet!" I said, peeking around the corner. "He could hear you!"

"So? Good! He should hear me. Go talk to him!" she squealed, pushing me toward 86. Go get 'em, tiger!" She and Jessica dissolved into giggles.

All my tables were almost done, so I decided to go talk to him. I hadn't seen him in awhile and it would be nice to do some serious flirting, in any case. I walked slowly up to his table. I could see him laughing about something with Casey. When he saw me, he stopped and cocked his head to the right. His curly ponytail bobbed up and down and his eyes sparkled. His face slowly broke into a smirky smile.

"Well, well, well, what do we have here?" he said, putting his arms out to hug me. His hands lingered on my waist for a long minute and he gave me a knowing smile.

"What do we have here?" Casey echoed, trying not to laugh.

"Hi, guys," I said. I could feel the blush creeping on to my cheeks. "Casey, that's the best you could come up with? No smart remark of your own?"

"Nope," Casey said, biting into a mozzarella stick. "I'm just here to watch the drama unfold." He looked back and forth to Ricky and me as if watching a tennis match. "Oh, hey, and get Jessica back here, I'm gonna need some popcorn for this, I think. This is gonna be better than a movie! Just pretend I'm not here."

I rolled my eyes as Ricky continued to look at me. He was ignoring Casey. "So I heard a rumor…" he began.

"A rumor about what?"

"A rumor that one specific Kilt girl might be in need of some…attention?"

"I'm always in need of attention."

"Yeah, but the sexual kind. From a boy. Excuse me, a man."

"Perhaps. Where did you hear this?"

"Doesn't matter. Well, perhaps I could help you with your…predicament?"

"Who says it's a predicament?"

"I do. Sounds like a predicament. Looks like a predicament."

"This is what a predicament looks like?"

"I'm not sure. But if it does, I must say, I like the way it looks." He looked me up and down approvingly. "How about this," he mused, tapping his fingers on the table "you finish up your work…quickly, get your hot little ass back here so I can buy you some drinks, get you liquored up, regale you with witty, funny and fascinating tales of life, liberty and the pursuit of happiness, then we get the hell out of here so I can start…helping you out."

"That sounds like a good suggestion."

"It wasn't a suggestion. It's happening."

"Well, you sound like a helpful kind of guy. Helpful and determined."

"I am. I like to help. Especially damsels in distress. It's the least I can do. I'm a gentleman that way."

"I might consider letting you…help me. I suppose. Are you any good at it?" I smiled at him.

Ricky looked up at the ceiling for a minute, as if thinking it over. Then he leaned in closer to me, put his fingertips on my hips, pulled me a little closer to him and looked straight into my eyes. "I am more than good at it. I'm outstanding."

"GUYS!" Casey shouted, throwing his hands up in the air. "Seriously? Get a room, already! I'll even pay for it. Just go. My God. Please!"

We both turned our heads in surprise when Casey started yelling. We had literally forgotten he was even there. We hadn't needed to pretend.

~

The next morning I was late to work. I am never late. I had texted Kelly when I woke up to warn her of my late arrival, and she had only texted back a smiley face. I wasn't sure how to take that. At least she wasn't mad. But I knew I was going to hear so much shit from the girls. I was starving, tired and extremely hungover. I bounded up the stairs and skidded right into the middle of the morning meeting. Kelly stopped talking as six pairs of eyes focused on me. Everyone was quiet. Sandra was the first to break the silence.

"OOOOHHH!!" she exclaimed, clapping one hand over her mouth, and pointing the other finger accusingly at me, her eyes growing wide. "You're wearing the same outfit as yesterday!"

"Walk of shame!" Jessica said. "Again, you're welcome."

Heather said "Damn, girl-you hooked up last night? With a guy? Gross!"

Pauline said "You do sucky sucky faw fif-y dollaas? You maay Pawrine prouw?"

Keri asked "Did you sit on his face? Tell me you sat on his face!"

And Kelly said "Details. Now." She sat down and crossed her arms over her chest and smirked at me.

I held my hands up in front of my face in embarrassment. "No, no, please continue with your meeting. I wouldn't want to interrupt."

"Oh no! You were late and we need to know what happened. This IS the meeting now," Kelly said with an evil laugh.

"How was the beard? Did it tickle?" Sandra asked, still wide-eyed.

Jessica said "Who cares about the beard? I want to hear how it went with THAT HAIR!"

Heather covered her ears with her hands very dramatically, stuck out her tongue, made a gagging motion and said "Ew!!! Guys!! Hairy guys! I think I'm going to be sick!"

Pauline said "Heather, you're so dramatic, shut up. We need to hear this!"

And Keri screamed "DID YOU SIT ON HIS FACE OR NOT?! JESUS CHRIST!"

I surveyed all of them and said: "Thank-you Jess, I owe you one. The hair was everything I thought it would be and more, Sandra, the beard tickled but it felt goood, Pauline, I'm not a Chinese prostitute like you so no money exchanged hands, and Heather, yes, I hook up with guys. It's not gross." I took a deep breath and looked at Keri who was looking at me expectantly. "And Keri, yes, the answer is yes. Three times, okay? Are you happy now?"

Keri jumped out of her chair in excitement. "I knew it! Yes! I'm so proud of you! My little Katy!"

Kelly shot up out of her seat and headed for the back. "Best meeting I've ever held," she said.

I just laughed.

~

I called Erin after work. I needed to fill her in on my latest escapades and wanted to hear how she was doing. She had heard about Ricky and about our flirting. I knew she would be dying to know what had finally transpired.

"HI!" she yelled into the phone when she picked up. "I was just thinking about you! What sort of trouble have you been getting yourself into in Chicago?"

"Well," I started, laughing already. "I kind of did get into trouble. With a boy." I was sure she could hear the smile on my face.

"Who?" she yelled, bursting with anticipation. "Wait! Let me guess…Robby!"

"You mean Ricky?" I said.

"The guy with the hair," she said loudly. "Whatever his name is. I thought it was Robby. But holy shit, Katy! How was it? Did you have sex with him? That hair! How was that?"

"Whoa, so many questions, slow down! And why does everyone ask about the hair right away?" I asked, knowing the answer.

"Because it's crazy hair! Was he good in bed at least? You guys have had that sexual tension building up for awhile now. I bet it all just came to a head. Get it?? Came to a head?? Did you give him head? You did, didn't you?"

"Yes, I did. No sex though. And yes, it was good. Really good, actually. The hair turned out to be some weird, freaky turn-on."

"I knew it!" she said, triumphantly.

"No you didn't! You said the hair was freaky!"

"Freaky hot. I like it. I'm so happy for you. I bet he's going to be so into you. I bet you'll be able to do whatever you want with this guy."

"We'll see," I said, musingly. "Maybe he won't be that into me."

"Not possible," Erin said. "He'd be crazy not to realize that he's so lucky to be banging an amazing girl like you."

"Well thanks, but not banging yet. We will be, though. We will be."

"I can't wait to hear about the hair sex!" Erin squealed. "You better call me immediately afterwards with all of the details."

"Oh, I will, you better believe it. And I need to hear about the details of your love life."

Erin sighed. "Oh, we'll get to that. I gotta run now, but we'll talk soon. I have stories for you."

"I can't wait. Okay, I'll call you soon. Love you, bye."

"Love you too!" And with that, she clicked off.

~

Ricky and I continued to hang out for a few weeks. Things were going really well. He was hilarious. All I would do was laugh when we were together. He made me feel happy and silly, and I needed that after my stint with Kevin. We spent a lot of time together, and he would come in to the restaurant frequently. I never knew when he and Casey would show up, though. Sometimes I'd be done with work and just about to leave, and I would see them come in. It was always a treat to see them, but I found it a little odd that Ricky would never give me a heads up. And if I was still on the floor, he wouldn't necessarily sit in my section. At first, this didn't bother me, he had been coming in to the restaurant for a long time before we started hooking up, but I felt now that we were hanging out, I felt he might want to make sure that I was still there. But he never did. It hurt my feelings a little bit, and I thought it was strange, but I brushed it off. He seemed to like me and I liked him so I didn't worry about it.

We never talked about what was going on with us. It was too early to determine what it was, and it seemed like things were going well. I would have liked to have known, though. I wasn't exactly sure what I wanted, but of course wanted to know what he was thinking. I hadn't brought it up yet, but in a weird, old-fashioned way, I felt like it was the guy's job to do that anyway. He was cool and funny. I could get past the beard and the hair. I found him interestingly attractive. I knew in the back of my mind that we were very different people, but I was more than open to the idea of a boyfriend. Probably too open. I was ready for someone to care about me the way I cared about him. I didn't know if Ricky would be that person, but I was willing to try with him. Whether that was the right thing for us or not.

One night, we met at The Tilted Kilt before going to a Mexican restaurant. As we left the building, Ricky turned right instead of left and heading toward the train.

"Where are we going?" I asked.

"I'm taking you to the news station. I wanted to give you a tour and show you where I work."

"Cool!" I exclaimed. This was going to be fun. A private tour of the news studio sounded great.

As we approached the building, Ricky held the door open for me and we ran into a security guard reading a magazine at the lobby desk.

"Hey, Frank," how's it going? Ricky asked him, putting out his hand to shake his.

"Pretty good, man, what's going on?"

"Not much. Just gonna show her around the place if that's okay?"

"Definitely, go right ahead."

I was about to stick out my hand and introduce myself so Ricky didn't have to. We were at the stage where introducing each other was getting weird. We didn't know if we were just supposed to use each other's names or say "friend" or what, so I thought I would spare him the trouble and just introduce myself. But Ricky beat me to it.

"And Frank," he said, sweeping his hand out towards me, "this is my girlfriend, Katy."

Oh.

Interesting.

I'm sure my face contorted for just a split second. I was definitely caught off guard. Girlfriend? Okay, then. Well. I guess I was. Or I guess he wanted me to be. I found it funny that we had never discussed it, and that he had just introduced me as that without saying anything, but I figured that was his way of doing things. He seemed strangely sure of himself. I hadn't pegged him as that way, but he was constantly surprising me.

"Hi," I said, shaking myself out of my reverie and putting my hand out. "Nice to meet you."

Ricky then started walking toward the glass doors in front of us, so I followed dutifully. He seemed calm, like nothing out of the ordinary had happened. I decided to just go with it.

He showed me the studio, which was beautiful. Like a dork, I took pictures of me behind the news anchor desk. Ricky showed me the lights and the teleprompter, and tried to explain what it was that he actually did. I didn't really get it, I was too busy looking around to pay attention, but I nodded and asked some appropriate questions. At least, I thought they seemed appropriate. Then he took me into the green room where two girls were watching TV. They looked up as we came in the door.

"Hey, Ricky," the prettier of the two greeted us. "What are you doing here?"

"Just showing her around the studio," he said, leaning on a desk. He looked at me and said "this is Theresa," he pointed to the pretty one, "and this is Carly. This here is Katy. My girlfriend."

Oh.

Interesting.

But this time I was ready for it. I said hi and we all chatted for a minute. After a few minutes, Ricky told them that we were headed to dinner so we needed to go. I told them it was nice to meet them and we exited the building. I left extremely confused and perplexed about what had just transpired, but also curious and excited to find out what that had been about.

And I realized I also felt quite happy.

~

The happiness waned quickly. Two weeks passed and Ricky refused to talk about it. I had brought it up a few days afterward and had simply asked him if we could talk about the fact that he had introduced me as his girlfriend. He said that we could, but was extremely hesitant about it. He gave me a weird look and then, after a pause had said "sure." It was not exactly the response I was looking for. I was more confused than ever and curious. The curiosity was killing me, actually. I had no idea why he would introduce me as his girlfriend, not bring it up again and not want to talk about it. Why not just introduce me as his friend or as simply "Katy" if he wasn't interested in me being his girlfriend? And if he was interested in me being his girlfriend, why wouldn't he bring it up? Did he just assume I wouldn't say anything about it? Was he now embarrassed? Had he changed his mind? Had I done something wrong? I thought it tremendously unfair of him to do that without consulting me and then not explain himself. I felt I deserved an explanation whether it was the explanation I wanted or not. We hadn't hung out as much after the incident. We had met up one time after work for dinner, but had mostly just chit-chatted about nothing. We had texted back and forth throughout the week, the normal silly banter, but it wasn't anything significant. I had tried to bring it up over text again, but he simply ignored my text. It was almost as if he was avoiding me. I felt like I was getting the brush off and I didn't like it. I decided to confront him within the next few days.

But I didn't have to, because the next day he and Casey came into the restaurant. I was with one of my tables as I watched them walk over to Jessica's section and sit down. I guess they weren't going to sit with me again. I was getting sick of the not knowing when they would come in, sick of the not knowing what was going on with us, sick of the not knowing anything. I was just getting done with my shift so I changed quickly and made my way over to their table. Jessica was just setting down what looked like their 15th shot. They were getting drunk. Great. I debated whether or not I should talk with him about this while he was intoxicated, but decided to try to go for it. I determined that some truth serum might actually help me in this situation. Jessica rolled her eyes at me as she set down their drinks and made a motion of putting a glass to her lips and drinking from it. "Drunk," she mouthed. Then she said "Good luck" aloud and headed to the back.

"Hey," I said, as I slid into a chair next to Ricky. "What's up, guys?"

Casey said hey and kind of nodded at me. Ricky said hello, then cocked his thumb toward me and looked only at Casey. "Well, well, well, look who it is," he said. "My girlfriend," he continued, sarcastically, raising the shot glass to his lips and motioning toward me with his head. He then drank the shot, slammed the glass down on the table, guffawed loudly and high-fived Casey, who also snickered quietly.

Excuse me?

What?

Assholes.

I leaned back in my chair, crossed my arms over my chest and glared at Ricky. "Yep, that's me," I said, just as sarcastically. "Your girlfriend. According to YOU, as a matter of fact. It's nice to see you, too, BOYFRIEND." Casey looked back and forth between us, much as he had that time only a month ago. "I sense some tension between you two. Boyfriend and girlfriend fight?" He stressed the words "boyfriend" and "girlfriend" and snickered again. Ricky tried to suppress a smile unsuccessfully.

"What is your problem?" I demanded, turning in my chair to face Casey. "I'd like to talk to Ricky alone right now if you wouldn't mind. Can you just give us a minute?"

"I'll do better than that," Casey said, standing up and throwing three twenties on the table. "I'm out, bro," he said clapping Ricky on the back. "Good luck with this one, dude," he said motioning to me and turning his finger in a circle next to his ear, indicating that I was crazy. "Good fucking luck." And with that, he was gone.

"What the hell is his problem?" I said, turning back to Ricky. "And what is your problem? Why are you guys being so mean to me and calling me crazy? I haven't seen you in a week, and now you come in here, sit with Jessica, and sarcastically make fun of me? That's awesome."

"Sorry," Ricky said, not sounding sorry in the least. "We wanted to get drunk, and we hadn't sat with Jess in awhile so we came in. It's not a big deal. Don't get all crazy about it."

That was the second time in four minutes that someone had insinuated that I was crazy, and I didn't like it.

"That's it," I said, shooting up from my chair. "We're going to talk. But not here. We're leaving."

"But I'd like to stay," Ricky said, sweeping his hand around the restaurant. "Shots, TV's, hot chicks," he said, physically pointing at Mary, one of the servers.

Now he was pointing out other hot women to me? My co-workers? My friends? Oh, no. That was it for me.

"Too. Fucking. Bad," I said, yanking on his arm and pulling him out of his seat. We're leaving."

He followed me down the escalator and out onto the sidewalk where we stopped in front of the building. He was about to open his mouth to say something, but before he could, I held up my hand and started talking.

"Here's how I see things, Ricky, and correct me if I'm wrong. You and I hook up, start having a good time, hang out. But you never come to see me specifically at my restaurant, you don't even give me a heads up when you're coming, and you never sit with me. Then you take me to your place of employment, introduce me as your girlfriend on two separate occasions, tell me we can talk about it when I ask, then refuse to talk about it, and shadily avoid me for over a week. Then you come into TK, get drunk with your friend, and both of you make fun of me and call me crazy. Does this sound about right?" I stopped and leaned on the gridiron fence at the edge of the sidewalk and looked up into his face, waiting for his explanation.

"I guess so," he said, trying to act uninterested and looking around.

"So would you just say that you're a pussy and that's why you're refusing to talk about what happened at the studio? You said we could talk about it and we haven't yet. Sounds like a coward to me." I was getting angrier by the second.

Ricky shook his head exasperatedly and blew up at me. "I'm not a coward! And I'm certainly not a pussy! Maybe it's just that I don't WANT you to be my girlfriend, okay? Maybe it's that you KEEP bringing it up and it's SO annoying! First you are always harping on me about how I never sit with you at TK and then you are always talking about how I introduced you as my girlfriend where I work. Just let it go, okay?"

I took a step back. It felt like someone had punched me in the stomach. It's never much fun to hear someone say he doesn't want you to be his girlfriend, even if you're not sure you want to be his girlfriend. I had questions for him. He wasn't getting away with anything this easily.

"Okaaay," I said, slowly. "If you don't want me to be your girlfriend then why would you introduce me as that?"

Ricky ran his hand through his crazy hair and sighed. "Because it was just easier for me, okay? I like to keep my work life separate from my personal life and I didn't want anyone asking a ton of questions about who you were and blah blah blah. And then you kept wanting to talk about it and it got old really quickly."

"Well of course I wanted to talk about it!" I yelled back. "You can't just say someone is your girlfriend without talking about it with them because it's EASIER for you! Did you even think about my feelings in this situation? That I might be confused or sad or hopeful or....whatever! Why didn't you just give me a heads up beforehand? Like you could have just said 'hey, I'm going to introduce you as my girlfriend?'" I said, growing more exasperated. "But no, instead, you just said NOTHING and continued to say NOTHING like a pussy. Like a coward. And now you're making me feel awful."

"Well, would that have been any better?" Ricky shot back at me. "So I'm supposed to say 'hey, Katy, I'm going to introduce you as my girlfriend even though I don't want you to be...just a heads up?'"

"No, I guess that wouldn't have been any better," I said, yelling now. "But you know what would have been better? If you actually WANTED me to be your girlfriend. And thanks for making it so clear that you DEFINITELY don't want that. Thanks for making it sound like the worst thing in the world for ME to be YOUR girlfriend." I was surprised to find that tears were welling up in my eyes.

Ricky looked at me and said "well, it wouldn't be the worst thing in the world, certainly, but I would like to keep my options open as long as we're being honest here."

I stood stock still. "Well, that's obvious," I said, quietly, the tears starting to spill down my cheeks. "Keep your options open," I repeated, the words sounding foreign to my ears.

"Well, yeah," Ricky continued, still acting standoffish. "I mean, I could meet someone better. I could meet someone at Starbucks or at some work function. I could meet someone walking down the street. I could meet someone right here in front of this building as a matter of fact," he said, looking up toward the second floor of the massive building in which TK was housed.

Now it felt like someone had punched me in the face. Had he really just said that to me? The tears were coming full force now as I repeated to him what he had just said. "YOU want to keep your options open with ME because you don't want me to be your girlfriend and you think you could meet someone BETTER than I am WALKING down the street or in FRONT of this BUILDING?! How DARE you say that to me? What the hell is wrong with you? Who says that to someone else even if they think it's true?" I was crying and I had started to shake out of sheer disbelief. "I thought you liked me! I mean, you were always trying to get me to ditch the other guys I was seeing and hang out with you, we were always flirting, we've been having a good time the past couple of weeks…" I trailed off. I just didn't get it. It was like he had done a complete 180. Like the tables had turned violently and without any warning whatsoever.

"We have been having a good time, and I like flirting with you and you're cool, but…well, I guess, I mean, I guess that's how I feel." Ricky said, not meeting my eyes. He seemed uncomfortable with the fact that I was crying. "But…you could, too, you know?"

"I could what?"

"Meet someone better. You could."

"Stop saying that! You're just trying to backtrack at this point to make that sound not so bad!" I yelled. "And I could, especially now since everyone is going to be better than you, asshole! But it's going to be kind of hard for you to meet someone better than me in front of this building, considering you and Casey are not welcome back at TK anytime soon."

Ricky's head snapped around and he finally met my eyes. "Don't do that," he begged. "Don't ban us from TK. Come on," he begged, clasping his hands together, pleading with me. It was tremendously unattractive. Finally, he seemed passionate about something. He seemed to care somewhat. Unfortunately, it was about not being able to go back to The Tilted Kilt and not about me or my feelings. As I stood there studying him, it hit me. I wasn't girlfriend material to him, I was a conquest. He had been coming in to the Tilted Kilt forever without landing any one of the girls and had jumped at the chance to hook up with me. He had succeeded in his quest and now he was uninterested. He had introduced me as his girlfriend at work selfishly and because it really was easier for him. He hadn't thought about my feelings and hadn't even respected me enough to talk about it with me when I asked. He just wrote me off as a crazy girl, one who wouldn't let up on getting an answer from him, one who got upset about his lack of caring. But he wasn't going to care about me. At this moment he only cared about being able to come back into a stupid chain restaurant. I realized all of this, and also realized he didn't deserve to come back into that stupid chain restaurant.

"Too bad," I said, wiping away tears from my cheeks. "I have never had someone say such asshole stuff to me before in my life so don't come into the TK. It's MY restaurant, so you stay away. I'm serious. I'll have every single one of my friends up there, those girls you think are so hot, hating you so fast you won't know what hit you. And if you or Casey ever set foot in there again, I guarantee that you will regret it. No one will take you to a seat, no one will serve you, no one will even look at you. And if you do come in, I'll know about it because every single girl in there will speed dial me so fucking fast your head will spin. So do me a favor and don't even think about it. Don't even attempt to entertain the idea of thinking about it. You and Casey think I'm crazy? How's that for crazy for you?" I finished.

Ricky just stared at me. "You can't be serious. What the hell is wrong with you?"

I stared back at him, done crying now. "I'm totally serious. What the hell is wrong with YOU? Good luck finding someone BETTER." And with that, I spun on my heel and walked away, leaving him standing on the sidewalk, alone.

~

That night, I poured myself some vodka on the rocks and lit a candle. I got out the phone and called Erin. I was still reeling from what had happened earlier. The minute she answered, I started crying. I was more upset than I had realized.

"Oh no! What's wrong?" I could hear the worry in her voice. "Is it something with Robby?"

"Ricky!" I wailed. "Ricky is a stupid asshole."

"What happened? What did he do?"

"He told me that he could find somebody better than me."

"He actually said that to you? No he did not!"

"He did." I sniffled. "He did. He said that to my face. He was being a jerk at the restaurant so I called him out on it. He doesn't want to be my boyfriend."

"The nerve!" Erin yelled, sounding very worked up. "How could HE not want YOU to be his girlfriend. Who is he going to find who's better than you? No one that's who! He's so lucky to even be able to bang you. To even be in your presence!"

"Thank-you that's nice," I said, tears still streaming down my face. "But he did. He's just an asshole. I totally had him pegged wrong."

"I just don't get this," Erin said. "You guys aren't even in the same league. You did him a favor by hanging out with him. And how dare he say that to you. I'm sorry, Katy. Forget him. Just forget him and his stupid hair. You deserve someone way better than him. Not the other way around."

"Thanks. I am going to forget him. But it still hurts, you know? It stings. I was so wrong about him. I thought he was a cool guy and so funny. But I have never been talked to like that before. And the hair, yeah. Gotta forget that, but it's not easy to forget."

"You live and you learn, though," Erin said wisely. "You will be more cautious next time. You will pick up on the jerkiness sooner. Trust me. You'll be okay. It's not like you were going to marry the guy, anyway. And please tell me you're not taking what he said to you to heart. You know you're the best. I'm going to come over there to Chicago and kick him in the balls for you. And cut off his stupid hair."

I laughed, finally. "Would you do that for me? I think that would help. And of course I'm not taking what he said to heart. But it still sucks. I'm still bummed. I was really starting to like him. And he made me laugh. That was what got me about him." I could feel the tears springing up behind my eyes again.

"I know," Erin said, quietly. "I know it sucks. But hey, no more crying, okay? Not over that stupid boy. Hey, I know what will make you feel better! Want to hear about this stupid jerk I met? I thought he'd be super great too, but you will never believe what he said to me…"

I laughed again. "I would actually love to hear about that. That would make me feel better. You always know how to do that."

"Great. Because this guy gives stupid Robby or Ricky or whatever the hell his name is a run for his money."

"Ricky who? Who's Ricky?" I asked, playfully.

"Exactly! That's what I like to hear. Now, you will never believe this…."

"Start talking," I said. I took a sip of vodka, smiled and wiped the last tear from my cheek.

Chapter 7

Chris

"So, I have a date tonight."

"You do?!" Jessica squealed, stealing a chip from one of the baskets on the ledge of the back pantry of the Tilted Kilt. She shoved the chip in her mouth and simultaneously grabbed for a cup filled with ice.

"Yes. I'm so not excited about it."

"Well, why not? Wait, who is this guy? Why have we not heard about him before?"

"Because I met him on Match.com."

"That's cool!" she nodded her head vigorously as she filled the cup with Diet Coke. "So you decided to do the online thing?"

"Yeah, I mean, you had told me you had some good experiences with it, so I decided to try it out. He's my first real date on it so far. We've been e-mailing back and forth and he looked cute, so I decided to meet him."

"I did like it," Jessica said thoughtfully, twirling her hair and reaching for a straw simultaneously. "The first Match date is always the make or break one, though. I had a really good first Match date so I kept up with it, but my friend Melissa, she had a bad one and she quit right after that."

"Well, thanks for the optimism and vote of confidence," I said, sarcastically.

"I didn't mean it that way!" she said, punching me playfully on the arm. "you know I liked Match, I met some really cool guys on there. Some really awful ones too…" she trailed off thoughtfully, then snapped back to reality. "But, mostly, it was fun! I'm glad you're on it!"

"Yeah, well, I decided to bite the bullet and just go for it. It's fun just looking at guys pictures and flirting with them over e-mail. But I went on Match to be social and to get out, so my first date is happening…tonight. I'm scared. What if he turns out to not look like his picture? Or if he turns out to be a weirdo?"

"Well, that's just the thing," Jessica said, stealing a chip herself and munching on it thoughtfully. " What if he's worse than a weirdo? What if he's a rapist? Or a murderer? Or worse yet, a rapist AND a murderer?"

"Who's a rapist and a murderer?" Heather had entered the back pantry and stood with her arms crossed, leaning against the wall.

"Katy's blind date tonight," Jessica said, pushing a straw down into the syrupy liquid in the plastic cup.

"Thanks a lot, Jess!" I exclaimed. "I'm nervous enough as it is, but now there's a chance he'll be a rapist and a murderer?"

"Why would you go on a blind date with a rapist and murderer?" Heather asked, obviously concerned.

"I'm not! He's not!" I swallowed the chip and attempted to defend myself. "It's not a blind date, I met him online."

"Hmmm," Heather mused thoughtfully, flinging her hair, "That's a blind date and he still could be a rapist and a murderer."

"I hate rapists and murderers!" Sandra exclaimed, sliding into the pantry and frowning. It was getting crowded back there.

"Okay, guys! Stop!" I yelled, slamming down the basket of chips and silencing them all with a wave of my hand. "His name is Chris. I met him on Match.com. He's cute. He asked me out and we're going tonight. I just don't know if he's like, a weirdo. He seems kind of weird, maybe."

"How so?" Sandra asked.

"Well, he just sent me this text right now. Let me know what you think." I held my phone out for everyone to see. Three heads bent down in front of me as the girls crowded in to read the text.

"Can't wait to see you tonight…wear something sexy for me," Jessica said aloud. She whipped around and stared at me. "You're kidding, right? This guy seriously just sent you this text?" She was aghast.

"Yeah, but that's not it. Look at this next one," I said, scrolling down to the next message and holidng the phone out again.

"A dress please, sexy?" Sandra read aloud. "What?!" she said, shaking her head in disgust. "He literally asked you to wear a dress? What a weirdo!"

"Yeah, that's weird, right? I mean, I thought so too," I responded, shoving my phone into my bra by my armpit. That's where we Tilted Kilt girls were forced to keep our phones. We couldn't keep them in our little purses that we wore around our waists. Those were for wallets and pens, and every once in awhile, a manager would check them. If we got caught with our phones, they'd get taken from us, and nobody liked that. So we put them in our bras to make sure we could have them at all times. We figured that if any of our managers checked for them there, then he or she would be faced with a huge lawsuit.

"Totally weird," Jessica said, stirring the ice in her glass around and around. "But…I once dated a guy who acted like that right off the bat. Like, he was trying to act all sexy and macho and kept saying "hey baby" and just basically being a weirdo. But I stuck it out because I was kinda into him and kinda curious, oh, and he was seriously gorgeous, and he actually turned out to be a really nice guy. It was just an act the whole time. His bark was bigger than his bite."

"So, you're saying I should go out with this guy tonight?"

"No! Absolutely not!" Sandra screamed, shaking her head and clasping her hands together.

"How cute is he?" Jessica asked, turning from us and punching her number into the computer.

"He's really cute," I explained, "and he seemed really nice and normal when we were e-mailing. He asked me a bunch of questions about myself and he seems really close with his family and has a dog and we had some really good talks over e-mail and text. I was getting excited about the date…until now. Now I don't know what to think."

"Well, here's the thing with a lot of these guys online," Jessica explained wisely, as the girls leaned in to hear better. "A lot of them are perfectly nice men who really want to be in a relationship and settle down. Why else would they be on match.com? But a lot of the other guys are only on it for sex. They're on it to get desperate girls to get some play. Judging from the way this guy is texting you, I'm going to guess that he's one of the latter examples, but, eh, who knows?. Give him a chance. He's probably harmless. If anything, you can go on the date, get stuff paid for and make fun of him with us later!" Jessica finished, pumping her fist triumphantly. "Just be aware that this guy might be a total creep-o."

"Yeah, I think I'm going to go," I said. "I might as well. I just think the whole thing is weird. And oh my God! What am I going to wear? I was going to wear a cute little sundress, but now?..." I trailed off.

Heather laughed and walked off toward her table. "Wear jeans. Definitely do NOT wear a dress now."

"She's probably right," Jessica said. "Wear jeans. Look cute but not too cute. Play it down."

"Have you met Katy?" Sandra asked, punching Jessica on the arm. "She couldn't play it down if she tried!"

"Okay, well, jeans, cute top, heels. Minimal makeup."

"Gotcha," I said. "I can do that. Now, what do I text him back?"

"You're on your own with that one," Jessica said, leaving the back pantry and pulling Sandra along with her. "I say nothing, but it's up to you. Don't give him too much to work with just yet. I mean, what if he's a rapist and a murderer?" she yelled over her shoulder as she retreated out of view.

I had recently, and very hesitantly, stepped into the world of online dating. It was a recent thing, and something that I had decided to try at the behest of my friends and family. My friends had all but insisted I join, and my family, surprisingly, agreed. While I was deciding whether or not to bite the bullet and delve into what I considered to be the "last resort" in dating, I polled almost all of the girls at The Tilted Kilt to find out if A.) They had ever done online dating themselves, and B.) If they thought, in their highly regarded opinions, that I should do it myself. I was shocked to find that a whopping 75% of the girls had joined an online dating community and participated in it at some point in the past two years, and that an even more shocking 100% of them agreed that I should try it. Most of my conversations regarding whether or not I should join went something like this:

> *Conversation A: Me: "Hey, (fill in the blank) have you ever tried online dating?"*
>
> *TK Girl: "Yes! I have! It was awesome! I was on it for like 6 months and met a lot of really cool guys. No one ever really stuck, per se, but it was so much fun just looking at people's profiles and e-mailing with them. The other thing was, I went out EVERY SINGLE NIGHT if I wanted to! It's a great way to just be super social and meet people!"*
>
> *Me: "Soo...do you think I should do it?"*
>
> *TK Girl: "Definitely."*
>
> *Conversation B: Me: "Hey, (fill in the blank) have you ever done online dating?"*
>
> *TK Girl: "No, I haven't but I always wanted to. My friend was on it, though. She said she met a lot of cool guys but a lot of douches too. Overall, she liked it, though. She was on it for 6 months and she went out with a different guy EVERY SINGLE NIGHT! Seriously, she was always out being really social and getting taken out and meeting people and getting all her stuff paid for."*
>
> *Me: "Soo...do you think I should do it?"*
>
> *TK Girl: "Definintely."*

Conversation C: Me: "Hey, (fill in the blank) have you ever tried online dating?"

TK Girl: Yes. I was on it for six months. Pretty much all those guys were only out to get laid. I met this one guy who looked nothing like his picture. He was really hot online and then I met him out and he was fat and bald and ugly. Total loser. But I met a lot of people and I was super social. I went out like EVERY SINGLE NIGHT with a different dude. Oh, and I got laid a lot. Which was good.

Me: "Soo…do you think I should try it?"

TK Girl: "Definitely."

From these conversations I discerned a few things: I should DEFINITELY go on an online dating site, and I should do this for six months exactly. I also concluded that I would be a ridiculous social butterfly for those six months if I so chose and would be able to go out EVERY SINGLE NIGHT. Because everybody had come to this consensus, I thought I couldn't go wrong, and what the heck, I should try it!

I had always been skeptical of Match.com and eHarmony and all of the other dating sites. I had been skeptical because, to put it bluntly, I was a snob about it. I didn't want the stigma of being on a dating site. I didn't want to HAVE to be on a dating site. And while I was embarrassed to say that I was at first, when I found out how many people had actually been on one, I loosened up a little and embraced it. I still wasn't entirely comfortable with saying that I was on Match.com, but it broadened my horizons if nothing else.

I'm a big believer in the phrase "don't knock it til you try it," and that went for online dating as well. So I decided to see for myself and bit the bullet. Match.com seemed like a good one to me. Yes, I had heard that Match.com was for the people who were only trying to get laid, but I didn't want to do eHarmony because I had heard that was for the people who were a little less fun. Match.com seemed harmless and fun and exciting and the guys who were on it looked cute.

Which is how I found Chris. He was on the bigger side, cute, friendly and seemed sincere. I'm not sure how one can seem sincere over e-mails and flirty cyberspace messages, but he did. I liked talking to him online, so I figured I would enjoy his company in real life. Either way, I was going to find out.

~

I met Chris at a restaurant at the edge of Chicago. He lived in the suburbs and I lived west of the city, so we decided we'd meet halfway in between. Per Jessica's request, I wore jeans, a cute top and heels, and arrived five minutes late. I always made it a point to be a few minutes late to my dates, but not too late; that would be rude. I liked to make an entrance and I have a phobia about walking in to bars by myself where no one is waiting for me. If I have to spend any amount of time sitting at a bar by myself, even if I'm waiting for someone, I don't fare very well. So I texted Chris to make sure he was there, and arrived a few minutes later. The texts from my friends began pouring in as I was driving to the restaurant. Jessica's said "hope you wore what I told you to wear you little slut," Heather's said: "keep me updated on the weirdo/rapist/murderer situation," and Sandra's said "be careful! Text me if you need anything! I love you!" I ignored all of them: they seemed quite dramatic, and silenced my phone as I entered the restaurant.

He looked just like his picture, thank God: cute, on the short side, sandy blond hair and stocky. He had a nice smile and was nervously twirling his thumbs when I caught his eye. He waved cheerily and patted the bar stool next to him. I made my way over to sit down next to him. He put me at ease instantly, and all thoughts of him being a weirdo, rapist or murderer vanished from my mind.

"I'm glad you could make it tonight," he said, signaling for the bartender. "I'm sorry I didn't order you a drink, but I didn't know what you'd like," he mentioned, apologetically.

"Oh, it's no problem," I answered, setting my bag down on the stool next to me and glancing at the menu. I already knew what I wanted: a dirty martini. "I know what I want, anyway."

"Let me guess," Chris mused. "You're probably a dirty martini kind of girl."

"How did you know?" I asked, incredulously, staring openmouthed at him.

"Lucky guess," he fidgeted in his seat. "Dirty martini for a dirty girl." He winked at me.

So much for him not being a weirdo. That statement was a little ballsy, I thought.

"Um, yeah," I replied, giving the bartender my order. "No, I just really like them."

"It's cool," he said. "Would you like something to eat?"

"No, I'm okay," I said, taking a sip of my drink. "We can just talk."

And talk we did. We both liked football, so we discussed that for awhile. He was gentlemanly and funny. We laughed and talked very naturally for close to two hours. I had two more dirty martinis and I was getting drunk. Which was bad, because I had driven. I mentioned this to Chris who seemed more than happy to come up with a solution to this problem.

"Well, I can take you home!" he suggested, very emphatically. "Or, better yet, you can come stay with me! I can get you up for work in the morning! What time do you have to be there? I can drive you! It's really no problem at all!"

Whoa. Okay, Chris was a little intense. I figured every guy wanted to hook up, but he reeked of desperation. It was not a turn-on. But, because I had had a little too much to drink, I didn't react the way I should have. I came up with a solution: He could drop me off at my apartment and maybe come up for a nightcap. So I suggested just that.

"Sounds great!" he said, emphatically, motioning for the bill. He was very eager to leave. I sighed. If I hadn't been drunk, I would never had offered for him to come up to my apartment. If I wasn't drunk, I would have just said goodnight and driven myself home. If I wasn't drunk I would have had to have decided whether or not I even wanted to see this person again. He was nice, he was cute, he was fine. But that was just it: he was FINE. Not great, not exciting, fine. Mediocre. At best. But I was drunk so all of these thoughts went out the window and I let Chris drive me home and come upstairs. I had, of late, been experiencing a little something called desperation.

Ahhh, desperation. The dictionary defines desperation as "recklessness arising from despair," which I believe is accurate. I am usually not one to act recklessly, per se, but I have had my reckless moments. And despair was something I had grown accustomed to. Despair is perhaps a touch dramatic, I wasn't hanging off the ledge of a thirty story building and I didn't have the knife up to my wrist, but, from time to time, I did feel in despair when it came to men. Men had been the source of my despair recently. No one seemed to like me. It was sad. I am a girl who needs a lot of attention: a lot of attention from males, more specifically and no one was giving me the attention I felt I deserved. No one wanted to be my boyfriend. A few dates were fun, a few hookups I could get, but as far as a relationship or any sort of commitment, I was batting 0. So, I suppose I could have been categorized as desperate. I was 29 years old, wanting a mate, a partner, a boyfriend, and I had to go on Match.com to search for one. I would practically do anything with anyone who would give me an ounce of attention, and if that's not desperate, I don't know what is. I was open about my "desperation" at that time in my life. When friends and others would try to tell me "oh, no! You're not desperate, Katy! You're just picky…you know what you want! You could have any guy in the world you wanted!" I would politely correct them with the phrase: "Thank-you, that's very kind…but, I am desperate. Like, literally. It's really okay. You don't have to sugarcoat it for me." After which, I would be met with silence. Cricket-chirping, awkward silence. I'd usually just shrug and walk away. No skin off my back. It was the truth. I owned my desperation and I was okay with that, but the problem with desperate girls is that you can always TELL. If a girl is desperate, she unfortunately wears it like a stamp on her forehead. She has an undeniable aura about her that screams desperation. She can't help it, but guys tend to pick up on it, and then they don't reciprocate or they get scared. So she becomes rejected and more desperate, and the vicious cycle begins again.

So that is why I took Chris home.

That turned out to be a mistake.

Not a terrible, horrible, irreparable mistake, but a mistake nonetheless.

I knew it was one, but the desperation caused me to act recklessly because of my despair. Let's blame it on that.

Because the first hook-up was good, and we seemed to click somewhat, I decided to give Chris a second chance with a second date. We decided to go to the movies and then have dinner afterward. I showed up in a long flowy dress and heels and you would have thought I was naked from the way Chris acted.

"Damn, girl!" he all but yelled as I strolled up to the theater. "You look fucking HOT tonight! What am I gonna have to do to take that dress off of you?"

Well. He was certainly trying to start off with a bang. Pun intended.

"Yeah, thanks," I replied. "Well, it's just an old dress."

"Old dress my ASS! YOUR ass!" he said, rubbing his hands together. "You look banging, girl!"

I wasn't exactly sure why he was coming on so strong. Maybe he thought it was impressing me or turning me on, but it was doing neither. I wasn't exactly sure why he had chosen to use the word "banging" either.

"Um…thanks," I replied, adjusting my purse strap over my shoulder. "Just a little dress," I repeated. I was already uncomfortable. "Sooo…should we get tickets for the movie? I'm really excited to see this one," I said to him, heading toward the door of the theater. There was no answer from Chris. I turned to look over my shoulder. He was just standing in the same spot, looking down at my backside. "Well, are you coming?" I asked, impatiently.

"Just admiring the view," he answered, licking his lips lasciviously. "Hey," he said suggestively, cocking his head to the side while still staring at my butt, "how about you give me a little peek?"

"At what?" I asked, innocently.

"You know what. That upper echelon rear."

"My what?"

"That sexy little ass of yours."

"Aren't you looking at it currently? I thought this dress showed it off pretty well."

"It does, for sure. But I mean, a real look. Come on, show me some cheek."

"Show you some what??"

"You know, some of that nice little round cheek."

"Right here? In the lobby of the movie theater?"

"Why not?"

"There are really too many reasons for me to expound upon the answer to that right now."

"Awww…really? I thought you were cool."

"I am cool. I am a very cool girl. That does not mean I am going to show you my ass in public."

"I thought you were adventurous. Where's your sense of adventure?"

"I am adventurous. And my sense of adventure also has nothing to do with me getting naked in front of total strangers."

"Not naked, just a little butt show."

"This conversation is over. Let's just go see the movie." I yanked open the door and stepped into the lobby. I was incredulous at what he had just said to me. I couldn't believe any guy would talk to a woman that way, nevertheless on the second date. I was somewhat disgusted with his words, but a part of me did feel flattered. My backside was, in my opinion, one of my most treasured commodities. I was used to being complimented on it and I enjoy attention from men, I require a significant amount of it from them, so his attentiveness did not go ignored, but I did not enjoy being told that I wasn't "adventurous" because I wouldn't moon some guy I barely knew in public.

Chris caught up to me and slipped his arm around my waist. "Well, if I can't see it, can I at least give it a little grab?" he asked, making a pouty face. I had to laugh, it he was just so pleading. And desperate. Maybe we were more alike than I had first thought. So I let him and he grasped my left cheek firmly. I didn't mind, it actually felt good, but then as he tried to let his hand linger there for more than a second, I firmly shoved it away. I laughed again. "Just for letting you do that, you're paying for the tickets," I said, teasing him.

"I was planning on it anyway, sweet cheeks," he answered, stepping up to the ticket booth. Chris was corny, that much was for sure, but there was still a sprout of hope that he was not a hopeless case. Something was telling me to look beyond all of his faults and keep trying. Maybe it was my optimistic nature. Maybe it was my desire to have the Match.com thing work out. Maybe it was simply desperation…still.

We wandered into the theater and looked around for two seats together. It wasn't difficult, seeing as the theater was almost completely empty. I craned my neck around the side of the railing and asked Chris "where do you want to sit?"

"In the back row."

"Oh, are you a back row kind of guy? I don't like to be too close to the front myself, but I'd say the absolute back row is a little…" I trailed off when I realized how naïve I was being. I looked back at Chris. "Wait a minute," I said almost accusingly, "WHY exactly do you want to sit in the back row?"

"To make out, obviously."

"You can't be serious."

"Why not?"

"Are you 15?"

"What? You don't make out during movies?"

"No."

"Even when you were 15?"

"Nope. Not even then."

"Why not? You don't like making out? What about your adventure side? I really thought you were the type of girl who was really outgoing."

"I love making out but I like watching the movie more! I am really outgoing but not in the type of way where I'm going to make out with you in the back row of a movie theater like we're a pair of teenagers, okay? Jesus, can you just drop the whole sex thing for one second? It's just not going to happen so get over it, okay?" I was becoming extremely frustrated. I wanted him to stop talking about sex. It was getting on my nerves and was annoying. I just wanted to have a normal date with a normal boy, a movie, some dinner and nice conversation. If it ended in a hook-up at the end of the night, even better, but I didn't even necessarily want that. I wished I wasn't on a date with someone who acted like he was a horny teenager just hitting puberty. I stomped down the stairs and picked a seat in the middle of an aisle four rows from the front. I did this to make Chris angry and to get as far away from the back row as possible. I slammed down my popcorn and soda in frustration and folded my arms across my chest.

Chris scurried down the aisle and tentatively took the seat next to me. He tapped me lightly on the arm and said, "Hey, I'm sorry. Are you okay?"

"Yeah, I'm fine," I answered. I toyed with the idea of telling him off again, but figured I had said my part and if he didn't understand, then that was his problem. Also, it was still only our second date so I didn't really feel like seeming like a crazy girl by yelling at him some more, even if he was being childish and stupid. So I said nothing more.

"I won't talk about your ass anymore, I promise. And we don't have to make out during the movie, either. We can just watch. I like your company. Would it be okay if I put my hand on your leg, though?" Chris looked at me with the puppy dog look again.

"Sure," I replied, smiling in spite of myself. "That would be nice. And appropriate," I finished, pointedly.

Chris placed his hand just above my right knee and rubbed it gently. As the lights went down and the screen blinked to life, I settled in to watch. Then Chris leaned in and whispered in my ear "when you said 'it's not going to happen,' did you mean like we're not going to have sex in general or were you just referring to making out during the movie?"

I sighed, pushed his hand off my leg and folded my arms in front of my chest yet again. As the previews began, Chris leaned over and whispered in my ear. "Hey, I'm sorry, listen, how about I take you somewhere fun after the movie? I have a place in mind."

I perked up at that. It was the least he could do after being such a hornball. I nodded. "Okay," I whispered back. "Where is it?"

"You'll see," he patted my leg. "It's a surprise."

We left the movies and headed back to his car. I was excited to see where Chris was going to take me. He turned right and headed down Michigan Avenue. I kept asking him where we were going but he refused to tell me. He just kept an annoying little smile on his face. It was driving me crazy. I hate surprises and guessing games but I was still trying to guess. Maybe he was taking me to the Signature Room! That was the bar at the top of the Hancock building with the best view of the city. It was romantic and expensive. As we passed Illinois and Ohio streets, I was sure. We were heading right toward it! I squirmed in my seat. It had been awhile since I had been there with a guy. Maybe Chris wasn't so bad after all…

Then we passed it. I swiveled my head quickly back in the direction of the Hancock building. I could see it looming behind us as the car continued to speed forward. "Wait, what?..." I said, opening and shutting my mouth a few times. "Where are we?..." Chris turned a sharp right and swung the car down Clinton Avenue. What in the world was on Cinton Avenue? I wracked my brain, trying to figure it out. A bar? A restaurant? A show?...And then it hit me. No, it couldn't be, I thought. There was no way. But it was. As Chris stopped the car with a flourish, I looked out the window at the pink neon lights that were glowing down on me garishly. It was a bar. And a restaurant. And a show. It was all three of these things.

It was a strip club.

The Pink Monkey was the biggest, most well-known strip club in downtown Chicago. Let's get one thing straight: I am not against strip clubs. I have been to plenty of them and I had even had fun at them. I had been with various boyfriends and his friends and was ridiculously drunk every time. This had been a good time every time. But being at a strip club with a guy I barely knew, on our second date and SOBER was highly unacceptable. Why in the world would Chris think that I would want to go with him to a strip club the second time we hung out? It seemed extremely offensive, not to mention presumptuous of him. How awkward! I had to get out of this.

"Uh…yeah…" I stammered, still sitting in the car and continuing to stare up out of the window. "THIS is where you're taking me?"

"Yeah, baby, is there a problem?" Chris asked, drumming his fingers anxiously on the steering wheel. "Best strip club in town! Only the best for you!" he said, punching me on the arm playfully.

"Ow!" I said, placing my hand on my shoulder, "and seriously? Why would you think that I would want to go to a strip club with you on our second date?"

"Thought it might be fun. We could get simultaneous lap dances together," he retorted, punching my arm again.

"Okay, OW! Again, and no, that would not be fun at all! Can you just take me home please?"

Chris looked crestfallen. "Really?"

"Really."

"No couples lap dances?"

"No couples lap dances! We're not even a couple!"

Chris looked lost in thought for a minute, pondering this. Then he said, "Alright, but you gotta promise me that some time you'll do your own little lap dance for me sweet cheeks. Deal?" He pulled back his arm to punch me again.

"OK!" I yelled, shrinking back from his protruding fist. "Fine! Whatever! I'll do it! Just take me home! And don't punch me again!" I rubbed my bicep as Chris started the car and sped away.

~

I ran up the stairs to my apartment. I was beside myself with happiness to be home after the disastrous date with Chris. We had barely spoken on the ride home and I had bounded out of the car the minute he pulled up outside my apartment. As I slammed the car door, I heard him call after me that he would call me later. I ignored him and hoped and prayed that he wouldn't. That way I wouldn't have to deal with him ever again.

I inserted my key into the lock and walked through the door. I was shocked to be greeted by none other than my roommate, the elusive Natasha. "Hi!" she greeted me, spinning around in the hallway, a granola bar in her hand. She was wearing workout gear and a huge smile lit up her face. "I'm home!" she said, almost triumphantly. "My flight got cancelled so here I am! I think this is the first time in almost two months we've been here at the same time."

"I think so, too," I responded, giving her a hug. "And I am so glad you're home. I just had the most insane date." I flopped on the couch and took off my heels.

"Do tell," she said, crouching on the floor and tossing me another granola bar. "That's dessert."

"Good, thanks, I'm starving because I didn't get enough to eat at the strip club tonight."

"Wait, what? Strip club? I thought you said you had a date tonight. Was it with the Match guy?"

"Yup. And you heard me right. Match guy took me to a strip club after the movie. Seriously. He wanted us to get couples lap dances."

"WHAT?!" Natasha squealed. "Um, wow. I don't even know what to say to that." She cocked her head and sat in silence.

I waited but she still didn't speak. "Well, please say something! I mean, that must warrant some kind of response, right?"

She thought another minute and chewed her granola bar. Natasha swallowed and then looked me straight in the eye. "I was about to ask you if you liked this guy, but I'm not going to because it doesn't even matter. Katy, obviously this guy is not for you. This Match thing may not even be for you. I mean, just the fact that this guy would take you to a strip club on your second date is unacceptable."

"I know!" I moaned, flinging my head against the back of the couch. "I don't like him! I'm not even that attracted to him. He's just somebody to…"

"Go out with?" Natasha offered.

"Yes. And he's just somebody to…"

"Fill time and pay for your dinners?"

"Exactly. And the only reason I am even considering seeing him again is because…"

"You're totally desperate?"

"Bingo." I put my head in my hands. I was at the end of my rope. At least Natasha understood.

"I understand," she said to me, as if reading my mind. "I get it. I'm desperate too. We all are a little bit. We just want people to like us and we like spending time with people. With men, specifically. But Katy, I am going to tell you something and please don't take this the wrong way."

"Okaaay," I said slowly and skeptically. "I won't."

"You are the type of girl who tries to make bad things work. You date all these guys who aren't right for you and you know that and yet you still hold on, you still try even when you shouldn't."

"I know."

"It's a very endearing quality and I love that about you. You never give up on anyone. But take it from me, sometimes you should. Sometimes you should just throw in the towel. Give it up. Give him up. Forget it. Move on. Who cares."

I sighed. "You're right. I know this about myself. It's just hard for me to do that."

"But sometimes you have to think of your self worth, you know? And is it worth it? What's the point of continuing to talk to or see this person?"

"I don't know. I'm going to stop talking to him."

"I think that's good." Natasha hauled herself up off the floor. "And if you choose to keep talking to him, you know I'd still love you. I'd never judge you." She started walking in to the other room. "But a strip club, really?" she yelled. "What a douche. I'm sorry." She poked her head around the doorway and all of a sudden her face scrunched up and she guffawed in laughter. "It's actually pretty funny if you think about it. I mean, it's hilarious! He took you to a strip club on your second date and wanted you to get couples lap dances! That's one for the books! You need to write that down!"

I looked at her and burst into laughter myself. "You're right. It is pretty crazy. It's so funny. I love it!" And we both dropped to the floor and rolled around in laughter for the next five minutes.

~

It was the Friday night after Chris and my movie date and almost strip club date. The Tilted Kilt was in full swing. There was a line of patrons snaking out the door waiting for a table and there was a fight on television. It was loud, hot and crowded, but I was making lots of money.

I was at the computer ordering another round of beers for my table who had had quite a few already when Heather ran up next to me.

"Can I get in there? Please?" she pleaded desperately.

"Sure," I said, stepping aside. "You okay?" she seemed almost out of breath.

"Yeah, I'm just in the weeds right now," she panted, putting in her order. "In the weeds" was our term for any time that we were stressed out or had too many tables to take care of.

"How come?" I asked.

"You mean you're not?" she said, glancing at me out of the corner of her eye.

"Not really. I mean, it's busy but I'm definitely not in the weeds. I'm cool."

"Fucking Dawns," Heather muttered under her breath. "They're trying to kill me."

I laughed. Dawn was the name we had given to the hostesses. Every hostess. Heather had come up with the name after the popular 1970s TV show "Tony Orlando and Dawn." Both women in the show were named "Dawn," but not separately: they were "Dawn" as one entity. So whenever the hostesses were aggravating Heather for whatever reason (which was all the time according to her) Heather called them "Dawn" to show how stupid she found them. She lumped them all together with that name. It was mean and not very politically correct, but we had all adopted the name in spite of ourselves, and it always made us laugh. It was funny and definitely creative.

"They're not trying to kill you," I comforted Heather. "You should stop complaining. At least you're going to make money."

"We're all going to make money," she countered, pressing end on the computer and closing her screen. I just wish I didn't have to bust my ass to get mine tonight. I hate these fight nights. It brings out all the ghetto tables."

"And all the WT tables," I reminded her, thinking of my table who was drunk. "Speaking of WT tables, I gotta go get their beers. Wanna come with me?"

"Can't, remember?" Heather said, running off in the other direction. "Fucking Dawns," she called over her shoulder.

I saw Jessica up at the bar. She turned to me while she was waiting for her drinks and twirled her hair. "So," she started with a wink, "how's it going with your Match date? What's his name?" she snapped her gum.

"Chris."

"Oh, right."

"He's…fine."

"Okay, what's wrong with him? That is not a good answer. Is he a murderer?"

"No."

"Then he's better than what we once thought."

"You didn't ask if he was a rapist."

"He's actually a rapist?" Jessica's eyes were wide. "Maybe you can be on Law & Order SVU then! And you can meet Detective Stabler! He's so hot." Jessica looked dreamily off into the distance.

"Jess, focus," I said "he's not a rapist…I don't think… he's just really…"

"Sexual?" she interrupted.

"Yes!" I said. "Exactly! How did you know?"

"Judging from that first text message he sent you asking you if you would wear a dress on the first date I could just tell that he might be a little intense. And like I said, he seems like one of your typical Match.com pervs. What has he done?"

"He asked to see my ass in the street outside the movie theater."

"Oh, Jesus."

"And he always sends me sexts. Like, constantly."

"Let me guess, he's always asking you for sexy pictures of yourself?"

"Well there's that and he always responds with some sort of inappropriate response to every single text. When he was talking about going out to dinner the first night I asked him what he would want to eat and he responded with 'You, baby,' you know, stuff like that. It got old." I stopped, debating whether to tell her that he had tried to take me to The Pink Monkey the other night. I was kind of embarrassed to tell her this, but Jessica was one of my best friends and I decided that she would understand, that she wouldn't laugh at me or make fun of me.

"And," I paused, still debating. "He took me to a strip club on our second date," I said very hurriedly.

"What did you just say?" Jessica asked, looking up in astonishment.

"He took me to a strip club on our second date?" I said, phrasing it as a question and looking up at the ceiling while grimacing and waiting for her response.

"WHAT?!" Jessica screamed, bursting into raucous laughter and pushing me backward by the shoulders. "YOU'RE KIDDING ME!"

"No," I said, regaining my balance. "I'm not. And why does everyone keep hitting me on the arm?"

"What?" Jessica asked, gasping for breath.

"Never mind. Yeah, he tried to take me to The Pink Monkey. I wouldn't go in."

"Were you guys drunk?"

"No, unfortunately. If I had been, I might have gone in."

"Oh, my God. This is insane. Who does that on the second date? What a freak. I mean, there are some freaks out there on Match, but this like, takes the cake. Jesus. Oh wow. I can't believe it. Like, ew, gross. Come on. Get a life, whatever his name is."

"Chris."

"Doesn't matter. Please tell me you're not going to see him again."

"I'm not. Natasha said the same thing to me."

"That's because she's right and she's smart and obviously gives good advice. Good call. Strip club on the second date. Jesus." She walked away in wonderment, shaking her head.

I walked away as well and dropped off my round of beers then took inventory of my section. I had three tables while everyone else had at least five. Two of my tables were six or more people so those constituted big parties, but I still wondered why the hostesses were shirking my section. I was just about to go over to talk to them when I saw a blond Dawn walking a two-top to my table number 56. I was happy about receiving another table, but only two guests at a table for four? Guess I was still making one or both of them mad for some reason. I squinted to see who was coming. They looked like two guys about my age. I could see the one in front who looked semi-good looking. As he rounded the post and sat down at the table, I saw his friend behind him who also looked semi-good looking, but also vaguely familiar. Short, sandy blond hair, stocky…no, it couldn't be…there was no way…

Yes it was.

Chris.

Speak of the devil.

Chris had showed up at The Tilted Kilt. This was great. Just great. Now Chris was probably going to go on and on about my outfit, sexually harass me, annoy me and pester me for the rest of the night and then want to take me back to the strip club. I was certainly not prepared for this. I decided to go hang out by the computer for awhile, make them wait. I needed to collect my thoughts anyway. Pauline and Sandra sauntered up to me and leaned against the back of the counter.

"What's up?" Pauline asked me, smacking her gum. "Sandra and I are bored. Fucking Dawns."

"Yes, I agree, fucking Dawns," I said to them.

"Are they not seating you, too?" Pauline asked, shooting a death glare in the general vicinity of the hostess stand.

"Well, kind of," I replied. "They just sat me with a two top at a four top."

"At 56? That's shitty," Pauline said.

"It gets worse."

Sandra craned her neck to check out the table. "Why? They look cute, actually."

"One of them is Chris."

"Strip club Chris??!!" Pauline yelled.

"SHHH!" I scolded her, clamping my hand over her mouth. "Yes, strip club Chris. Keep your voice down. Fuck, news travels fast."

"I just talked to Jessica," Pauline said, but my hand was still covering her mouth so it sounded like "mwah mwah mwah mwah memica."

"That's him," I said, removing my hand from her mouth.

"Shut up."

"I swear."

"He's cute!" Sandra exclaimed.

"Sandra!" Pauline slapped her thigh emphatically. "He tried to take Katy to a strip club on their second date. That makes him not cute."

"He DID?" Sandra turned to me with wide eyes.

"Yes, he did, okay? I don't want him here!" I whined, stomping my feet.

"Oh, but it's perfect because now we get to meet this freak. Come on-this'll be fun!" Pauline tapped the back of the counter, grabbed Sandra and my hands and dragged us along toward the table. Before I knew it, we were standing in front of Chris and his friend. Because they were sitting and we were standing, both sets of the boys' eyes locked directly onto our midsections, then traveled up slowly to our chests, lingered there for awhile, traveled back down to our stomachs, even lower to our legs, then back up slowly, finally reaching our faces after lingering again by our boobs. We were used to these sorts of looks, we all received them ten times a shift, but Sandra crossed her arms over her chest, Pauline rolled her eyes and I placed my hands on my hips before forcing a smile and saying:

"Hey, Chris, fancy meeting you here."

"Hey, babe, wanted to come see you at your place of work." He pinched me on my stomach and winked. "Nice abs. HOT! Looking good, sweetheart."

Babe? Sweetheart? I didn't realize we were at that point in our "relationship." I was assuming our "relationship" was over. "Thanks," I deadpanned. "Chris, meet Pauline and Sandra," I swept my hand to my right and left.

"Ladies," he said, extending his hand to both of them. "Very nice to meet you. This is my friend Brandon." Brandon held out his hand as well. "Nice place you got here," Chris continued. "Never been here before. Lots of TV's, nice open space, plenty of titties." He slapped Brandon on the back and rubbed his hands together.

Great. Lovely.

"Did you just say 'plenty of titties?'" Pauline asked him.

"I did."

"Observant, aren't you?"

Chris beamed at her, obviously not picking up on the sarcasm in her voice. "Okay," I interrupted both of them. "Are you here to watch the fight?" I asked Chris.

"To watch the fight, yes, and to see you and your tight little ass. I told you. You wouldn't send me any pictures so I had to come in and see you for myself in that little skirt. Which, may I say, you are looking damn sexy in it, girlie."

Oh, man.

"Thanks," I said.

Brandon swung his neck around and looked at my "damn sexiness." Sandra by this point, had already run away in terror and Pauline said "you both are some really classy guys, aren't you?"

Before anyone could answer that question, I asked them what they would like to drink, the boys ordered beers and Pauline and I all but ran from the table. "So, that's him!" I said, feigning excitement and clapping my hands together. "Isn't he the best?!"

"Yeah," Pauline said, heading toward the kitchen. "Just like every other douchebag that comes in here. I think it would be better if he was actually a murderer. Didn't you like, break it off with him, though? I mean, why is he here?"

"I honestly have no clue. I didn't invite him. And I haven't spoken to him in days."

"Ah, well, that doesn't matter," Pauline remarked. "Guys are idiots. They never get a clue. He probably thought you've been pining away for him for days. Loser."

"Probably," I said, walking off to grab their beers.

The thing about restaurants is, gossip and drama spread like wildfire. If one of the servers or hostesses or bartenders boyfriends or girlfriends or parents or friends came in to the restaurant, everyone would know about it within five minutes. And then everyone would flock around the table where they were sitting to check them out, analyze them, introduce herself. And that's what happened with Chris and Brandon. The next time I looked at table 56, about three girls were gathered around. Even one of the Dawns was there. I wasn't surprised, and it was actually kind of great for me because then I didn't have to get sexually harassed more. Soon, the girls dissipated, and it became clear that I would have to go over there again. Chris caught my eye and waved me over.

"Hey guys," I said. "How are the beers?"

"Not as good as the scenery. This place is the best! It's so awesome that you work here. All these hot women! I told Brandon to get with one of the Kilt girls. How about that sexy brunette over there? Brandon loves brunettes, don't you buddy?" He turned to me. "You know her? Can you bring her over here?" He was pointing to Jessica.

This was going to be good.

"Sure," I said. "No problem." Just let me go check on my tables and I'll bring her right back.

"Thanks, baby," he said, giving my ass a slap as I walked away.

It was then that I decided I was definitely never going to go out with this person again, once and for all. Besides the whole strip club thing, I didn't even like him that much. He was way too overtly sexual, he made me feel uncomfortable and he was ridiculous in his actions. I didn't need to prove anything to anyone about Match.com or what I did in bed or in public or otherwise. The fact that he would come into my work and make a mockery of it and me spoke volumes. I expected that from the typical stranger douchebags that came into the restaurant, but not from someone who I was supposedly dating. I was desperate, but I wasn't that desperate. Thank God. Natasha had been right and I decided to heed her advice. It felt like a weight had been lifted off of my shoulders.

I checked on my tables, everyone was doing fine, and went to collect Jessica. I knew she'd have fun with this. I found her hanging out with Heather in the back pantry. Even better. Heather would want to fuck with them as well.

"You guys ready to meet Chris?" I said, waggling my eyebrows suggestively.

"Strip club?" Heather asked. I nodded. "I heard he was here!" she said excitedly. "Hell yes, let's go!"

"This oughta be fun," Jessica said, bounding out of the pantry. "Can't wait to fuck with this perv."

"He just slapped my ass," I mentioned, following them to the table.

"Oh, hell no, here at work?" Heather said. "What an asshole. Tell me you're not going out with him again."

"Definitely not. He is acting a fool here. He's just kind of pathetic. And so is the friend."

Jessica had reached the table and was standing in front of the boys. "Hi there," she said. "I'm Jess. I've heard a lot about you," she said staring at Chris.

His eyes lit up. "Good things I hope," he said.

"Not really."

Chris's face fell and Brandon laughed.

"What are you laughing at?" Jessica asked Brandon.

"Nothing."

"Good."

There was an awkward silence. "Um…Chris and Brandon, meet Jessica and Heather," I said, because I didn't know what else to say. I thought introductions seemed in order.

"Nice to meet you ladies," Chris said. "Aren't you two a pretty pair? Not as sexy as this one here, though," he said motioning toward me and trying to get me to sit down. When I refused, he continued. "So…what do you ladies wear underneath those kilts?"

"Good one," Jessica countered, putting her hands on her hips and taking a defensive stance. "That's an original question, we've never heard that one before."

"Sorry just curious," Chris said, narrowing his eyes and jerking his thumb toward Jessica. "You've got an attitude don't you? A little mouth on you, sugar tits, huh?"

"What did you just call her?" Heather asked, taking a step forward.

Jessica just smirked. "Heather, it's fine," she said, putting a hand out in front of her. "Again, typical," she said, turning back to Chris. "Heard that one before too. I thought you were an ass man anyway."

"I am. But only for this one's upper echelon ass," he said, putting his hand protectively on my left cheek.

"I don't believe the lady asked you to put your disgusting hand on her ass," Heather said, placing her hand on my right cheek. So now I had Chris and Heather's hand on my butt and Jessica and Chris were basically in an all out brawl. This WAS fun. I was enjoying this.

"Oh, and she likes yours there?" Chris sneered back.

"Much better than yours."

Jessica said, "don't touch the girls here you may get in trouble. Especially if you say and do douchebag things."

"What the fuck is this anyway? A strip club?" Chris asked, removing Heather's hand from my right cheek and giving my butt a little squeeze.

"It might as well be a strip club," Brandon said.

"AGAIN! ORIGINAL!" Jessica said very loudly. "And let's talk about strip clubs for a minute, here. Taking Katy to a strip club on your second date? Seriously? Gross. Were you raised in a barn? Is that really the way you think you're going to get laid?"

"Yeah, well, try telling your girl here to be more adventurous. I thought she was fun and up for anything. She's on match.com for God's sake. Tell her to stop being such a prude. Tell her to put out or something."

We all just stood there in silence. My jaw dropped. Chris was getting angry. And even more inappropriate.

"I would never tell her to put out for someone like you," Jessica said, balancing on one foot and then the other. "But I can tell you to get out."

"You can't kick us out," Chris said. "We're paying customers. Just want to see some tits. What's wrong with that?"

Heather said "You're really gross you know that?"

"You wanna suck my dick, honey?"

"I'd rather die, actually, but thanks."

"You a lesbian or something?" Chris asked, chuckling

"I am." Heather looked at him in all seriousness.

Chris looked surprised for a minute and then checked her out again. "Never seen such a hot dyke before," he mentioned, leering at her.

"THAT'S IT!" Jessica yelled. "Where's Donald?" She looked around quickly for our security guard. Luckliy, he was a couple of feet away talking to Sandra. He ran over as soon as he heard his name.

"Is there a problem here?" Donald asked, glaring at Chris and Brandon.

"Yeah," Jessica said, "these guys are harassing us."

Chris looked at me pleadingly. "Baby, you're not gonna let them kick us out, are you?"

I looked back at him. "Let's get one thing straight. I'm not your 'baby.' Never have been so I have no idea where you got the idea that it was okay to call me that. We've been on two dates, one of which you asked me to show you my ASS on a street corner. Now, you roll up in my restaurant and start acting like an idiot? Listen, you can call me whatever derogatory name you want. I don't care, because I'm never going to see you again and I don't give a shit about you. But you call my friends 'sugar tits' and 'dyke,' your ass is getting thrown out of here. They don't like that. Sorry. See ya."

I nodded at Donald and he dragged the boys up by their arms. "Let's go guys," he said. "You're gonna need to pay first though."

The boys each threw a twenty dollar bill down on the table. I smiled. Their beers had only been five dollars each and I wasn't about to offer them change. I had just made out like a bandit.

As Donald led the boys out of the restaurant, we all stood at the table and waved goodbye.

"I'll text you!" Chris yelled to me over his shoulder as he was escorted out. "I'll take you to the Signature Room next time! How's that, baby?"

"No!" I yelled back. "Don't text me and no, thanks!" Chris frowned, and just like that, he was gone.

I turned to Jessica and Heather. "Well, that just happened," I said. "You guys were awesome! Now I don't have to go out with Chris anymore!" I sighed with relief.

"Yeah, um, don't ever go out with that guy," Jessica said, shaking her head. "Typical douchebag match.com guy…but worse. That guy was awful. Total pervert. You were right."

"You were great, though!" I said, snatching up the twenty dollar bills. "I wouldn't have the guts to say all that stuff that you just did."

"I've dealt with so many of these guys before," she explained, helping me clear off the table. "They're all the same. Total losers."

"Guys are all losers!" Heather said, laughing at the memory of what had just transpired. "When are you two gonna become lesbians?"

"Heather, you say this every time," Jessica said. "Just keep waiting, it might happen." Heather crossed her fingers and made a wishful face.

"So, are you going to stay on Match.com?" Heather asked, putting down her hands.

"I don't know," I replied. "I didn't have the best first experience, but I don't hate it. I guess I'll keep on it for awhile, its kind of fun. Besides, I have to be on it at least six months. That's what everyone does, right?"

"Yeah," Jessica said. "Just stay on it until it becomes not fun. Or until you find someone," she suggested hopefully. "You really never know. But don't stay on it just because someone tells you to," she continued, seriously. "It doesn't make you desperate, you know." She winked at me.

"Thanks, girl," I said, giving her a hug. "This whole thing has definitely been a learning experience if nothing else."

"Just like this place," Heather pointed out, straightening her back as a hostess walked up to our group.

"Uhhh…" she said, stupidly, staring at us blankly and twirling her hair.

"Can we help you?" Heather asked acidly.

"Yeah, um…do you know where Heather is?"

"You're kidding, right? I'M Heather."

"Oh…uh…cool. You, uh…have a table….at 86."

Heather looked around her. "There's no one at 86."

"Oh…uh…I meant 87. No, 85."

"Heather sighed. "Okay. But what is it with you Dawns? I get sat again? Seriously? How is this happening?"

The hostess looked at us blankly again. "Um… you got sat again because it's the…eeeehhhh….rotation." She turned to me. "Are you Dawn?"

I stifled a laugh and Jessica guffawed. "No, I'm Katy."

"Oh…then I have a message for you."

"And what is that?"

"Some guy wants you to call him."

"The guy that was just thrown out of here?"

"Uh…yeah. That guy. He said 'tell Katy to call me.'"

"Okay, thanks I'll get right on that."

"Okay. And don't forget about table 86. I just sat it."

"That's MY table!" Heather yelled. "And it's table 85!"

"Oh, right."

We watched the hostess walk away in wonderment.

"This is quite a night," I remarked.

"I'll say," Jessica said. "Katy, don't forget to call Chris. And Heather, don't forget to take table eighty…something. Dawn wanted to make sure you got them."

"I'm on it," Heather said, walking away. "Fucking Dawns," she yelled over her shoulder.

Chapter 8

I suppose being Vice President of The Jerk Magnet's Anonymous Club doesn't automatically give me the right to say that I'm a Jerk Magnet myself. I suppose being the best friend of the President of The Jerk Magnets Anonymous Club doesn't give me that right either. But I do suppose that if I tell you about my luck with dating men, or lack thereof, then you will believe me, in case you were ever skeptical, so let's start this off right.

Hi. My name's Erin and I'm a Jerk Magnet.

Here's the part where you all say "Hi, Erin!" and then I launch in to my tales of woe. I am going to assume that each and every one of you said "Hi, Erin!" back, so now I will begin. I am going to prove to you that I am also a magnet for jerks and that I have a right to present myself as such.

I dated Travis in college, right after Katy and I were roommates freshman year. Travis was good-looking, fun and exciting. He was also abusive. Mentally, physically, emotionally, you name it, he was messed up and he took it out on me. And I took it, for years. I let it go on and on, turning a blind eye to the pleadings of my family and friends who begged me to get away from him. My self worth was destroyed while I was under this man's spell. My life was basically in shambles for months. I was young and naive and in love. No, these are not excuses, they were just how it was. My reality. Until one day, I had had enough. Something took hold of me and I up and left. I never looked back and I set off to find the person who would give me my dream.

My dream was to find a husband, and my dream was to have children. Those things were always what I wanted most in this life. Always. I had my wedding planned ever since I was two years old. I started wanting children of my own not long after that. I love children and am wonderful with them. I understand them and they understand me. I have been a kindergarten teacher and a pediatric nurse and nothing gives me greater joy than to be around little ones. So I set off after Travis, just knowing that right away, I would find the man of my dreams, settle down, marry young and start having babies.

What I got was date after date with a string of losers.

After Travis, there was Curtis. And what do you know? Curtis had a little girl of his own. A blond haired, blue eyed, beautiful, smart, kind, amazing four year-old creature who fell in love with me at first sight. And the feeling was mutual. Curtis and Cara and I would go out and everyone would compliment me on what a beautiful daughter I had. Of course, she wasn't mine, but I loved her like she was. And I loved Curtis, too. We worked for awhile. I thought maybe he was it, maybe he was the one. I had it all planned. We could raise Cara, have a few children of our own and be blissfully happy. Curtis seemed to approve of this idea as well.

And then Curtis got selfish. He started to put everything but me first. His daughter came first, which I expected and respected. But then his ex-wife started to come before me. Work came before me. His whole life seemed to become more important than I was and I put up with it as long as I could. I was confused and jealous of everything around him because he wasn't paying me the attention I felt I deserved. He seemed to be taking me for granted and I couldn't have that. It all came to a head when we went on vacation. I wanted to go to a nice restaurant which required Curtis to purchase a suit jacket, which he didn't have. He wouldn't do it. All I needed from him was to buy one stupid, lousy, goddamn suit jacket (something he should have had in the first place) for cheap (I found a great sale at Kohl's) and he would not do it for me. He flat out refused. We got into a huge fight about that jacket and I broke up with him. Now, some may think that that may be a stupid reason to break up with someone, but it honestly wasn't about the suit jacket. That was only a catalyst for the breakup. It was about Curtis' inability to see me, to recognize my needs, however big or small they may have been. And while I know it was the right thing to do, I was still sad. I missed Curtis somewhat, but, to be honest, I missed his little girl so much more. I still miss her to this day.

Then I tried the online dating thing and that's where the string of losers really came into play. I found out I had a "three date curse." I would go on a date with a guy, and we would hit it off. The date would go well, we'd see each other again, and then a third time. And then WHAM! He'd never call. Three dates was all I got with everyone. Three strikes and I was out. This happened four times in six months. I got the hint. I threw in the towel. While online dating was something I am glad I experienced, I decided it was not for me.

And then I met Danny. Danny was who I thought I had been waiting for all this time. He was much older than I with a high-school age daughter but those things didn't matter. We clicked. We fell in love. We talked about our future together. Even though he had been married before and already had a child, he swore to me he would marry me and give me the children I so wanted and needed. I made him promise me that, and he assured me he would. I was elated. I was set. For the three years we were together, I was happy. I was content. I was reassured that things were going to be okay. I would finally have the life I always wanted with Danny. He seemed to be the answer to my prayers.

And then it happened. On the evening of his daughter's graduation from High School, as we were standing on the lawn, waiting for the graduates to appear, he turned to me and told me that he couldn't do it. He looked straight into my face and said that he couldn't give me what I needed. Could not marry me and could not be the father of my children. He told me he was still in love with me, but that he just couldn't continue on with me. The sad thing in this case, though, is that "could not" meant "would not." "Cannnot" meant "Will not." He was choosing not to do these things, it wasn't that he was unable. His face registered nothing. Not a frown, a wince or a tear crossed his face. He was blank. And I was numb.

I can't truly remember what I felt at that moment. I was in shock. He had lied to me all of those years, never intending to follow through with the huge, life-altering promises he had made to the woman he loved, or claimed to love. Either that, or he had simply changed his mind. I don't know which one it was because I never cared to ask, and to this day, I cant' decided which is worse. As I stood there, the fog slowly started to clear and I caught sight of all of the young men and women around me throwing their graduation caps high up into the summery night sky. Here were people excited for all of the magic that life was going to offer. Here were people with nothing but possibilities in front of them. Here were people smiling and laughing and shouting because their lives were just beginning. And there I was crying because I felt like mine was ending.

I stood there for a minute, listening to Danny beg me to say something, anything. Listening to him apologize and repeat himself and stutter and blubber. I looked into his face one more time and then I turned and simply walked away. I never looked back and I never spoke to or heard from him again. Walking away seemed effortless at the time. The hard part came after.

For one week I did nothing but sleep and drink and talk to Katy. And cry. I cried more than I ever thought possible. I would wake up crying and go to sleep crying. And in between I would cry as well. I would leave my bed only to go to the bathroom or to fetch a bottle of wine, and sometimes I wouldn't even need to do that because my roommate at the time would bring it to me. I drank a bottle of wine a day for two weeks. For two weeks I sobbed and wept and cursed Danny's name and got drunk and allowed myself to miss him and be devastated and depressed. I felt sorry for myself and I asked God "why?" and all of that super fun stuff. And then, after fourteen days, I stopped. Quit all that super fun depressing stuff cold turkey. I got out of bed, dusted myself off and started living again. I went back out into the world and continued on. I had had my time to mourn and it was enough. I'm not so sad anymore. But I'm still a Jerk Magnet. Now do you believe me?

Katy lived the Danny saga with me. Even though she was not physically there through it all with me, it felt like she was. Even though she couldn't truly understand what I was going through, it felt like she did. She hated Danny for me. I should have hated him, wanted to hate him for what he did to me, but for some reason, I could not. So Katy hated him instead. So I didn't have to. Because that is the job of a best friend, is it not? To be sympathetic and empathetic.

To feel the feelings and do things for the other. To listen and support and cry with the other. To want something for the other person just as much or more as you want that something for yourself. Especially love. I think Katy wanted love for me more than she wanted love for herself.

And isn't it funny when we, as people can't have what we want? We do things we never thought possible. We turn into people we never thought we could become. Especially women. With women it's worse, because we want so much. In a good way. We want love and comfort and respect and to be wanted and needed. We want back all that we give, simple reciprocation, and this is not always what we get. Men want things too, but men are taught to go after the things they want. Women are expected to want in a wishing sort of way, to recognize what they want and then sit back and wait for it to happen. To simply hope that it will happen. And if it doesn't we are told there is nothing to be done about it, that that's simply how it is. Better luck next time. Sorry.

That is why we mourn the loss of the things we wanted more than men do. We put so much thought and effort and time and love and understanding into other people, into men, and then when they turn out not to be what we wanted, or cannot give us what we want, we are devastated. It's not that we think we deserve these things, necessarily, although that is certainly something we are told time and time again. How many times did Katy say to me or did I say to Katy "Erin/Katy you DESERVE someone who is good to you. You DESERVE someone who makes you happy and cares about you." And while I said it and she said it, and a million other women say that to each other every single day, and while some may think this is actually true, I think that the basic emotion of WANTING is enough. I think we all should just be able to say that we want and in return get what we want without needing to deserve it. That should be enough for us as human beings, that should be acceptable, and that should be true.

So when the time came around for Katy to have her heart broken, I was there. Not physically, but there nonetheless. I listened to her, I felt for her and I hated him when it all came crashing down. I reciprocated. Her situation was very different than mine but the heartbreak at the end was the same. Heartbreak is always the same. It's the experiences leading up to the heartbreak that differ completely.

Katy wanted him. More than she wanted anything in a very long time. I could tell that much. There was something in him that she saw that she liked immediately. She met him at her local bar on Father's Day. Katy was with a friend and he was drinking alone. He was exactly her type: big. Football player big. Handsome and gruff-looking. She told me he looked pensive, distracted and a little lonely. And while her friend was busy talking with their friend, the bartender, Katy, feeling bold and quite tipsy decided to take a chance. She was sick of waiting for someone she wanted to come up to her so she took matters into her own hands. She yelled out "I like big guys!" The exclamation was seemingly random, but it had a purpose. Katy had an agenda.

His head snapped up and he smirked a little, not quite a smile, but almost. And then he looked at her. She looked back, out of the corner of her eye and then looked away.

"What did you just say?" he asked.

"I like big guys!" she tried again.

"What a random thing to yell out at a bar."

"Not so random, you're here."

"Are you calling me a big guy?"

"Yes. Are you going to deny that you are one?"

"Most definitely not."

"Did you play football?"

"Yes."

"I knew it. What position?"

"Running back."

"What school?"

"Nebraska."

"Excellent. That is a good answer."

"It's a true one."

"That is sexy."

"Most girls seem to think so and then I try to talk to them about football and they don't know a damn thing about it."

"I do."

"Prove it. Can I come sit next to you?" He motioned toward the empty chair next to her.

"Absolutely." She patted the seat. "How am I going to prove my knowledge about football to you?"

"Talk to me about Florida."

"Love them. Love that they beat Ohio State for the national championship because I hate the Buckeyes. My dad went to Florida so I'm a fan. Saw them crush Western Michigan at The Swamp last year. Coolest stadium ever, besides The Big House but Gainesville is hot as hell. Steve Spurrier is a great coach, but I've heard he's an asshole in real life. Tim Tebow is obviously an outstanding quarterback but there's no way he's a virgin in real life, I mean, give me a break. Their running game is amazing, and you really can't go wrong if you're the number one pick in both the Associated Press and Coaches' polls at the beginning of the season, and it certainly doesn't hurt if you're the only Division I team to have straight back-to-back thirteen win seasons, in the Southeastern Conference, no less, which is the toughest one. They're sure to go into this season just as strong if they can get past Oklahoma's offense, but I see them dominating anyway. Dan a na na na… GO GATORS!" Katy finished and looked at him smugly.

He stared at her in stunned surprise, speechless for a few seconds and then said "Okay, I'm buying you a drink. Or 10. And then can we please have sex?"

Katy laughed. "Vodka on the rocks, please. And…we'll see."

~

Katy did go home with him that night, but they did not have sex. They woke up awkwardly in the morning, as most people do who have just hooked up for the first time, and he got her number. Then he called her later that morning to ask her out on a proper date. Katy was overjoyed. It had been some time since someone had asked her out on a proper date, and only a few hours after hooking up, no less! In her cynical mind, she had figured that he was just going to hook up with her and then be on his merry way. That's what girls like us had come to expect from guys, but not him. He called and set up a date; dinner and drinks for Friday. He wanted to take her out. He wanted to see her again.

Katy told me the date went fabulously. He was 35 years old and from North Dakota. He had never been married, didn't have kids, and had a good job working as a salesman for a large-scale equipment company. He lived just down the street, and had only been in the city for a few months. He had told her it was nice to meet someone who seemed normal and fun and down-to-earth and smart, and he had also said that he had had a hard time finding women like that to date. Katy found him to be the same: interesting, funny, intelligent and charismatic. They found they were both extremely sarcastic people. There was never an awkward moment, they talked incessantly, and both enjoyed the other's company. Besides, she was very attracted to him and he seemed to be quite attracted to her. They finished their meal and headed back to his place where she stayed the night.

And then, two days after their first date, he left for a two week vacation. This would be the first in a string of vacations and trips for work that he would take over the next year and a half. You see, he was always leaving. He was never around. He warned her that he traveled a lot for work, which he did, but he failed to mention that he also traveled a lot for fun and these trips would take priority over pretty much anything else. The first vacation he took was back to North Dakota to see family and he was gone for two weeks. Katy whined to me that he had taken her out on this wonderful first date, they had had a great time and then he had disappeared for fourteen days. But then she received a text from him on the night of the Fourth of July. She was walking home from work and looked down at her phone and his text read: "I miss you is that weird of me to say?" Katy replied "no, not at all because I miss you too," and after that, they began dating.

Katy told me that she believed he missed her from the very first moment they met. When they parted after spending that first awkward night together, he kissed her and she could tell that he would be contacting her, even though everything inside her told her not to get her hopes up. He left but called her hours later to make sure he could see her again because he missed her already. He was gone so much that Katy got used to the fact that he was just constantly missing her, because he wasn't around enough not to. From the very first text that read "I miss you," until the very last one that stated the same notion, he and Katy were always saying that to each other because they were usually apart. And because it was true.

Missing someone is a complicated thing because there is no one way to miss someone. There is also no correct way to miss someone. When I think about Danny and how I miss him now, I'm pretty sure I miss the possibility of what could have been more than actually missing him as a person. I miss the excitement of anticipating him being my husband and father of my children. I miss the security I recognized in believing that he would be that husband and that father, and I miss the innocence I felt when I was confident he would follow through with the promises he made. Everyone misses innocence to some extent, they miss the idyllic time before someone or something vitiates them, the harmonious time that comes before reality slaps you in the face. Everyone misses that blissful period of ignorance preceding corruption, like the calm before the impending storm.

But during those first few months, Katy missed him more physically. He became such an immense and powerful presence in her life, both literally and figuratively, that when he wasn't there she felt a void, a large one at that, and she felt the disappearance of his proximity very acutely. When he wasn't there, she felt like her life was lacking in some odd way. It was curious, but she accepted and embraced it as well as she could. He missed her for her. He didn't miss the idea of her, or the idea of having a girlfriend or someone to come home to when he was finished with whatever it was that he had to do. He never necessarily wanted a girlfriend or needed anyone by his side; that wasn't the kind of person he was. He was fine by himself, or more likely, better off by himself. He enjoyed Katy when they were together. She entertained him and made him smile and made him happy, and he missed those traits when he wasn't around. He simply wanted to be near her and when he couldn't be, or more accurately, chose not to be, he felt that void as well.

I hadn't met this person. I had only heard the stories about him. And they were usually not good stories. But that is another job as best friend. To hear more bad stories than good ones. To be a sounding board. To sympathize and empathize with our best friend when her boyfriend is being a jerk? To say "you can do better than him," "you ARE better than he is," "you don't need him," "you shouldn't be treated like this." I said all of those things many times to Katy during the course of her relationship with him, but I assume they fell on deaf ears. I know she listened and I know she values my opinions, but something was holding her back from believing the things I told her.

I told her that he sounded like a jerk sometimes. That he seemed more interested in being a loner and doing his own thing. He made it clear to her that he was going to do his own thing, no matter what, always, and that it would behoove her to just let him because he was going to do what he wanted to do. If he wanted to take off for home to visit for two weeks to go hunting, he would, even though he had literally just gotten back from a business trip the day before. Then the two weeks out of state would turn into three weeks without warning. Then if he wanted to visit friends in Florida for two weeks after that, he would, and those two weeks would turn into three without warning as well. And Katy would be there, waiting for him to get back, holding herself back from meeting other people because she was so into him, even though he was never there.

One night about seven months into their "relationship," I got a call in the middle of the night from Katy. Calls in the middle of the night from your best friend are never good. Just like calls from a family member in the middle of the night are never good. Ever. They always mean that someone has died, or is hurt, or is in jail or in some other predicament. No best friend calls her best friend to tell her how much she values her friendship and what a good person she is and to re-hash the events of the day after midnight. It just doesn't happen. So I picked up the phone in a state of panic. She was crying.

"Hello?" I said. "What's wrong?"

"He's moving."

"What do you mean? Where? Why?"

"I don't know. He just told me."

"What do you mean 'you don't know?'"

"He said he's either moving back home or back to Florida."

"Is it for work?"

"No. He said he can work from either place, though."

"Why would he just up and move when he has you? When he has a life and a job there?"

"I don't know. I guess he's not happy." She started crying harder.

"He just sprang this on you?"

"Yeah. We had an awesome day. We spent all day together and had a great time. Then he picks a fight with me. Just out of the blue. We were both kind of drunk, but he starts yelling about how I always put my wet towel down on the bed and he wants me to hang it up in the bathroom. When I try to apologize and say that I won't do it again, he keeps yelling at me about how the bathroom is so dirty and it's all my fault because I use his stupid bathroom all the time. But where the hell else am I supposed to use the bathroom when I'm over here? And his bathroom is so dirty because he's a disgusting boy."

"Sounds like he was picking a fight. Sounds like a scapegoat to me."

"I know. That's what I thought, too. So I ask him why he's so upset and there must be something else going on and that's when he just tries to break up with me and tells me he's moving. Just like that." Her sobs became louder.

"He tried to break up with you and then tells you he's moving? After you guys had had a good, normal day together?"

"Yes."

"I can't believe it. I'm so sorry."

"I know. He's just like 'I don't know if this is working out,' and I said, totally confused, 'wait, are you breaking up with me?' and he said 'well, I think it's best, I'm going to be moving in a couple of months.' WHAT?"

"Did he ask you to go with him?"

"No. He didn't ask me anything. He didn't ask for my opinion, he didn't ask me to go, didn't ask what I would think about it, nothing. He totally disregarded my feelings and basically my existence as a whole with this stupid, spur of the moment, random plan that he made. He didn't even bother or care to factor me in to the whole situation."

"I'm sure he did. I'm sure he had to have been thinking about you when he made this decision."

"I asked him if I was even a factor at all in his plan to just up and leave and the only thing he said was 'I'm sorry, this is just something I have to do.' He never even told me that he was thinking about this until now." She wailed again.

"Well, what are you going to do?"

"There's nothing to do. He's going, I guess. I am so sad. Erin, I begged him not to leave me. I literally begged him. How pathetic is that?"

~

He left two months later and went back to Florida. But instead of breaking it off with Katy and moving on like he said would be best for both of them, he wouldn't let her go. He was thousands of miles away, but he still called her. Still texted her all the time. Still told her he missed her and gave her attention and told her that he wished she was where he was. Katy loved the attention, relished the attention, but was confused because he had CHOSEN to be away from her. He had always chosen not to be where she was. And he had never apologized for that. That was just what he wanted to do, so that's what he did.

Katy knew he wasn't the right guy for her, that this "relationship" was going nowhere, that he was a jerk. She knew he was stringing her along because he liked to have someone there. To keep her close, but not too close. That's what he had done when they lived in the same place, so that's what he was doing when they lived a thousand miles apart. But it takes two to tango, and Katy let him string her along. She let him text her and call her and miss her because she was head over heels for him. She tried not to be, but she was.

The relationship was one-sided. He held all the power, he made the decisions. He got to do what he wanted to do while having Katy by his side even from far away. He had somebody to listen to him, to support him, to love him, to care about him, and he didn't have to do much of anything. He didn't open up to her, he didn't give her enough credit for being the person she was to him. He took it for granted. He didn't have to call her his girlfriend because he wasn't comfortable with it, and he didn't like long distance (or long term, for that matter) relationships.

He did say she was the only one, still. He said he wasn't seeing anyone else, wasn't dating. He told her he wasn't interested in anyone else and that she could trust him. I think Katy did trust him. She believed that he had moved away in haste and then realized he didn't know what he had until it was gone. They were far away, so it would have been easy for one or both of them to lie and cheat, but Katy didn't think he was lying or cheating. She had to believe that he would give her the respect not to be doing anything behind her back. She gave him chances to call it quits; to just move on and date other women, to find somebody else. But he refused. He said he didn't want to.

She told him she loved him and his response was that he didn't think he had the capacity to love a woman in that way. He said he had thought he had been in love before, but he hadn't been and now he didn't think he could be in love at all. He told her that he cared about her very much, but he wasn't in love with her. He told her she was his best friend, the person he cared about most, and that IF there were someone he would want to be his girlfriend, it would be her. IF there was someone he could fall in love with, it would be her. But he didn't want to be her boyfriend. And he wasn't able to fall in love with her so she shouldn't expect it and she should stop hoping for it to happen.

I told her to run away. Run far away from this person immediately. I told her he was damaged, sad, a loner, emotionally unavailable and selfish. Anyone who says he "cannot" do something, actually means "does not want to." I thought of Danny and his reasons for not being with me: "I CAN'T be your husband." "I CAN'T give you children." "I CANNOT give you what you deserve, want and need." Those things translate into "I WON'T be your husband." "I WON'T give you children." "I WILL NOT give you what you deserve, want and need." He chose not to do all of these things. And I recognized that same problem in him. And I told her to get away from him. I didn't want her to go through what I had already experienced.

But she didn't listen to me. I wouldn't have listened to me if I were her. What did I know? These were just my educated guesses about what was going on. I didn't know him, I only knew what Katy had told me about him. So I let her go and I waited. I knew one of a few things was bound to happen. She was going to come around in her own time and become tired of him and the situation. She was going to find someone else who treated her better, was willing to be with her fully, and who lived where she did. Or something awful was going to happen to make it all end. I hoped for one of the former options and not the latter, but I knew which one it would be. It's always the latter.

He came back to visit her a few months after he had moved. They went to a baseball game, they stayed in a hotel, they hung out at the bar at which they had met. They had a wonderful time and I heard all about it. Katy was sad to see him go, but she got the chance to be close to him again and feel close to him again. He seemed positive and upbeat when he left. He told her he missed her and he would see her soon and reiterated what a great weekend he'd had.

Katy called me the night that he left to tell me all about it. I told her I was happy for her and that I was glad that she'd had such a great time. I hung up and went to sleep. The next night she called again. That was odd because we usually didn't speak two days in a row. I wasn't expecting anything bad, I just figured she had forgotten to tell me something. Maybe he had professed his love for her, maybe he was coming back. Maybe he'd apologized and come around and they were going to live happily ever after and she was just calling to tell me that. Nah. That wasn't it.

"Hello?" I picked up the phone again.

"I did something bad." Katy's voice was eerily calm.

"What did you do?" I asked, my voice panicky with nerves.

"I saw something I shouldn't have seen. I knew by looking I might see something I wasn't supposed to, and that's what happened."

"What did you see?" I was getting anxious. I couldn't even tell if it was a good or a bad thing by the tone of her voice.

"He left his e-mail up on my computer when he left. All signed in and everything. I tried not to look, to sign him out, but I couldn't do it. I had to snoop. I just had to."

"It's not your fault. He was the stupid one who left it up. It's not like you stole his password and snooped around like that. It was his fault and he deserved to have his shit looked at. I would have done the same thing."

"You would have?"

"Absolutely."

She sighed. "I found an e-mail."

"Well, I would assume so, in his e-mail inbox and all."

"It was a draft of an e-mail."

"About what?"

"I'll read it to you," her voice was deadpan, void of any emotion at all. I heard her open her computer and clear her throat. She paused and then began.

"It was really great to see you again after all this time. It had been too long. I truly enjoyed the time we spent together and I need to see you more. You looked amazing. You are so beautiful. You are also such a caring person with a wonderful heart. I love being around you and I wish I had told you that more.

I am in love with you. I have been for a long time. I would do anything to be with you. There are some things I have to take care of here right now, but I would move anywhere so we could be together. I would understand your hesitancy in this, I know this is kind of coming out of the blue, but I think if you gave it some thought, you would see that we should just go for it. We should try for this, because

I really think we could be something great together. I hope you feel the same way. Please write back."

I sat in silence on the other end of the phone for some time, processing what I had just heard. I couldn't believe it. I was shocked. That e-mail sounded nothing like what I had heard about him. But I supposed people could change, they could come around. It gave me hope to hear that e-mail. He had written her something she needed to hear, finally. Something that she deserved to hear. But above all, it was something she wanted to hear. He had finally realized his feelings and opened up. He wasn't emotionally unavailable anymore. He truly had cared about her this whole time and he loved her. I was so happy and I was so glad that Katy could finally hear him say those words to her.

"This is great!" I said, excitedly. "This is what you've wanted! He FINALLY realizes that he loves you and he SAID it! These are the words you have been begging him to say to you for SO LONG. I guess he just needed some time to come around. I'm surprised, but I'll be the first to admit that I guess people really can change. I guess not all guys are jerks."

There was a long pause and I could hear Katy sniff and then whimper in the background. I heard her close her computer and then bring one hand up to her mouth to bite her nail. I could hear the clip clip of a nail being chewed off.

"Are you going to say something?" I asked. "This is good, right? What's wrong?"

"Do you know when this e-mail was written?" she asked quietly.

"I'm assuming today or right after he left you?"

"It was written two months ago."

"Well, maybe he wrote it and just didn't have the courage to send it to you. You said it was a draft." There was more silence again. "Katy, what is wrong?"

I could hear her start to cry then on the other end of the line. It was quiet tears at first, but it was crying nonetheless.

"Erin, you don't understand. It was written two months ago. It wasn't about this weekend at all. It's not…for me." She choked back a sob.

I was so confused and she sounded so upset I almost started crying myself, not even knowing why. "What…I don't get it, what do you mean? Of course it's for you. You're…you are…of course it's for you. Who else would it be for?"

"This e-mail is for another girl."

"That is not true, there is no way. No. Possible. Way."

"Erin, listen to me, I swear to you, it's true. It's for someone named Heidi. He lied to me. He had us all fooled."

I felt a tear roll down my own cheek as I tried to imagine this actually being the truth.

"No, it has to be a mistake. It's for you, it has to be for you. He wouldn't do that to you. After all of this, he wouldn't do that to you." I was just talking, repeating things, trying to convince myself at this point.

She paused and sniffed again. There was silence that seemed to go on forever. Then she burst into tears.

"It's addressed to someone else, Erin. This letter is not for me."

Epilogue

So, those are my jerk tales. Some definitely worse than others, but all of them, jerks. There are a few good things that have come out of my encounters with jerk people: I finally caught on to the phenomenon and began to observe and learn. Sounds corny, but I did. I learned to spot a jerk coming from a mile away. There are definitely specifics on what makes one person a jerk, or more of a jerk than another, but I found that many of their qualities overlapped. Such as, most of them were tight with their money. Most of them cared way more about themselves than they did about me or anyone else. Most of them lied to me at some point, and most of them never really cared about me the way I wished they would, or if they did, they couldn't show it or didn't admit it, and that's just as bad, if not worse, as not caring at all.

I also learned to give up on people quicker. Sounds sad, and it is, but I got much better at recognizing when not to waste my time. I got better at throwing in the towel, at giving up the ghost, when I realized things weren't working. I learned not to care so much about the people who didn't truly care that much about me. Was it hard?

Almost impossibly so. Was it worth it? To give up on jerks? Absolutely.

But Jerk Magnets Anonymous helped me through all of that. The girls encouraged me to persevere when things were going well. On the other hand, they encouraged me to give up when things weren't. Erin and Natasha were my biggest cheerleaders and my most trusted advisors. To have women as your best friends who are going through the same thing as you is priceless. To hear their advice, and be able to lean on them, to talk to them and cry to them, to hear their stories and be able to laugh with them was, for me, literally a necessity. Indescribably so.

Am I jaded? Bitter? I guess you can decide that for yourself. I don't think I'm such a jerk magnet that I automatically assume anyone who comes my way is an asshole. But I am skeptical. I do think twice. I take everything with a grain of salt. I go into every relationship knowing there's a possibility that it all could be a lie, that it could all crumble and fall, that things could turn out the way I never expected them to. But I do still think that this possibility is a small one. I do still hope for the best and try to be optimistic.

Because of course, I'm not without blame. God knows I've said and done jerky things. I've hurt people, I've blindsided them, I've lied to them. I've been selfish and self-centered and used people myself. I have been a victim but I have also been the perpetrator. I never claimed to be perfect. I'm not. I know this is shocking to read, but it's true. We all have a little jerk in us, and that's okay.

But Sam, John, Serena, Rob, Kyle, Ricky, Chris and He have that little extra in them. The jerk gene. So they can't help it either, I suppose. It's in their DNA. But they're not all bad, of course. Because even though this book is about the jerky things they said and did, they also did some good, non-jerky things. I had fun with each and every one of them. I try to remind myself to remember the good times more than the bad when I think about them, which I do, frequently. Every single one of them holds a special place in my heart and always will. Every single one of them brought something irreplaceable into my life, and for that, I am grateful. Do I regret any of it? Not at all. Would I do it all again if I could? Absolutely. In a heartbeat.

So in my mind, they are all attending Jerk Club meetings while I was writing this book. They are drinking their scotch and smoking their cigars and laughing at me mercilessly. They are comparing their stories and deciding who was the bigger jerk, trying to one-up each other. But then, in my mind, every once in awhile they cease their laughter and their mockery and become quiet as they remember the good times, too. They stop and think to themselves: remember that girl? The one I used to hang out with? She was fun, I liked her. She was cool, we spent some good times together. But she thought I was such a jerk that she wrote a whole book about it. She was crazy. Totally insane. This is what they'll remember and stop and think about, fondly, just for a minute.

And smile.